two birds
/one stoned

ABOUT THE AUTHOR

Neville Thompson was brought up in Ballyfermot in Dublin. Having spent some time in Corfu, he now lives in County Westmeath with his wife, Jean. His first novel *Jackie Loves Johnser OK?* was published in 1997 by Poolbeg.

the whispering crowd, the screech of the siren, there was so much noise.

The hospital waiting-room was packed. There were drunks lying everywhere and three fellas with bandages on their heads. Every time they looked at each other they started fighting.

The doctor was young, too young. His eyes were sad as he approached me slowly –

"Mrs Kiely? Perhaps you'd like to come into the office for a moment?"

I stared at him blankly.

"Please, Mrs Kiely, this way."

Mrs Kiely, any other time I'd have loved for someone to call me that. To call me by the name I'd always wanted. I used to sit at me desk in school practicing it. Sometimes I'd write Mrs Jackie Kiely, other times Mrs John Kiely.

Even bills wouldn't have mattered once they were addressed to Mr and Mrs Kiely, they would have seemed like a statement of our togetherness.

One time I bought a raffle ticket and put Jackie Kiely on the stub. I was out with the girls from work and some eejit was annoying us to buy tickets and, even though I didn't want the first prize of a teddy bear, I bought one.

Ann said I was mad, what would I want with a big ugly teddy bear? The fella who was selling the tickets said that teddy bears were all the rage, "collectors' items".

"Collectors' items?" says Ann, "The only person who'd want teh collect that fuckin thing is a bin man, an even then he'd want it well-wrapped."

I felt sorry for the poor fella –

"Ah Jasus, it's not that bad."

"Would yeh stop, it's fuckin brutal." She turned to the fella. "Did yeh make it yerself or what?"

"Ah leave him alone, will yeh? It's for a good cause."

Ann looked at the ticket –

"A good cause? It's fuckin Anfield Football Club, what kind of a good cause is that? They're not even a decent team."

I bought the ticket anyway. At the end of the night someone was walking around with a board showing the winning tickets and there was Jackie Kiely in first place. At first I didn't even cop it, I'd never won anything in me life. If I'd thought I might win I'd have put me proper name on it. I wasn't going to say anything but Ann saw it –

"What are yeh like, Jackie Clarke? It's bad enough havin teh use their names when yer married teh them without playin Mr and Mrs when yer only goin out with them."

The doctor led the way into a cluttered office. He sat me down on a plastic chair, offered me tea and told me I could smoke if I wanted to. I wanted him to stop, I didn't care about tea or smoking or anything else. I just wanted him to do whatever he had to do, tell me whatever he had to tell, so as I could get the fuck out of here and back home to Johnser.

Johnser needed me. He needed me to be by his side, to hold his hand, to tell him that everything was going to be all right. He always acts so bloody brave, but I knew that deep down he was as terrified of dying as anyone else.

"Mrs Kiely, you've suffered a terrible shock. Your husband has just been shot . . . "

"Yeah, I know all that. I know he was shot, I was there . . . that's why I want teh go fuckin home!"

"I'm sorry Mrs Kiely . . . "

I walked out of the office, there were police everywhere. "Jackie Clarke? We need to ask you a few questions."

The doctor appeared at me side –

"Not now, gentlemen, this woman is in no fit state to answer questions."

"But we need to speak to her now. If we leave it too long the killer will have fled."

The doctor turned to me –

"Are you up to it?"

The detective tried coaxing –

"He may strike again, Jackie. How would you feel if another innocent person was to lose his life?"

Bastard, I thought. Did he really think I came down in the last shower? This wasn't a serial killer – Johnser wasn't an innocent victim. This was business. This was some calculating bastard settling an old score. The gun-man was long gone, they weren't going to find him. He'd let me live, cause he knew I wouldn't rat him up. Besides, he hadn't been paid to kill me. This was a pro, not some loony who was just passing by and seen the key in the front door.

I walked past them, towards the matron –

"I want to go home."

Johnser would hate this. He'd hate them to see this emotion. To see someone who loved him in so much pain.

"Never show emotion to your enemies," he used to say. And as far as Johnser was concerned, the police were his enemies.

I turned away. The matron, sensing what was going on, took control –

"Come with me Jackie, I think we could both do with a cup of tea."

TARA

Chapter Seven

I started going out with Slash. He was a bit of craic and after the disaster of his hair I thought it was the least I could do. For all his talk and Mr Big attitude, he was really quite shy. He definitely wasn't as experienced as me in the kissing department. He was like a mullet fish, all mouth. I swear he had it open before we even touched.

I never said anything. Ma had told me that men were funny about this kind of thing. They wanted to be told they were the best but I couldn't tell Slash that cause he wasn't anywhere near the best. In fact, he was a crap kisser, so I dreaded to think what he'd be like at anything else.

* * *

They say you never forget your first time. I'd done loads of wearing and even a bit of petting, now I was ready to go all the way. We were on holliers in Blackpool. It was brill. Well, as brill as any holiday could be when you were with your parents.

The place was packed but, thankfully, there were as many teenagers as old folk.

24

On the first morning I was up at the crack of dawn. I wanted to get down to the beach early in order to get a deckchair and a good spot in the sun. I had a lovely new white bikini and was determined to show it off. Ma had bought the bikini for herself but, these days she wasn't doing too well in her battle against weight. So she'd decided on a swimsuit instead.

I was well settled by the time they arrived. Da was wearing his George Webbs with a pair of white sports socks. He had his trousers rolled up to his knees and was still wearing his vest under his shirt. He was carrying a huge striped beach ball. I tried to hide behind me magazine –

"Jasus, if I'm seen sittin with him, I'll never get a fella."

Ma must have been embarrassed too, cause she was walking miles behind him. Ma spotted me and made her way over to sit down. Da called her –

"Com'on Pauline, don't fall down on me yet, she has teh be around here somewhere."

I peeped out from behind me magazine.

"Wha . . . " He came running back. "What deh fuck are yeh doin dressed like that? Jasus Christ, Pauline, cover her up with somethin."

"Daa . . . yer embarrassin me! Ma, will yeh tell him?"

I could see people starting to look at us.

He was stuttering and stammering, he always started this when he got flustered –

"You're not . . . she's not . . . she can't . . . ah Jasus, Pauline . . . "

"Will yeh sit down, yeh big eejit."

He was wiping his face with his hanky –

"Pauline, tell her teh put some clothes on."

"She's grand the way she is. There's no one even mindin her."

"I was bleedin mindin her! Yeh can't fuckin help it with those . . . things stickin out like that. It's not right."

He was pointing at me boobs.

"Will yeh ever stop, yeh fuckin eejit. She's no different teh any other young one sittin on the beach."

I got fed up listening to them. I jumped up and grabbed me beach bag.

"Where deh yeh think yer goin?" he asked.

"I'm goin teh get a drink."

"Yer not goin anywhere dressed like that, girlie."

I stormed off ignoring him.

Da was the same about everything I wore.

"Luv, I know what them fellas are like. Believe me, I was young once."

"Hasn't yer father got a great memory, Tara?" Ma would say.

Every night was the same. Dinner in the hotel at seven, drink in the bar at eight and off to the cabaret at nine. The band weren't bad, but they played the same songs in the same order every night. I tried to get Ma and Da to go to some of the other shows but they liked this one because they could get a late drink and Da was always called up to sing.

Gerry, the drummer, took a fancy to me. He never let on in front of Da, he'd talk to him all night about football and Chuck Berry. Da loved Chuck Berry and could answer any question Gerry threw at him.

"What did Chuck Berry train as?"

"Hairdresser."

"Where did he grow up?"

"Easy. Saint Louis, Missouri."

"Who did he give a demo to in 55?"

"Muddy Waters."

"Wrong. It was Leonard Chess."

26

"No, Chuck gave it to Muddy, Muddy gave it to Chess, who owned Chess Records. And that led to Chuck recording 'Maybellene'."

You couldn't catch Da out. All the while Gerry had his hand on me leg.

He showed up everywhere. When I'd go for a drink on the beach, he'd be there. When he sang his solo, "Summer Loving", he always looked directly at me.

We started seeing each other but he told me that we had to keep it a secret. I said I didn't care if the whole world knew about us. But, Gerry said, if the management found out the whole band would be out on their ear. He told me that if it was just him he wouldn't give a shite but Dave, the singer, had three kids to support and couldn't afford to lose this job. He was so thoughtful, always putting other people first.

One night he told me that he couldn't take it any more, we just had to be together. He wanted to wine and dine me, show me off to the world. I said no. I didn't want him losing his job because of me. Instead, we agreed that I should go to his hotel when Ma and Da were gone to bed. I thought they'd never go. Christ, Ma could put away some amount of drink. Eventually they went and, as soon as I heard Da snoring, I snuck out.

I was dressed to kill in me favourite outfit, a pink top and black skirt. I was wearing a new pair of sexy lace knickers that I'd robbed from me ma. I knocked on his door and he opened immediately –

"Hi, Tara, you know Brian and Dave?"

They smiled at me, they were lying on their beds. I turned to Gerry –

"I thought we'd be on our own?"

"Ah, don't worry about them."

Before I could protest, he kissed me.

27

"Would you like a real drink or do you always only drink shandy?"

I had a vodka, then another. Gerry was certainly eager, we were on his bed and he was kissing me between sips. "Let's get in."

I looked across at the others.

"Don't worry about them, they'll be asleep in no time."

I thought I heard a muffled laugh but Gerry said it was Dave snoring.

He went into the bathroom and came back naked. I couldn't believe it. I grabbed me drink. Gerry was pulling at his thing and every time he did this it got bigger.

"Com'on Tara, let's get to it."

I didn't like his tone –

"Ah no, I have teh go, Gerry." He grabbed me and took the glass from me hand –

"But Tara, I love you. I've never felt this way about any one before."

He was pulling at me top.

"In fact, I'm writing a song about you."

Me top was off and me bra open.

"*I can't live if living is without you, I can't give, I can't give any more . . .* "

The snores from the other side of the room got louder. I lay naked in his arms. He was on top of me, we were kissing and he was trying to enter. He handed me a condom telling me to put in on for him. I opened the packet. I'd never held one before, I didn't like the greasy feel of it. I put it on the top of his micky.

"Well, don't just leave it there, roll it all the way down."

I felt really stupid.

"Tara, is this your first time?"

"No," I lied.

He tried to enter, but I cried out in pain. He put his

28

hand between me legs and began touching me. I wanted to go to the toilet –

"I need the loo."

"In a minute," he said pushing hard against me. He was moving up and down, grunting, forcing himself inside me.

It hurt. Not as much as a few minutes before, but it still hurt.

As his movements became more frantic the covers fell off the bed. His body was shaking and I could feel his thing wriggling inside of me. I asked him did he still love me –

"Yes, yesss," he shouted as he rolled off me.

As I leaned out of the bed to retrieve the covers, he lit a cigarette, took a long hard pull and then handed it to me –

"Blimey, that was something else."

I didn't say anything, I was glad it was over.

I wrapped meself in a sheet and ran to the bathroom. As I was sitting there, I heard him cursing –

"Ah, fuck! Look at the state of the bed!"

I came out –

"Gerry, what's wrong?"

"You stupid bitch, why didn't you tell me it was that time of the month for you?"

"It's not."

"It was your first time, right? Christ, why didn't you say? The sheet is ruined."

Jasus, I was scarlet. I didn't know what to say.

"Tara, I think you better go."

I gathered me clothes and went back to the bathroom, only to discover I'd no knickers. Jasus, what was I going to do? I'd have to walk all the way back to me own hotel with no knickers, cause I was fucked if I was going to ask him to look for them.

As the door closed behind me I could hear the other two roaring laughing but Gerry wasn't seeing the joke –

"The stupid little bitch. I'll tell you, virgins aren't worth the hassle."

I never spoke to him again.

When we got home Ma missed her knickers but, I convinced her that she must have left them in the hotel.

So like I say, Slash wasn't the first.

JACKIE

Chapter Eight

The media had a field day, the day Johnser died. They were all there, the press, the TV, the radio. If it wasn't happening to me, if they weren't parked outside my door, I'd have lapped it up. I'd have been dug into the telly, listening to every news bulletin, waiting for more information.

But this wasn't about someone else, this was about me. It was real, it was all happening outside my front door. It was my wall that the photographer was sitting on. It was my family that the tabloids were interested in. And that nosy bitch in number four was loving every minute of it. Acting like we were best friends, telling anyone who was willing to listen all about me and Johnser.

The lying bitch, she knew fuck all about me or Johnser. I wanted to scream at her to shut up, to stop telling lies. If she wanted to talk about Johnser, then tell the truth. Tell them how she used to flirt with him, how she used to parade up and down the garden in her dressing-gown waiting for him to pass. How she'd use the most ridiculous excuses to try and lure him into her house –

"Howya, Johnser, yeh couldn't help me bring in this bin, could yeh?"

"Would yeh have a look at me telly, the stations are all gone off?"

"Johnser, do yeh know how teh change a plug?"

But Johnser never brought in her bin, or looked at her telly, or changed her fucking plugs, because Johnser couldn't fucking stand the stupid wagon.

But I didn't scream at her because I didn't go outside the door. I sat peeping out the curtains and feeling guilty. Guilty for all the times I'd scrutinised the fuzzy pictures taken of celebrities when they were in the privacy of their own homes. Guilty for listening to all the mindless gossip their so-called friends were always ready to spill to the highest bidder. But now, with the media parked outside my house, I had some idea about how they felt and, I swore to God that I'd never again read another tabloid, if He'd just make them go away.

Did they honestly think I was going to tell them anything? Did the fella sitting on me wall seriously think I was going to pour me heart out to him? What made him so special? He didn't know us, he didn't care about what had happened to Johnser. All he wanted was his story and his big fat pay packet at the end of the week. And there was no way I was going to talk to the police either. Who did they think they were coming around here asking me all sorts of questions –

"Did you recognise the killer?"

"What height was he?"

"Had Johnser any enemies?"

"Was Johnser involved in anything illegal?"

If they thought they were going to get anything out of me they were mistaken. They'd promised me protection and said that they'd get Johnser's killer but, I knew. I knew there was more chance of me winning the lotto than there was of them catching his killer, and the chances of me winning the lotto were very remote.

I'd never even got three on the same line. As far as I was concerned it was all a big fix. I mean, did you ever see the smirk on your man's face, "The Independent Observer" when Ronan Collins introduced him? He had a smirk that said –

"Hello, you fucking eejits, so did you all buy your tickets? Good, cause I'm here to tell you, you haven't got a hope in hell of winning!"

Then he'd look straight out of the telly into me sitting-room and whisper to me –

"And as for you, Jackie Adams née Clarke, you haven't a whore's hope in heaven of even getting three and the bonus."

But the real reason I didn't want to cooperate with the police was Johnser. I knew he wouldn't have wanted me to. I'd heard Johnser talk about fellas who'd gone to the police, fellas who were scared shitless of some bastard who'd half killed them and were only going to the police looking for protection. But that didn't wash with Johnser. As far as he was concerned, it didn't matter what happened, you just didn't go to the police. The only people who went to them were snitches, grasses and the scum of the earth. I could never understand his mentality but, out of respect for him, I was saying nothing.

Besides, his killer had looked straight into me face, letting me have a good look at him. He hadn't tried to hide behind a mask because he knew he was above the law. No one in their right mind was going to rat him up. So, the police could go and shite. Me mind was made up, I didn't care what they promised. Me kids needed a mother, not a martyr.

When they seen I wasn't going to be swayed by

promises, they tried bullying. Big mistake, I hated bullies. I remember when I was in school, Mary Nolan was the bully then. The big fat cow. You'd see her coming and scarper. If you didn't, she'd do something terrible, something one girl shouldn't do to another. Like pull your sanitary towels from your bag in front of the fellas and throw them all over the yard. The fellas would think this was great craic –

"Are yeh in yer rags?"

Jasus, I hated that. It made us sound like something out of the Dark Ages. I'm sure that's where that saying originated from. Although those thick fuckers in the school yard wouldn't have known that. And it wasn't the kind of thing you could discuss in class. It's not as though you could put your hand up in the middle of a history lesson and ask –

"Miss, does the saying 'in your rags' date back to the Victorian times or the Dark Ages?"

There were other times when that bitch Nolan would rob the girls' bras when they were in the shower after a PE class. And, as if that wasn't bad enough, she'd then give them to the fellas who thought it was great to hang them on the school railings. She was a wagon, she knew you'd have to own up to the fact that it was your bra. Cause you could hardly go home without it, could you? And if you did admit it was yours, the dirty bastards would spend the rest of the day staring at your chest. But like all bullies she got her come-uppance in the end. And from the most unlikely source.

There was a new girl who came into our year. And, as was the normal with new girls, she was to become Nolan's number one victim. Nolan broke eggs on her head and robbed her lunch money. Poor Aisling was terrified. She was tiny. They used to say that I would break in a strong breeze, but she would have broke if you blew on her. I'd

34

just started going with Johnser so Mary Nolan had finally stopped annoying me. In fact, she even asked if I wanted to be part of her gang. I thought it would be great but it wasn't. I couldn't get used to all the standing around doing nothing, except smoking and acting tough. I hated what was going on but at least it was going on with someone else now. It wasn't my bra hanging on the railings, or my towels floating around the yard any more.

Every day was the same and all the subjects were stupid. Everyone was a fucking eejit except the fellas in sixth year.

We all dressed the same – gaberdine macs, our left hand tucked in between the centre buttons, and our brogue heels click-clacking as we walked. Sister Aileen went mental. As far as she was concerned –

A mac meant you were part of a gang.

Hand tucked in made you a member of a cult.

And brogues . . . well, obviously you were a daughter of the devil.

But we didn't care. We were cool.

And the number one rule of the gang was . . . "Never look excited about anything".

I would have liked to talk to Aisling. She'd just come to our school from London. London, imagine living somewhere like that? I wanted to know all about the Queen's Palace and Harrod's and Madam Tussaud's. I'd read about these places and they seemed real exciting. But Mary Nolan said that all Brits were scum. She wrote, "Up The RA" on Aisling's schoolbag and was forever going on about what they'd done to us –

"Me da says the Brits tried teh starve us teh death."

Then one day she went too far. We cornered Aisling behind the bike shed and, as the sixth years looked on, Mary Nolan grabbed Aisling's bag and started flinging her stuff all over the place.

35

"Give it back . . ."

When Mary found Aisling's purse she no longer had any use for the bag so she threw it up on the bike-shed roof.

"I said give it back . . . there's no money in it."

Mary pushed her face up against Aisling's –

"Shut the fuck up . . . yeh English wagon . . . where's the fuckin money?"

"I told you, I don't have any money."

Jasus, I pitied her. I knew Aisling was trying her hardest not to cry.

Mary took a photo out of the purse –

"So who's the dog?"

"Give it to me."

"Not till yeh tell us who he is."

Then she laughed and holding the photo high in the air continued –

"Lookit everyone, borin aul Aisling has a boyfriend."

I didn't like where this was going –

"Com'on Mary, give it back teh her."

She turned on me –

"You butt fuckin out. Right?"

She held the photo in both hands, as if she was about to tear it in half –

"Who is he?"

I shouted at Aisling –

"Aisling, just fuckin tell her. Will yeh?"

"It's my father."

"Ah, isn't that nice. Daddy's little girl."

The sixth years laughed and Mary took that as encouragement.

"An' what does Daddy do then?"

Aisling lowered her eyes towards the ground.

"My father is dead."

The sixth years stopped laughing.

"My da says that the only good Brit is a dead Brit," Mary Nolan said as she tore the picture in half.

Before anyone could move Aisling had her on the ground and was banging her head off the bike-stand –

"Bitch, fucking bitch!"

It took three of us to pull her off Mary. And even as we did she kept on kicking her. Mary Nolan was lying on the ground, crying like a baby.

So like I say, no one was going to bully me. Not even the police.

TARA

Chapter Nine

I knew the main reason Slash was going out with me was because of me boobs. I had a nice face, good legs, but I knew me boobs were me greatest asset. And it wasn't just the fellas who were obsessed with them, it was the girls too. We were always comparing sizes. Linda used to say she'd kill for a cleavage. Mandy was a size 36A but she was always complaining that it was all in her back. Donna told her to stuff her bra with cotton wool but she said no, she wanted the real thing –

"Jasus, imagine if Baldy tried me up an got a handful of cotton wool? I'd die of shame."

"But what about Farah Fawcett?" argued Linda. "She hasn't got a tit teh her name yet all the fellas fancy her."

"Try tellin that teh Baldy. As far as he's concerned the only difference between his chest an mine is five fuckin hairs."

"Jasus, he didn't say that, did he? I wouldn't go out with anyone who said that about me," I told her.

"Yeah, but I luv him," she sighed.

So I was glad that mine were big. Although I hadn't always felt that way.

I remember going to Madam Nora's on O'Connell Street to be fitted for me first bra. Jasus, I was scarlet. All these grannies were fussing around and talking about me as if I wasn't there –

"Isn't she lovely . . . she has your eyes . . . "

"An me problem," Ma said, cupping her own diddies for emphasis. "I was only ten when I was brought in here."

"Really?" said one of the ladies.

And they were ladies, real ladies, upright and proper with their measuring tapes and soft voices.

They measured me diddies everyway imaginable. Under me arm, over me arm, up, down and all around. Eventually, three new bras later, we left the shop. Ma insisted that I carried the bag meself –

"Yeh should be proud carryin that bag, Tara. Let everyone know where yeh buy yer lingery. None of that chain-store rubbish for you, we don't want yeh looking saggy by thirty."

I hated having tits. They were reefing itchy all the time. At night I'd scratch the living daylights out of them and squeeze them till they were black and blue. But it was no good, two minutes later they'd be itching the life out of me again. Ma said it was growing pains and that one day I'd be grateful –

"That's what men like, Tara. Men like girls with big boobs."

I didn't give a shite about men or what they liked. I just wanted the itching to stop.

Da gave out shite. He said I was too young to be wearing a bra but Ma said this was a woman thing and unless he wanted to tell me all about the birds and the bees, he'd better butt out. He just looked at her and said nothing more.

What bugged me most about me new-found-figure was

that it stopped me playing girlie games. I used to be the best skipper on our road. I often wished they had skipping in the community games cause I knew that I'd have easily won the gold medal.

I was never caught out, not even in Teddy Bear, Teddy Bear. Even jumping in backwards, something no one else could do, I never faltered. I could do all the actions with me eyes closed.

"Teddy bear, teddy bear, touch the ground,
Teddy bear, teddy bear, twirl around,
Teddy bear, teddy bear, show off your shoe,
Teddy bear, teddy bear, that will do.
Teddy bear, teddy bear, run up the stairs,
Teddy bear, teddy bear, say your prayers,
Teddy bear, teddy bear, switch off the light,
Teddy bear, teddy bear, say goodnight, goodnight."

So I stopped playing skipping. Not because I wanted to, but because suddenly skipping became more interesting to the fellas than football and they all stood watching as we played. I knew the reason they wanted to watch had nothing to do with admiration, it had to do with me diddies bouncing up and down. No one ever said anything, they weren't that brave but I stopped anyway.

Ma said I was stupid and that I shouldn't be minding them. But it wasn't her they were gawking at. I stopped playing with the girls on me road. I wouldn't go out and when they called for me, I told them that skipping was for kids.

I discovered make-up and, spent all me time sitting at Ma's dressing-table trying to perfect the art of application. I'd plaster me face with Max Factor foundation, Mary Quant eye-shadow and lipstick, only to scrub the lot off again using her Anne French cleanser. I had no idea how much cosmetics cost. And when I'd finished with me face, I headed for her wardrobe. Opening Ma's wardrobe was like walking into a Mirror Mirror boutique, it had everything. Jumpers, skirts, blouses, trousers, cardigans, dresses, suits and any amount of shoes and boots. I tried everything on, even the clothes I knew wouldn't suit or fit me. I soon learned what colours best suited me hair and what styles best suited me figure.

Finally the day came when I was ready to face the public (the public being Ma). I had me face made up to perfection and was wearing a long straight wine skirt with a pink ribbed jumper. All from Ma's wardrobe of course.

I braved the thirteen stairs in me wedged heels and, taking a deep breath, strolled into the kitchen. Ma done a double-take when she seen me –

"Tara . . . "

"Well, Ma, what deh yeh think?"

"So that's where all me make-up's goin, I was beginnin teh think yer father was wearing it."

"Ah Ma, stop. Seriously, do I look alright?"

"Yeh look lovely, Tara."

"So does that mean I can wear these clothes teh deh dance on Saturday night?"

"Yeah. But, just make sure yer father sees yeh before yeh put yer make-up on."

That Saturday night I went to the disco. It was great. I felt like the new girl in town. Fellas who wouldn't have even looked at me a few months ago were now asking me to dance. I felt the gear. And for the first time I realised how lucky I was to have big tits.

JACKIE

Chapter Ten

The night Johnser was shot was one of the longest nights of me life.

I wanted to lie down and sleep. But how could I? How could I possibly sleep when the man I loved with all me heart had just been blown to bits in me sitting-room?

Besides, there was so much to do, so many people to talk to, so many questions to answer, so much tea to drink.

Me mind drifted back to the last time I'd drunk this much tea. It was the night Johnser had rescued me from that bastard Robert who'd tried to rape me outside the disco. God, I used to think that was the worst night of me life. But, compared to this it was nothing. And besides, what happened with Robert that night was what finally brought me and Johnser together . . .

"Jackie, Jackie . . . "

Someone was talking to me but I didn't want to listen. I wanted to think about Johnser.

"Jackie, Jackie . . . "

I looked up, it was Ann. She was saying something about me having to leave the house. I didn't want to leave me house, this was me and Johnser's home. I couldn't leave. I sat staring at the kitchen wall, remembering back to the day he'd arrived home with the new wallpaper. Jasus, I'd nearly gone mad when he'd told me it had cost nine ninety-nine a roll. Did he not realise that would be nearly a hundred quid just to paper the kitchen, and what about paint? That would be at least another thirty quid. God, I could've paid the ESB and phone for two months with that money. But Johnser was having none of it, sure hadn't he already organised two fellas to do the job. I tried to convince him that we could do the decorating ourselves but he said no. He hadn't spent that money on wallpaper just so as he could make a pig's ear of it. So eventually I agreed and when it was done I was delighted. It looked lovely, worth every penny. Even the clock on the wall reminded me of Johnser, he'd brought the kids shopping to buy me a Mother's Day present and that's what they'd come home with. It was an awful-looking thing but, I couldn't tell them that. I had to pretend it was just what I'd wanted. And the carpet in the hall, that had been another big event. We'd managed to bargain the knackers down from a hundred and forty quid to seventy-five. We were delighted with ourselves. That was until we opened it out and discovered that the pattern on the edges wasn't the same as the one in the centre.

This house was full of memories. Every room had a tale to tell, even the bathroom. I remembered the time I'd come home from work and found Johnser up to his ankles in water. Edward had left the taps running in the bath and flooded the place. Johnser didn't want him getting into trouble so he'd tried to clean it up before I seen it.

I had to get out of the kitchen. There was too much noise, too many voices all talking at once. I stood up.

"Jackie, are you all right? Where are you going?"

"To the toilet."

I went upstairs and into the kid's room. I stood looking at the posters on the walls. Johnser had bought most of them. My Johnser had bought almost everything in this house, how could they expect me to leave? I wanted to lock meself away from them all. Just me and me boys and me memories.

I froze. Where were me boys? I hadn't seen them downstairs. Who had them? What had they done with me boys?

I ran back to the kitchen –

"Where are me babies? What have yous done with me babies?"

"Jackie, Jackie, calm down. The boys are at my house. They're alright, remember? Tommy brought them over teh our house after . . . "

"After what, Ann? After someone came inteh me fuckin house an shot Johnser. Why don't yeh say what yeh mean, Ann?"

A policewoman put her arm around me shoulder –

"Com'on, Jackie. Sit down and have a cup of tea. The boys are fine, your friend's husband is looking after them. You can go and see them whenever you like."

"I don't want teh go an see them. I want them here."

"I don't think that's a good idea . . . "

"I want me boys . . . here . . . in this house . . . with me."

The policewoman persisted –

"Now listen, Jackie. Listen carefully. You can't bring the boys back here, it wouldn't be fair. What with all the reporters outside and the police coming and going. And what about the mess? You wouldn't like them to see that, now would you?"

"She's right, Jackie. It wouldn't be fair." Ann said holding me hand. "Why don't yeh pack a few things and come an stay with us for a few days? Just till we get this place sorted out. What deh yeh say?"

I glanced towards the sitting-room. She was right, it was a mess. I couldn't bring the boys back here. I went upstairs and packed a bag.

I stood in Ann's hall. The boys had come down the stairs like a hurricane the minute she'd opened the door. We stood hugging each other as though our lives depended on it. Tommy stood looking on. I half-expected him to say something smart but he didn't. He asked quietly –

"You OK, Jackie?"

I just nodded, I couldn't trust meself to speak. Ann took me bag –

"I told Jackie her an the kids could stay here for a few days."

"Yeah, sure. Yeh know yer welcome teh stay as long as yeh like." Tommy smiled.

The kids clung to me like leeches. They wouldn't let me out of their sight for a minute. Once when I came out of the bathroom, I found Edward sitting on the landing sucking his thumb. Something he hadn't done in years. I sat down and put me arms around him –

"Com'on luv, yeh don't have teh worry, Mammy's not goin anywhere."

45

The floodgates opened and he sobbed his little heart out.

That night after I'd put the kids to bed, I sat with Ann and Tommy drinking vodka and reliving the events of the previous night –

"They say that they have teh have a post-mortem teh establish the cause of death. It doesn't take a fuckin state pathologist teh tell me the cause of my Johnser's death. He was shot twice in the head, at close range. Who gives a fuck whether it was the first or second bullet that killed him? He's dead, shot by a fuckin madman an all the pathologists in the world won't bring him back."

They tried to change the subject. Ann started talking about the supervisor at work but I didn't want to hear about her. I wanted to talk about Johnser.

"Thank God the kids were in bed. Imagine if they'd seen what happened," Ann said trying to humour me.

"But maybe the killer was a family man. Maybe if he'd seen the kids he wouldn't have shot Johnser."

I knew I sounded pathetic but I couldn't help it. I also knew deep down in me heart that nothing would have saved Johnser. After all, the gunman must have gone to a lot of bother to track him down. I hadn't expected Johnser home for another two hours. So, how could the gunman have known he'd be there unless he'd followed him all day? It was obvious he'd wanted Johnser to die at home. If he'd wanted to, he could have shot him anywhere. Cornered him in a pub carpark, dragged him down an alleyway or even bundled him into a car and brought him up the Dublin mountains.

But no, he decided to do it in the house. Just walked in, no mask, no hiding, and shot him in front of me. Sure the kids may as well have been sitting watching the telly, it wouldn't have made any difference.

Tommy gave up, his eyes were closing and he had work in the morning. Work. Christ, I hadn't even thought about me job. I knew I'd have to contact them. Ann must have read me mind –

"Don't worry about work, I'll ring in for both of us in deh mornin."

"Jasus, Ann, yeh can't be takin time off cause of me."

"Course I can. Sure it's ages since I took a sick day an anyway, I'm due a few days' holidays."

She was a brutal liar. I knew she'd used up all her holliers and she couldn't afford to be taking time off – none of us done the cleaning for the love of it. But I didn't argue. She was a good friend and I needed her to be here with me. It was selfish, I know, but I couldn't help it.

Eventually Ann had to go to bed. But, I didn't mind I still had half a bottle of vodka. Vodka had been a good friend to me in the past. It had got me through the last time when I couldn't have Johnser and it looked like it was going to do the same again.

* * *

I was standing in the kitchen ironing when he walked in –

"Jasus, Johnser. what are yeh doin here?"

He answered while he spread jam onto a piece of bread –

"What deh yeh mean, doin here? I live here, remember?" He was laughing as he stuffed the sandwich into his mouth.

"But, Johnser. Yeh were shot . . . The doctor said yeh . . . "

47

As he made his way down the hallway, he looked back over his shoulder –

"Yeh wouldn't wanna believe them doctors, luv."

I woke with a start. It had all been a dream, a wonderful wonderful dream.

TARA

Chapter Eleven

There were a number of different reasons why me and Johnser got together. It wasn't only because I hated Jackie Clarke.

Da had started talking about some young fella who was the apple of the Brush's eye. Ma hit the roof. Why was Da allowing some young fella to come in and take over, after all the hard work me da had put in over the years? Da said it wasn't like that, that the new fella was no threat to him, he was just some kid that Brush was fond of. But I could tell he wasn't convinced. You can imagine me surprise when I heard that this new kid was Johnser. So, Johnser Kiely had become a member of a real gang, the crafty little fucker. Christ, and he never said a word, told nobody, not even Slash. From that day on Johnser Kiely went up in me estimation. I mean to say, he wasn't just another spotty teenager trying to make himself sound important in the hope that he might get into some young one's knickers. No, he was different, he was a man. A man who knew where he was going.

I began to see him in a completely different light. All his standing around and saying nothing wasn't because he was as thick as two planks, it was because he had a secret. And now I knew that secret too, but I said nothing. I figured that if Johnser was moving on, maybe it was time I thought about doing the same.

I was getting bored with Slash, he couldn't piss without the rest of the gang. We couldn't even go to the pictures unless his mates wanted to go and because they'd seen all the Kung Fu films, they said that going to the pictures was crap. I wasn't particularly mad into the pictures meself but it would have made a nice change every once in a while. I mean to say, if I had to choose between *Star Wars* and wet grass, *Star Wars* would have won every time. But no, Slash couldn't make a decision without asking his mates first. With the result we never went anywhere.

Leanne was always telling me about the disco bars and nightclubs she went to at the weekend and it all sounded very exciting. Meanwhile what was I doing? I was sitting in wet grass sharing cigarettes and cans of warm beer. And, if I was lucky, I might get to see Fat Larry's shrivelled-up micky when Froggy pulled his towel off. I was nearly qualified as a hairdresser and wanted something more out of life.

I started going out with Leanne and it was great. The hairdresser lot were all posers but they were good craic. We went to different places and drank different drinks. Christ, I used to think that cans of Harp and bottles of cheap cider were the only drinks on the market.

For two weeks I didn't go near Slash or the rest of the gang. I went instead to every disco bar and nightclub in Dublin and danced with every Tom, Dick and Harry who asked. Gloria Gaynor's "I Will Survive" became me anthem. The world was me oyster.

Then one night when no one from me "new set" was going out I decided I might as well go up and see Slash. I met them outside Quinnsworth. Nothing had changed. We gave Johnser our money and he went in and got the drink. Even though we could have got served ourselves, we couldn't break the habit of a lifetime, could we? Anyway, Johnser came out and handed the bags to Froggy and Fat Larry who carried them down to the canal. When we got to our bridge, Johnser distributed the drink, lit the first cigarette and then passed it around. First Slash, then Jackie, then me. And when Fat Larry got back from collecting the firewood, he was given the butt. Once the fire got going the slagging started –

"Well fatso, what d'yeh have for brekkie?"

Christ, how pathetic. Then they started on Froggy about never having a girlfriend –

"So Froggy, d'yeh have a wank before yeh came out?"

Froggy's answer was always the same –

"No, I'm callin round teh yer aul one later. She said she'd do it for me."

And when they got bored with each other, they started on us girls.

If one of us went to the toilet they'd shout –

"Hey, did yeh wet yer hair?"

Fucking comedians, the lot of them. On this particular night when they started, I freaked.

Johnser had handed out the drink. Harp for the girls and cider for the fellas. I was sick of it –

"Why'd fuck d'yeh get me Harp?"

"Cause yeh drink it."

"An say I wanna change?"

"But yous girls only drink Harp."

"Says who? Who fuckin says that us girls only drink Harp? D'yeh not think that maybe we might like a change?"

"Sometimes we do get different beer."

"Yeah, only when it's some fuckin cheapo brand. How com'yeh never get Heineken or somethin like that?"

51

Slash looked at me like I'd two heads –

"It's dearer."

"I'd pay deh fuckin difference."

I looked over at Johnser –

"An how come you always do deh shoppin, eh?"

"If *you* wanna do deh shoppin be me guest."

He wasn't getting off that lightly –

"An why do deh others always have teh carry deh bags? Are you too high an fuckin mighty teh be seen carryin a bag in public? An tell me somethin else, how come yeh always get first drag of the cigarette?"

Johnser was getting annoyed –

"Wha'deh fuck's up with you, yeh stupid cunt? If yeh want yer own cigarettes I'll fuckin give yeh them."

He grabbed me head and stuffed a packet of cigarettes into me mouth –

"Now, now yeh have yer own cigarettes. Are yeh happy now?"

He pushed me so hard that I fell off the log I'd been sitting on. I looked at Slash –

"Are yeh gonna let him away with that?"

Slash reached over and pulled me up –

"Will yeh give it up, yeh stupid wagon. What's wrong with yeh, are yeh in yer rags or what?"

I pushed his hand away and walked off.

Why did they always have to say that? Why did men always think you were in your rags just because you had an opinion that was different to theirs? It really annoyed me.

Well, they could all fuck off, especially the girls. They should have supported me but they didn't. They stayed with their fellas instead.

JACKIE

Chapter Twelve

What was I going to tell Ma and Da?

They hadn't known Johnser, they'd only met him once or twice and that was only in passing. So how was I going to explain to them that he'd been shot in me sitting-room? For fuck sake, I still hadn't told them we'd been living together.

When we'd been together as teenagers, I'd never brought him home to meet them. Johnser wasn't exactly what Ma and Da had in mind for their only daughter. He looked rough. He was the type of fella Da would cross the road to avoid. The type he'd threaten with the guards if he stopped outside our gate for more than ten seconds. And there was no point in trying to convince them that Johnser was a nice fella because as Da would say –

"I know his sort."

The main reason I never told them about Johnser back then was I knew they'd want me to bring him home to meet them and no teenager wants to do that. Besides, knowing Johnser, he'd never have agreed and even if by some miracle he had, I'd have been a bundle of nerves for days and, whenever I got nervous, me stomach would act up and I'd spend the day on the toilet.

Johnser would probably have said the wrong thing, not on purpose, it was just that he had a habit of always saying things he wasn't supposed to. I could just picture me da asking him what he thought about James Bond and Johnser would say –

"No, I don't like him. He's shite."

And that would have been the end of Johnser's visit. He'd have been shown the door and I'd have been carted off to the nearest home for wayward girls.

And if Da didn't ask Johnser about James Bond, he'd ask him about his family –

"What's your surname?"

"What do you do for a living?"

"What does your father do for a living?"

If you asked Johnser questions about his family he immediately became defensive and told you to –

"Fuck off, an mind your own business."

I could imagine Da's reaction. The whole thing would have been a nightmare. So in order to avoid all this, I never invited Johnser home to meet them. In fact, I never mentioned him at all.

Eventually we split up and I married Jeffrey. So, that was the end of that.

And when Johnser re-entered me life, I still didn't tell them too much about him. I mean what was I supposed to say?

"Da, this is Johnser . . . no, you haven't met him before . . . because he's been in prison for the last eight years . . ."

We all know what would have happened then.

So I always made sure that Johnser was going to be out before I invited them around. At first this wasn't a problem as Johnser only stayed with me the odd night. And when we moved into the new house I still didn't tell them. Because, me being me, I hoped that with them still living in Kimmage and us living in Clondalkin, they'd never find out.

The kids loved having Johnser around and why wouldn't they? He spoiled them rotten. They were always talking about him so I'm sure they must have mentioned him to Ma, because she still minded them while I was at work. But, Ma being Ma, she never said anything. Jasus, whoever coined the phrase "like mother, like daughter" must have had us in mind.

I hated the whole situation, all this cloak and dagger stuff. Praying that Johnser would be out of the house by eleven and not back before seven. Making sure that there was nothing belonging to him in the bathroom, no shoes under the couch, no jackets left on the back of chairs and no bookies' slips behind the clock on the mantelpiece. Needless to say I always missed something. I remember the day Da came back from the toilet with a disposable razor in his hand –

"Has Jonathan started to shave, Jackie?"

"No he hasn't. That's for me legs."

"I thought you women had cream for that kind of thing?"

"Yeah, we have, but that takes too long and besides, it's too expensive. The razors are much cheaper and quicker." Why I hadn't just told them the truth I don't know. I mean, it would have made life so much easier not having to be continually on me guard while they were there and worrying in case Johnser decided to come home early. But I hadn't. I'd kept putting off telling them until another day. And now with Ma and Da standing in Ann's kitchen, I knew that day had arrived.

"Well girl, what have you to say for yourself?"

I started to cry. Ma put her arm around me –

"Jackie love, it's OK."

"It's not fucking OK." I'd never heard Da curse before.

"It's far from OK. I want to know exactly what it is you're involved in. Do you hear me?"

I took the tissue Ma offered –

"I'm not involved in anythin . . . "

Da gripped the table –

"Oh, I see. So you're telling me that this . . . man . . . who was blown to smithereens in your sitting-room had nothing to do with you? That you didn't know him? Isn't it bad enough that your mother and me are going to be the talk of our neighbourhood without you telling us lie after lie?"

I couldn't even answer, I was crying that much.

"And you can forget about your whinging, that won't work on me."

"Peter, please!" Ma whispered. "Let her be."

"No, woman, I won't. You've mollycoddled this one for far too long. I've no intentions of leaving here until I get some answers."

So I told them all about Johnser. How he'd spent eight years in prison for robbery. Da said that was a long sentence for robbery. So, I had to tell them about the two old people who'd died during the robbery. And even though Johnser hadn't killed them, he still got the blame. I told them about his nightclub business, about him selling drugs, but that he never sold them while he was with me. I knew I was wasting me breath, I could tell by their faces that they

56

didn't believe a word I was saying. When finally I'd finished, they said nothing, just stood staring blankly at me.

"I swear, that's it."

"What do you mean, that's it? Christ Almighty, Jackie, have you no consideration for anyone other than yourself? Did you not think about the effect that madman would have on your children? Did you not consider your mother and me in all of this? By God, Jackie Clarke, I never thought I'd hear meself say this, but I'm ashamed to call you me daughter." He turned to Ma. "Com'on Betty, I've heard enough lies for one day."

As he marched towards the front door Ma took me by the arm –

"Jackie, give him time. Your father's upset. This has been a big shock to us, it's hard to take it all in."

I'd had enough –

"A shock for you! An how the fuck deh yeh think I feel?"

Da swung around –

"Don't you dare curse at your mother like that. It's easy knowing the kind of company you've been keeping. You're not fit to rear children!"

"Get the fuck outta here, deh yeh hear me? Get out! How dare yeh say I'm not a fit mother. I may not be the perfect daughter but don't dare tell me I'm not a good mother . . . don't yeh fuckin dare."

I couldn't stop crying. Ma hugged me, pulling me close to her like she used to do when I was a little girl. But I wasn't having any of it –

"Just leave me, Ma, please, just go."

She brushed me hair back off me face –

"Jackie, Jackie shush, love. Listen, listen to me. I'll stay with you for a few days and we'll sort everything out together . . . "

"No, Ma. I'm grand, honestly, I'm grand . . . "

"Jackie, you're not grand . . . "

"Ma . . . "

"OK, OK. But if you change your mind, well . . . you know where I am."

TARA

Chapter Thirteen

As I was leaving work one Thursday night, I noticed a big fancy car coming towards me but I didn't pay it too much attention. I was too busy feeling sorry for meself. I hated Thursdays because I had to work late and me feet were hanging off from having to stand all day. I swore that if I got varicose veins I'd sue Marcus.

"Hey, Tara. Want a lift?"

I nearly jumped out of me skin –

"Fuck yeh, Johnser. Yeh nearly frightened the life outta me. What are yeh doin in a Saab?"

"Jasus, Tara. Keep yer voice down an get in."

I jumped in and sank into the soft leather seat –

"Very nice, Johnser. Where'd yeh get it?"

"College Green. I was walking past the bank and this suit jumped out to go to the night safe. So I thought to meself, I fancy a drive in that an here I am."

I laughed –

"Jasus, Johnser. Yer fuckin mad."

He smiled, looking very pleased with himself.

"So, are yeh goin straight home or deh yeh fancy cruisin for a while?"

"No, we'll cruise. But, I'll have teh take me shoes off cause me feet are killin me."

He waved his hand in front of his nose as if trying to get rid of a bad smell.

"Fuck off, Kiely. Me feet don't smell."

He put the car into gear and screeched off down the road.

"What music have yeh got?"

"I don't know. Have a look in the glove compartment."

I looked inside –

"Ah, for fuck sake. Chris De bleedin Burgh an some aul fella called Verdi!"

"I'm so sorry, Tara. In future I'll only rob cars whose owners like Status Quo an Queen."

I turned on the radio and tuned into Radio Dublin. The DJs were crap but at least they played decent music. I sang along to the song that was playing –

"Yeh ain't seen nothin yet. I said, baby yeh just ain't seen nothin yet . . . "

I was having a great time until I spotted the squad car –

"Oh Jasus, Johnser. What'll we do?"

"Don't worry. They'll never catch us in that heap of junk."

He took off like a bat out of hell. The squad car gave chase. I was getting nervous. Suddenly, there were two squad cars and they were coming straight for us. Johnser put his foot down on the accelerator. I screamed –

"Jasus, Johnser. What deh fuck are yeh doin?"

"Playin chicken . . . "

He drove straight at the police. I could see the look on the guards' faces, they couldn't believe what he was doing, that he wasn't going to back down. The music was blaring and I was screaming about how I was too young to die. At the last minute the guard who was driving spun the steering wheel to the right. The squad car screeched to a halt on the footpath, inches from the playground railings.

As Johnser sped off I turned on him –

"Fuck yeh, Johnser Kiely. What deh hell deh yeh think yer doin? Yeh could of fuckin killed us. Yeh mad bastard!"

The second squad car was still giving chase.

We drove down Le Fanu road and across the canal bridge, heading towards the Naas road. Once we got to the dual carriageway we lost the police. He headed out to Tallaght, taking corners so tight that I'm sure he cut the grass on the edges. He continued driving like a maniac all the way up the old Blessington road until we reached the lakes, where he finally stopped the car.

We sat in silence for what seemed like an eternity. Eventually, he broke the silence –

"I love it up here."

"Deh yeh really?"

"Yeah. It's real peaceful. Yeh can really get yer head together up here."

"Well, it obviously doesn't do yeh any good."

"What deh yeh mean?" He looked puzzled.

"Johnser! Have yeh forgotten what just happened back there? Yeh nearly fuckin killed us. Now, maybe I'm wrong, but yeh didn't strike me as someone who had his head together. And there was nothin peaceful about deh way yeh drove up that fuckin bendy road."

He laughed and, leaning towards me said –

"Well now, Tara. Maybe yeh could make me feel peaceful?"

I moved closer –

"Did yeh ever bring Jackie Clarke up here?"

"No. I always com'up on me own."

He pulled me towards him and we kissed.

His hand was on me tit, mine was on his zip. I could feel

61

him getting aroused. He opened me blouse and pushed me bra up, his hands felt cold against me bare tits. I unzipped his jeans and his micky popped out. I nearly laughed, it reminded me of a Jack in the Box, the way it sprung up. I squeezed and his breathing grew heavier, his hands tightened on me tits.

"Let's get into the back."

He didn't need to be asked twice. We struggled to get out of our clothes. The Saab might look like a Love Machine but it definitely wasn't built for action. However, despite the delay, Johnser lost none of his enthusiasm. We kissed again, then he was on top of me, trying to enter. He wasn't managing very well. I reached down and taking him in me hand, directed him towards the spot. It didn't last very long. One, two, three . . . and it was over. We got dressed, smoked nearly a full packet of cigarettes then drove home.

He hadn't said it was all off between him and Jackie, but, he hadn't said it was all on either. So, I figured the only way I was going to find out if she was still on the scene was to take a trip down to the naller.

JACKIE

Chapter Fourteen

I knew the minute I came down the stairs that morning that there was something wrong. Ann was being unusually quiet and Tommy scuttled out of the kitchen the minute I walked in. I felt uncomfortable –

"Ann, what's wrong?"

"Nothin, Jackie. I'm just a bit tired, that's all."

I didn't believe her –

"Ann, I'm not fuckin stupid, I know there's somethin wrong. Is it me? Have I worn out me welcome? Does Tommy want us teh go?"

"Don't be stupid, Jackie. It's nothin like that, I swear. I'm just a bit tired, I didn't sleep very well. I got me period in the middle of the night an yeh know how I suffer with cramps. I had Tommy walkin the streets at half six this mornin lookin for tablets an he's still fuckin moanin about it. I swear he thinks I do it on purpose."

"Oh, I see. Well now that I'm up why don't yeh go back teh bed for an hour? I'll tidy around an get the kids their brekkie?"

"Go'way outta that. I'm grand now, honest."

I asked Ann where the morning paper was and she

mumbled something about Tommy and the crossword. I immediately became suspicious – there was definitely something wrong. Tommy never did crossword puzzles, he hated them. I wasn't a big fan of crosswords meself, I was more into the problem page. I loved reading about other people's misery, it helped to take me mind off me own. But, Jasus, some of the letters she got were mad –

"*Dear Diana,*

My husband and I have a great sex life but recently I came home to find him wearing my bra and knickers. What should I do?"

I would have loved her to have replied –

"*Dear Reader, I think you should go on a diet. Cause, if your undies fit your husband you must be too fat.*"

But needless to say she never did. She usually advised the reader to confront her husband and try to get to the root of the problem.

Jasus, I'd have died if I'd come home and found Johnser wearing me knickers.

Johnser, Johnser, Johnser. I just couldn't stop thinking about him. As I watched Ann getting Tommy's breakfast, I thought of him. Johnser never ate a breakfast. His breakfast consisted of a cigarette and a cup of tea. In the evening, when Tommy left the house at ten o'clock to go for a pint, I thought about Johnser – if he was going for a pint he'd have been gone by eight. He never seen the point in getting all dressed up to go out for the last hour. As far as he was concerned, it was a waste of aftershave.

Anyway, I cornered Tommy and asked him for the paper. He looked at Ann.

"What's wrong, Tommy?" I asked.

He directed his answer at Ann –

"She's gonna find out sooner or later . . . "

"Find out what?"

Ann sighed, walked over to the couch and, lifting the cushion produced the morning paper –

"It's a stupid article, I wou . . . "

I grabbed the paper. I couldn't believe the headline –

"MURDERED DRUG BARON'S WIFE OPENS HER HEART."

As I read the article I could feel the blood drain from me body. How could she? How could Tara do this to me? And more to the point, why? What had she to gain by telling these lies?

She'd given a four-page interview. Telling how Johnser had been having an affair, and how she'd only just recently found out about it. How devastated she'd been at first but once she'd got over the initial hurt she'd been prepared to give Johnser another chance, because no matter what he'd done, she just couldn't stop loving him. Besides, children needed a father.

She admitted that, yes, Johnser had been an active drug dealer, and no she didn't agree with drugs. But, she'd done everything in her power to try and convince him to give it up.

How could she say these things? It was all lies. How could she say that her and Johnser had been happily married? They'd never even lived together. He'd gone to prison straight after the honeymoon. And by the time he'd come out, they were finished.

The fucking cheek of her, trying to maintain that I'd only been some bit on the side. And the apartment she'd been photographed in, that wasn't their love nest. It was her fucking alimony.

And why was she saying that Johnser was still a drug dealer? She knew he'd given all that up a long time ago. He'd given it up because he'd wanted to be with me. So why was she blaming me for trying to wreck her marriage?

Telling how I'd visited him every week in prison. And, how I'd tried to lure him away when he got out. She even suggested that the only reason Johnser had the affair with me was because he needed somewhere to keep his drugs. They'd even printed a photograph of me house. I'll fucking kill her. How dare that bitch suggest that I'd allow drugs into me house! The lying little cunt.

I finished the article and sat staring blankly into the fire. I couldn't speak.

"Don't mind them, Jackie. It's a load of rubbish. Sure nobody ever believes a word they print in them rags."

But that was it, it had been printed. And people would read it. People loved reading about crime in Ireland. And, they'd believe her story, because people always believed the Poor-Little-Wife. And they'd all say –

"Jasus, that Jackie Clarke one is a right little wagon."

Suddenly a thought struck me. Maybe she wasn't lying. Maybe what she was saying was true. Maybe Johnser had been the liar?

I began thinking back to all the nights when he'd had to go out unexpectedly. He never went into detail about where he was going, he'd just say it had something to do with work. Sometimes he wouldn't come back till morning, and he never needed to catch up on the sleep he'd missed. How did I know he hadn't been dealing drugs? Just because he'd told me he'd given it all up didn't make it true. And what about Tara? What proof had I that he wasn't still seeing her? None. Because I wasn't with him when he went out. No, I was at home playing happy families.

"Here, Jackie." Ann handed me a drink.

I read the article again. When I'd finished I poured meself another drink, knocked it back and poured another.

What was Tara talking about when she said that Johnser had kept drugs in me house? Did she think I was stupid?

That I wouldn't notice if someone was stashing little parcels of drugs in me house? I mean where would he hide them? Despite what she might think, I did clean the place from time to time. I would have seen something, wouldn't I? Unless . . . the garden . . .

I jumped up.

"Jackie, what's wrong? Where are yeh goin?"

I didn't answer. I opened the door and went out onto the street.

"Jackie, come back . . . put a coat on . . . you'll freeze!"

I ran towards me own house. A camera man came towards me but, I pushed him away –

"Fuck off, yeh bastard."

I took the key out of me pocket and let meself in. I walked straight through the kitchen, opened the back door and went out into the garden. I found a shovel and started digging. The ground was hard but, I didn't care.

Suddenly, I was exhausted. I fell to me knees. What was I doing here? I knew there were no drugs, I knew Johnser hadn't been living a double life. Why was I letting that bitch, Tara Coyle, get to me? How could I have been so stupid as to doubt Johnser? My Johnser. "Well, fuck yeh, Tara Coyle. Yeh rotten cunt. May yeh never have a minute's happiness in yer poxy life."

TARA

Chapter Fifteen

On Friday night I went down to the naller. I knew the minute I arrived that Johnser and Clarkie were still an item. But, fuck it, I could wait.

Slash was delighted I was back, he was all over me like a bad rash. Not that I minded, I was loving every minute of it. I was watching Johnser on the sly and, when I knew he was looking, I'd start wearing the face off Slash. I wanted to make Johnser jealous, wanted him to remember the night before, when we'd been together.

Eventually, him and Clarkie headed off to the long grass, and me and Slash snuggled up by the fire. The rest of the gang had gone to get chips, so we had the place to ourselves for a while.

I was sitting staring into the fire listening to the muffled voices of the other two, they sounded like they were having a row. I looked at Slash –

"Jasus, do them two ever stop fightin?"

"Mmm . . . "

He was trying to get his hand up me bra and didn't really care what Johnser and Clarkie were doing.

"Well," I continued, "for a couple who're supposed teh be in love, they don't seem teh get on very well."

I gave up. He wasn't listening to me. He was more interested in trying to get me bra off.

The others were coming back. I could hear Froggy shouting –

"Com'ere yeh big fat pig. I'm gonna fuckin . . . "

Fat Larry came running out of the bushes and tripped over Slash's legs. Slash nearly jumped out of his skin. He'd been so engrossed in me tits that he'd forgotten where he was –

"What deh fuck . . . gerroff, yeh fat fucker." He jumped up grabbed Fat Larry and, giving him a kick up the arse shouted –

"Watch where yer goin, yeh dozy fuckin bollox."

Slash sat back down and put his arm around me but the moment was lost. Jasus, they were a shower of fucking eejits.

I'd just told Slash that I was going home when Jackie Clarke went running past, screaming at Johnser over her shoulder –

"Yer only a fuckin bollox, Johnser Kiely."

Jasus, I thought. This was turning into some night.

A few minutes later Johnser emerged, rubbing his balls. He sat down at the fire –

"Any drink left?"

"Here." Slash threw him a can.

He opened the can and sat staring into the fire. No one spoke. Fat Larry and Froggy started giggling. Johnser looked at them –

"Wha'are yous two fuckin eejits laughin at?"

"Nuttin Johnser," they said in unison.

Johnser stared at the flames for a few minutes –

"Ah, fuck this. I'm off." He stood up, kicked the can into the air and walked off.

I jumped to me feet –

"Here, Johnser. Hold on an I'll walk with yeh."

Slash made as if to follow us but changed his mind. Typical, I thought, he'd rather stay with his mates.

When we got to the shops I pulled him down an alleyway and gave him his first blow-job.

* * *

Johnser couldn't get enough of me, we had sex every night for a week. It was great, I didn't think life could get any better. But, it did. One night while we were standing at the corner of the shops, a bus went past. I don't know what made me look up but, I did. And lo an behold, there was Jackie Clarke sitting in the front seat all dressed up to the nines. She was staring at me, I smiled back. Poor bitch. Had she really thought that Johnser was going to sit around waiting for her to come back? At that minute Johnser put his arm around me. I smiled up into his face and he kissed me. She didn't get off the bus.

That's right, Jackie, I thought. Keep goin, yer not wanted here any more.

JACKIE

Chapter Sixteen

I went to the hospital to sign the papers for the release of Johnser's body. They'd done their post mortem. Opened him up and had a good look inside. Talked into their fucking dictaphone about haemorrhaging, loss of blood, loss of tissue . . . loss of fucking face. And, now that there was nothing left to poke at, they no longer had any use for him.

I asked the receptionist if I could see the body and, she scuttled off to ask one of her superiors. Ann had come with me but we didn't speak. We sat in silence waiting for the receptionist to come back. Ann hadn't wanted me to come here. She thought I should wait until the body had been embalmed before I saw it. But, I couldn't wait. I had to see him, I wanted to spend time alone with him, to comfort him, to hold him. I wanted to tell him how sorry I was for having doubted him, for allowing that bitch, Tara Coyle, to cloud me judgement of him. I wanted to say goodbye.

I was starting to get irritable. We'd been waiting for what seemed like hours and the receptionist still hadn't come back. Ann obviously felt the same, she jumped up –

"Ah, here. I've had enough of this."

She stormed over to the office –

"Scuse me. But, we've been sittin here for the last hour

waitin teh see a body. Surely teh Jasus, it doesn't take that long teh find a bleedin corpse. I mean teh say, it can't have gone very far!"

She didn't wait for an answer, just turned on her heel and walked back to me. Her outburst seemed to do the trick, because five minutes later an older-looking man, wearing a grey suit came through the swing doors –

"Ms Clarke?" he inquired in a whisper.

"Yes."

"Well, Ms Clarke. I'm sorry to have kept you waiting but we've been trying to locate the body of Mr Kiely. Unfortunately, he's no longer with us. His body was released at nine this morning."

"What deh yeh mean he's been released? I didn't give anyone permission teh take Johnser's body anywhere!"

He looked sympathetic –

"It was his wife – Mrs Kiely – who gave the instructions for the removal."

I turned and walked out. I could hear Ann asking him questions but I wasn't interested in his answers. Me legs were like rubber, I felt so weak. I leaned against the wall, its roughness cut into me face but I didn't care. I needed this pain, anything to keep me from fainting.

I opened me bag and took out me cigarettes. The pack was empty –

"Fuck, fuck, fuck," I shouted as I trampled the empty packet into the ground.

An old couple frowned as they tried to sidle past me. They probably thought I was a drug-addict or something. But fuck them. I didn't give a shite what they thought. Ann came rushing out –

"Yeh OK, Jackie?"

"Giv'us a smoke, Ann."

She took out two cigarettes, lit them both and handing me one said –

"I know what funeral home she used. We can go up there now if yeh like?"

"What I want teh do now is teh go for a stiff drink."

"For fuck sake, Jackie. It's only a quarter to twelve."

"No one's askin yeh teh come, Ann. In fact, I'd rather yeh didn't. I need a bit of space."

I marched off down the road, not bothering to wait for her answer.

I went into the first pub I met and ordered a large vodka and orange. The barman looked at me but, said nothing. I took me drink and made me way towards the little snug at the side of the bar. I'd forgotten to get cigarettes. So, I went back to the bar, asked for twenty Rothmans and ordered another vodka. I'd only just sat down for the second time when a scruffy-looking face peeped round the side of the snug –

"Fancy sum company, luv?"

I looked up. I couldn't believe this dirty little aul fella was trying to chat me up –

"NO."

He obviously had a hearing problem because he sat down beside me –

"Hey, luv. Yeh know wha dey say, a problem shared is a problem haffed."

"Why don't yeh just fuck off?"

I turned away from him and took a large gulp of me drink.

"Hey," he said putting his hand over mine, "Yeh don't mean dat."

I kicked him on the shin –

"Get yer filthy paws offa me an fuck off."

He jumped up holding his shin –

"OK, OK. Yeh fuckin dyke. I was only tryin teh be friendly."

The barman came over and asked me to leave.

"What? I didn't do anything . . . it was him . . . "

"I said I'd like you to finish yer drink an leave."

"But . . . it wasn't me . . . "

Ah, fuck it, I thought. What's the point? I drained me glass and got to me feet –

"This place is only a fuckin kip, anyway."

I made me way home, stopping at the off-licence on the way. I thought about going back to Ann's, but decided against it. She'd only start moaning at me and I wasn't in the humour for listening to her. So, I went back to me own house instead.

Someone had cleaned the place up, probably Ann. But, despite the overpowering smell of air freshener, I still got the stench of blood.

There was a dark circular stain on the settee and, although the walls had been washed, they still looked dirty. I opened me bottle of vodka. Jasus, I thought, I'll have to get this place redecorated. Then I settled down to drink meself into a stupor.

I woke to the sound of banging. It was a few minutes before I realised the noise was coming from the hall. Someone was banging the door down. I struggled to me feet and made me way down the hallway. I barely had the door open before Ann started –

"What deh fuck deh yeh think yer doin, Jackie?"

Her raised voice was like an explosion in me head –

"For fuck sake, Ann. Don't start, I'm not in the mood."

"Don't start. Is that all yeh can say? Yer turnin inteh a fuckin alcholic before me eyes an yer tellin me not to start, cause yer not in the mood!"

We were in the sitting-room. I held up the bottle –

"Deh yeh want a drink?"

"No. I don't want a fuckin drink."

"Well, yeh don't mind if I have one?"

"Yeah, Jackie. I do fuckin mind."

"Well, tough shite Ann. Cause it's none of yer fuckin business what I do in me own house."

She grabbed me hand and tried to take the bottle from me. She pulled at me fingers trying to loosen me grip but I wasn't letting go. I pushed her in the face with me free hand, me fingers found her eyes. She let go. Her hands went to her face –

"Yer a fuckin bitch."

"Yeah. Well, yeh shouldn't have tried teh take the bottle."

I sat down and poured meself a drink. Ann sat opposite me, rubbing her eyes in her sleeve –

"What deh fuck are yeh like, Jackie?"

"Oh, scuse me for bein fuckin human, Ann. How dare I sit here drinkin when I've just lost the man I loved. He was taken from me in the prime of his life by some fuckin lunatic with a gun, something yeh seem teh have forgotten. So, don't sit here and tell me that's no reason teh have a drink." I took another swig – "Did yeh know we were gettin married? Yeah, big weddin, with all the trimmins. Did yeh know that?"

She nodded –

"Yeah, Jackie. I did know, yeh told . . . "

I didn't let her finish –

"We were gonna have the dinner in the Burlington. Jasus, Ann, can yeh imagine that? The Burlington? But I told him, I said, 'Johnser, you'd have teh take out a mortgage teh buy a pint in that place.' He said he didn't care what it cost, cause nothin was too good for me. Jasus, it would have been great. He was even gonna hire the band Smokie teh play at the reception, can yeh believe that? I told him they'd be too dear but he said they wouldn't cause they hadn't had a hit in years. An the cake. We weren't havin a currant one cause he hated currants. No, we were gonna have a five-tier Black Forest gateau with . . . "

"Jackie, stop. Stop doin this teh yerself. Johnser's gone an he's not commin back. But, yeh have teh go on, life has teh go on."

I started to cry –

"I don't want teh go on. I don't want life teh go on without him."

Ann knelt in front of me and took me hands in hers –

"Listen teh me, Jackie. Yeh have teh pull yerself together. I know yer hurtin, but this isn't just about you. Yeh have the boys teh think off, they're hurtin too. What good will it do them if yeh fall apart? Who'll they turn to? Yeh have teh be strong for them, Jackie, they need yeh now."

I fell into her arms –

"Oh, Ann, I'm sorry. I'm so so sorry. I'm tryin teh be strong but I feel so empty without him."

"Yeh don't have teh apologise teh me, Jackie. I know yer doin yer best. I also know there's nothin yeh wouldn't do for yer boys. So, tell me that you'll be very brave and strong, for their sake."

I wiped me eyes –

"Oh, Ann. Yer the best friend a woman could ask for."

She smiled. "Yeah. I suppose I am."

I laughed and a big bubble came down me nose –

"Yeh dirty bitch, Jackie Clarke. Get yerself a hankie."

I put me arms around her and hugged her tight –

"Thanks again, Ann. Now I think it's about time I reintroduced meself teh Jonathan and Edward."

"They'll probably be in bed by now, Jackie. Besides, yeh look a sight. Why don't yeh have a good night's sleep and, come over all glammed up and ready for action in the mornin? And, if yeh feel up to it, we'll go and see Johnser. What deh yeh say?"

"Yeah, right Ann. That's what I'll do."

TARA

Chapter Seventeen

Johnser was really starting to move up in the world, he even had his own car now. And, money didn't seem to be a problem either.

Having the car was great. It was getting close to Christmas and the weather was freezing. So, it was nice to sit in the car with the heater on full blast listening to music. Instead of trying to keep warm sitting huddled around a fire in the middle of some poxy field.

It also gave us the privacy we needed to be able to have sex. I no longer had to worry about Fat Larry or any of the rest of the little pervs getting their rocks off while they were peeping at what me and Johnser were doing.

Sex was still a novelty for him, he couldn't get enough of it. But, I didn't mind. Regular sex had its advantages for me as well. Before I'd let him near me, I'd drop all kinds of hints about the lovely coat I'd seen or, the new LP I'd heard or, the gold bracelet Leanne had told me about. And, bingo, he'd give me the money to buy whatever it was I was after. I always made sure to get me shopping list in early cause he still wasn't one for conversation. As soon as the sex was over he'd want to take me home so as he could go back to his mates. I didn't really hang around with the gang any more. They were a shower of fucking eejits that I'd outgrown. So on the nights that Johnser went drinking with them, I went out with Leanne.

* * *

Marcus had organised a Christmas party for the staff. He'd collected twenty quid from everyone over the last twelve weeks and booked a cabaret with Christmas dinner. This was going to be the best Christmas party ever, so Marcus said.

Needless to say, it wasn't.

The meal was cold, the band were crap and as for the comedian? Well, the less said about him the better. Anyway by eleven o'clock I'd had enough –

"Ah, fuck this, Leanne. I can't take any more of this shite. Are yeh on for goin dancin?"

"Jasus, Tara, I thought you'd never ask."

"Great. What about the others? Will we ask them?"

"Hey everyone, we're goin dancin. Does any of yez wanna come?"

They didn't need to be asked twice. We were out of there and organising taxis in record time.

We agreed on a disco and piled into our taxis. Me and Leanne were the first to arrive and as soon as we'd put our coats into the cloakroom, we headed for the bar –

"Scuse me. Two Bloody Marys please," I shouted over the noise of the music.

"What about me, Tiara? Do I not get a drinkie-poo?" Marcus and the rest of the gang had arrived.

"Make that three Bloody Marys."

I handed Leanne and Marcus their drinks and we went off to find a seat. After me fourth drink, I was ready to dance the night away. I grabbed me handbag and strutted out onto the floor. Marcus followed.

The girls in the salon were always going on about how good-looking Marcus was but, I never got involved. I'd never really paid too much attention to Marcus or what he looked like. But now as he faced me across the crowded dance floor, I had a feeling that was about to change. Jasus, he looked so cool. He was wearing a white suit with a red shirt opened almost to the waist. His gold medallion sparkled as it caught the light. And the way he moved that beautiful bronzed body of his. Jasus, he was gorgeous. And judging by the way he was looking at me, he obviously thought I was a bit of all right too. He moved closer, tripping over me bag on the way –

"Tiara, you are looking very lovely tonight."

"Yeh don't look too bad yerself, Marcus." I laughed, trying to hide me embarrassment.

"Pleeze, Tiara. I am being serious. Tonight I can look at no one else. You are, how you say, beautiful."

"Jasus, Marcus. Yer not in the bleedin salon now, so yeh can cut the crap."

"But, Tiara. It izz true. You are like a star in the night sky, shining only for me."

"Will yeh fuck off, Marcus. Yer makin me scarlet."

The DJ began a slow set and Marcus put his arms around me. As we swayed in time to the music, he whispered –

"Tiara, I want us to spend dee night together."

We kissed. God, I thought. He's somethin else.

When the lights came on I pulled away from him –

"Jasus, Marcus, I'm parched. Let's get another drink."

As he made his way to the bar, I went back to our table. Leanne was the only one there. She was dug into some fella and didn't even notice me arrival. It was only when Marcus came back with the drinks that she came up for air –

"Tara, where were yous two? I was lookin everywhere for yous. The others are all gone home an I was left sittin here on me own like a fuckin gobshite."

"Well, yeh don't look very alone teh me," I said nodding at her companion.

"Fuck off, Tara. He was only keepin me company for a few minutes. He's a friend of me brothers."

"Yeah? Well we're here now, so shurrup moanin."

By the time we'd finished our drinks, Leanne was nowhere to be seen. So when Marcus suggested we should leave, I agreed.

We collected our coats and left the disco. The air hit me like a slap on the face, it was freezing –

"Jasus, Marcus, hurry up an get a taxi before I die of cold."

"We'll never get a taxi here, Tiara. Let's walk as far as dee corner."

As we made our way down the road he pulled me into a shop doorway.

"Fuck off, Marcus. What deh yeh take me for?"

"Tiara, I am sorree. But, I can't keep my hands off you, you drive me crazee."

"Yeah, well yeh can keep yer fuckin craziness till we're in a taxi."

Having stood for nearly an hour in the freezing cold we still hadn't got a taxi. It had started to snow and me feet were like stones. I couldn't even feel me toes anymore. And me coat certainly hadn't been designed for warmth, it was paper-thin. I was thinking about how awful it would be to freeze to death when Marcus had a brain-wave –

"Tiara, I can't believe how stupid I've been. My apartment izz only about fifteen minutes from here, why

80

don't we walk there and I will get my car and drive you home?"

"Jasus, Marcus. Yer right. Yeh are fuckin stupid. Yeh stand here for an hour before yeh remember that yeh only live a few minutes away."

He put his arm around me and we hobbled off in what I hoped was the direction of his apartment.

When we got to his apartment he tried to coax me inside, but I wasn't having any of it –

"Marcus, just get deh bleedin car an bring me home."

When he eventually found his keys and opened the doors I hopped in and turned the heater to full. Marcus got into the driver's seat and leaned towards me. Jasus, he was like an octopus, his hands were everywhere.

"For fuck sake, Marcus, will yeh calm down. Gimme a chance teh get warm."

"Tiara, it izz your own fault. You have me all a titzy."

"Tizzy. The word is tizzy, yeh fuckin eejit."

But, he wasn't listening. He was too busy mauling me lovely white dress, trying to get it off.

"Marcus, calm down, for fuck sake. What's yer hurry? Yer not in a bleedin race, yeh know."

He buried his head in me chest –

"Oh my Tiara, I think I am in love with you. We will get married, yez? I will change the name of the salon, it will be called, *Marcus and Tiara's House of Hair* you would like that, yez?"

He opened the buttons at the front of me dress, pushed me bra up and took me tit in his mouth, at the same time pushing his hand between me legs. I started to laugh and his head jerked up –

"Tiara, what izz so funny?"

"It's yer moustache, Marcus. It's tiddling the life outta me."

He went to move his hand away but, I stopped him –

"No, Marcus, don't stop. I like what yer doin." But it was no use, I couldn't stop giggling.

He got annoyed –

"Tiara! How am I supposed to concentrate on your body with all diz laughing going on?"

"I'm sorry, Marcus. Really."

I leaned over and kissed him, while at the same time putting his hand back between me legs. I was just going to come when he moved his hand –

"Don't yeh dare move, Marcus!"

Suddenly, I was coming and it was better than ever before. I pulled him on top of me –

"Com'on Marcus. Give it teh me, nice an hard." While he fumbled with his clothes I got a Durex out of me bag –

"Here, put this on." But it was too late, he was in.

"Well take it out before yeh come, right?"

"Yez, yez. Of course I will, my little love." He groaned and his body stiffened. He pushed deeper into me as I tried to push him off –

"Marcus. Take it out. I told yeh not teh come inside me." But it was too late and I knew it. "Gerroff me, yeh bastard." I grabbed his hair and it moved. I jumped up –

"Oh Jasus, Marcus. What deh fuck happened teh yer hair?" He didn't answer. He sat back in his seat and started the car.

As I straightened me dress I noticed it was scruffy. It was streaked with browny coloured stuff, like shoe polish. I bent me head forward and sniffed at me hem. I recognised the smell, and it wasn't shoe polish –

"You're wearin false tan!"

He didn't answer. I rubbed me hand down the side of his face –

"Yeh are. Yer wearin false fuckin tan!"

82

"Fuck off, yeh stupid bitch."

I grabbed his hair and it came off. I started laughing –

"Yer a fuckin fake, Marcus. Fake hair, fake tan . . ."

I patted his trousers –

"Are yeh sure that's not fake too, Marcus?"

"Fuck off, Tara."

I stopped laughing. His accent had disappeared too. He stopped the car –

"What deh yeh think yer doin?"

"I'm gettin fuckin rid of you. That's what I'm doin."

"Well I'm not gettin out. Yeh have yer shite if yeh think I'm walkin home at this hour of night."

"OK, but if yeh keep fuckin sniggerin, ye'll be walkin home."

I didn't say anything. I sat in amazement and watched as he twisted the rear-view mirror towards him and put his hair back on. Jasus, I could almost feel sorry for him.

We drove for about ten minutes before he spoke –

"Me name isn't Marcus Sinelli, it's Mark Simpson. I used to have a salon over in Coolock, that's where I'm from. Anyway, the only clients I ever got were aul fellas looking for short back and sides. I was twenty years of age, bald as a coot and covered in freckles. It wasn't fair. I knew I was a good hairdresser, much better than all them posers with fancy salons packed from one end of the week to the next. But, the problem was, I didn't look right.

"One night when I was moaning about me lack of looks to me sister, she suggested I wear a wig. At first I just laughed and told her not to be ridiculous. But she set me thinking and, the more I thought about it, the more sense it made. Eventually, one day, I worked up the courage to buy a wig. I couldn't believe the difference it made, I felt great, full of confidence.

"The next thing I needed to change was the colour of

me skin. I tried a session on a sunbed but, that only made me freckles worse. Then I discovered false tan, and the rest was easy. I dyed me moustache, changed me accent and rented a salon on the south side of Dublin where no one would know me. I changed me name to Marcus Sinelli and I became a hit.

"Me new salon was packed day and night. Aul ones, who wouldn't have let the baldy northsider anywhere near them, were now flocking to have Marcus the Italian run his fingers through their hair."

I sat looking at him, I didn't know what to say. I did pity him, but I would have pitied him a lot more if he hadn't just rode me. Jasus, I couldn't believe I'd had sex with a baldy. No, correction, I'd had sex with a freckly baldy. Jasus, what would I do if anyone found out? I had to think quick –

"Right then, here's the deal. When we go inteh work on Monday, you'll still be smarmy Marcus, the Italian stud, OK? But, if yeh ever tell anyone about tonight, I swear I'll reef that bleedin wig offa yeh in the middle of the shop. Do we understand each other?"

Needless to say, he agreed. The thought of his wig flying across the salon was enough to make him promise anything. But Christ, he was a cheeky pig. As I was getting out of the car the fucker tried to kiss me –

"Fuck off, baldy. Don't push yer luck."

JACKIE

Chapter Eighteen

When I woke up the next morning, I thought I was going to die. Me head was pounding and me mouth felt like gravel. I dragged meself out of bed and staggered down the landing to the bathroom.

I looked in the mirror –

"Jasus," I thought, "yeh look like a fuckin sixty-year-old slapper."

Yesterday's eye-liner was caked in the corners of me eyes, me hair was all stringy and greasy and me face was as white as a sheet. I thought me head was going to burst, it felt like there was a brass band playing inside. I opened the bathroom cabinet and found the tablets. I couldn't find a glass so I bent down and drank straight from the tap.

As soon as the tablets hit me empty stomach, it heaved and I had to dive for the toilet. Thank God, the lid was up. I must have thrown up about five pints of liquid. When finally there was nothing left in me stomach, I dragged meself up off me knees and took more tablets. I turned on the shower, the water wasn't exactly warm but, I didn't care. I just stood there letting the water wash over me. The cold water had some effect and I started to feel a bit better. I got out of the shower, brushed me teeth and gargled twice with some vile-tasting mouthwash.

I went into the bedroom and sat down at me dressing-table. I put on a bit of make-up and dried me hair. Now for something to wear. I'd promised Ann that I was going to make an effort, so that ruled out the usual jeans and jumper. I opened the wardrobe and took out me navy suit, me only suit.

The jacket was a shade darker than the skirt cause I often wore them as separates and washed the skirt in the machine. The lable said *Dry Clean Only* but that was all me arse. I couldn't afford to pay four pounds twenty for dry-cleaning every time I wore the fucking thing. Besides, the suit had only cost me forty-nine pounds ninety-five.

When I was ready I went downstairs and into the sitting-room. I drew back the curtains and opened the window. The smell of cigarettes was disgusting. I looked at the coffee table, the same table that Johnser used to use as a foot-rest. There was a quarter bottle of vodka sitting looking back at me. I walked over to me old friend and poured meself a small one. One wouldn't do me any harm, it would just help me to relax. I was about to raise the glass to me lips when there was a knock on the door. I put the glass down and went out into the hall –

"Who's there?" I called.

Jasus, what was wrong with me? I'd never done that before. I usually just opened the door without thinking about it, even late at night. But not now. Now I stood well back shouting for the caller to identify themself. It suddenly dawned on me that I was afraid. Ever since Johnser's murder I'd convinced meself that I was safe, that there was no way the gun-man was going to come back for me. But, now I wasn't so sure, I was nervous. The flap on the letter box opened and I nearly jumped out of me skin.

"Jackie, will yeh open the bleedin door."

I grabbed the latch –

"Ann, thank God, I didn't know who it was."

She walked into the sitting-room and looked at the glass of vodka –

"Jasus, Jackie, yer startin early."

I could feel meself going scarlet. I avoided eye contact as I grabbed the bottle and the glass –

"No, that was from last night."

She helped me tidy up and then we went over to her house to see me kids.

Jonathan was very quiet. He didn't seem to care whether I was there or not. I tried to talk to him but he said he was watching the telly. Edward gave me a big hug and seemed pleased to see me.

"Ma, why are yeh all dressed up? Where are yeh goin?"

"I have teh go out for a while but I promise I won't be long."

"Can we come with yeh?"

"No, Edward, not today." His eyes filled with tears.

"Ah, Edward, com'on now, don't cry. Yeh haven't heard me plan yet. When I get back we'll get a video and a pizza and we'll have a lovely night together, just the three of us."

His face lit up –

"Can we get the *Babe* video?"

"Yeah, yeh can get whatever yeh want. What deh yeh say, Jonathan?"

"*Babe*'s not out on video yet."

"Well, we'll get some other video then."

He didn't answer. Edward cut in –

"Ma, where are we gonna watch the film?"

"At home, in our own house."

Jonathan got up and walked towards the door –

"I'm not goin home." He left the room, slamming the door behind him.

"Jonathan!"

I went to follow him but Ann stopped me –

"Leave him, Jackie. Give him a bit of time."

I thought me heart was going to break. Jonathan and me had always been so close, and now he wouldn't even talk to me. Sweet Jesus, would I ever get me family back to normal? I could understand him not wanting to go home after all that had happened there. Jasus, I didn't want to go back either. But I couldn't let him know that. "Right," I thought, it's time you became a mother again, time you took control.

I walked out of the room and found him sitting on the stairs. I sat down beside him –

"Now listen, Jonathan, I know this isn't easy for yeh, but yeh have teh understand that it's not easy for me or Edward either. We all miss Johnser, we all want him back, but we know that's not goin teh happen. The only way we're goin teh get over losin Johnser is teh go home and try teh get back teh normal. I mean teh say, we can't stay here forever. Besides, you and Edward have to go back to school soon and I have teh go back teh work. Anyway, I know yeh hate sharin a bed with Edward, you'd much rather have yer own bed all teh yerself."

I squeezed his shoulder –

"Isn't that right?"

He gave a watery smile. I put me arm around him and gave him a hug. He didn't pull away.

I told him me and Ann had to go out for a while and that while we were gone, him and Edward were to get all their stuff packed and be ready to go home.

We walked back into the sitting-room together. Ann looked up from the paper she was reading –

"Everything OK?"

"Yeah, everything is goin teh be fine."

"Good." She sounded relieved.

I kissed the kids goodbye and told them I wouldn't be long.

Now for the business in hand. It was time to say goodbye to Johnser.

TARA

Chapter Nineteen

When I got into work on the Monday after the Christmas party, Leanne was waiting to interrogate me –

"Where did yeh get teh on Saturday night?"

"Did Marcus leave yeh home?"

"Did yeh let him wear yeh?"

"For fuck sake, Leanne, give me time teh get me bleedin coat off!"

"Right, now yeh have yer coat off, tell us what happened."

"Nothin fuckin happened. I felt sick so I went home. End of story."

"Well, Marcus must have felt sick too cause he went missin at the same time."

"So?"

"So, did yeh get off with him?"

"Will yeh fuck off, Leanne."

"Don't act like yeh don't fancy him, Tara, I saw yous dancin together."

"Leanne, I danced with you too but that doesn't mean that I fancy yeh."

"Oh, very fuckin funny, Tara."

At that minute Marcus walked in –

"Tiara, may I speak to you for one momento pleeze?"

Leanne muttered from behind the towel she was folding –

"Ooh, Tiara, I can't get enough of you . . . "

I laughed –

"Goway, yeh spa!"

I followed Marcus into what he called the canteen. What a joke. The canteen consisted of a kettle, a few cups, a box of tea bags and a few packets of biscuits. There was barely enough room for two people in there. He slid the door across –

"What were yeh sayin teh Leanne?"

"Nothin."

"I don't believe yeh."

"I don't give a fuck what yeh believe."

"I swear, Tara, if yeh breath one word about the other night I'll . . . "

"Don't fuckin threaten me, Marcus. I told yeh I wouldn't say anythin, so I won't."

I slid back the door and stormed out.

Jasus, I thought the day would never end. Marcus kept watching me and, Leanne kept pestering me with questions –

"Ah, com'on Tara, tell us what happened?"

"There's nothin teh fuckin tell."

"Don't be such a fuckin bitch, Tara. I always tell yeh about me fellas. I even told yeh about the time I went off with that black fella in Zhivagos."

"Leanne, I told yeh, I went home sick, I swear."

"Well then, why does Marcus keep lookin at yeh?"

"Leanne, he's not fuckin lookin at me, he's lookin at you. Cause he's told yeh three times teh sweep the floor and yeh still haven't done it."

Marcus shouted –

"Leanne!"

She grabbed the brush –

"OK, Marcus, keep yer hair on."

He glared at me.

"Marcus, I swear, I haven't said a word."

* * *

I was never one for keeping track of me period date. I could never remember if it was twenty-eight days from the day it started or twenty-eight days from the time it finished. I often used a whole box of Tampax waiting for it to start. And God knows, it's bad enough having to use those things for five days never mind two fucking weeks. Although they were better than those fucking pads. I remember when I started me period me ma gave me a packet of sanitary towels –

"Now Tara, put these away in yer press and let me know when yeh need more."

Jasus, it was a nightmare. It was like wearing a nappy. I was afraid of me life it was going to work its way up the back of me knickers and fall out. And as for the bulge, I was convinced the whole of Palmerstown could see it.

So, like I say, I never had any idea when me period was due. As far as I was concerned the longer it stayed away, the better.

Johnser used to get real narky when I had me period. He'd get all huffy and wouldn't see me until I was finished. I swear he thought I did it on purpose just so as I wouldn't have to have sex. The fucking eejit, he hadn't a clue.

One morning I woke up feeling crap. I was as sick as a dog. But I thought nothing of it. I'd been out drinking three nights on the trot so I put it down to that.

Ma wasn't as convinced –

"Tara, did yeh get yer period this month?"

"Yeah, of course I did."

"Well, how come there's no Tampax in yer drawer and I haven't seen any empty box in the bathroom basket?"

"Jasus, yer like Sherlock fuckin Holmes, I used the last one in work. Sooo . . . I threw the box into the bin in the salon . . . no big deal . . . no big mystery. Satisfied now?"

She believed me.

I thought back to the last time I'd had a period. It was the week before the Christmas party. I remembered because I'd been moaning about it to Leanne and she'd said I was lucky cause at least I'd be finished for Christmas. She was due hers the following Friday so that meant she'd have them for Christmas. And then she went on about the straight pencil skirt she'd bought to wear on Christmas day and now she wouldn't be able to wear it cause her belly would be bloated and she'd look like a pregnant duck.

That made it seven weeks since I'd had a period. I'd better go to a doctor.

I thought about getting one of those home kits but decided against it. I couldn't risk Sherlock finding it. I knew even before the doctor told me that the test was positive. But, I still couldn't believe it. Fuck it, I thought. The one time I'd done it without a frenchie and I'm up the fucking pole.

* * *

Johnser hit the roof when I told him the happy news –

"What deh yeh mean yer pregnant? How did it happen?"

I knew he'd react like this. But, I'd have to brazen it out. There was no way Mark "Marcus" Simpson was going to be the father of me child.

93

So I explained –

"Well, Johnser, it's like this. Yer a man, right? An I'm a woman. You put yer man's thing in me woman's thing and when all yer little tadpoles swim up me passage, they join with me eggs and, hey presto, I'm preggers."

"Don't be so fuckin smart, Tara, I know how it happens. But, yeh can't be up the pole cause I always wear a rubber."

"Well, Johnser, yer fuckin rubber musta burst cause I'm up the pole whether yeh like it or not."

He lit a cigarette –

"What are yeh gonna do?"

"Dunno."

"Are yeh gonna keep it?"

"What deh fuck deh yeh mean, am I keepin it? I'm no bleedin killer."

"I didn't fuckin say yeh were a killer. I just thought . . . yeh know . . . maybe an abor . . . "

"Thank's a fuckin bunch, Johnser. Thank's a fuckin lot for all yer support." I pointed to me stomach. "There's a baby in there, your bleedin baby. So what are yeh gonna do about it?"

"I'll stand by yeh."

"Jasus, that's big of yeh. What does that mean, Johnser? A few bob every week and a visit whenever yeh fancy a ride?"

"No, that's not what I mean."

"Well, what deh yeh mean?"

I started crying. Jasus, I should be in the fucking films. I could cry at the drop of a hat.

"Ah, for fuck sake, Tara, don't start bleedin whingin. I'll do whatever I have teh, whatever yeh want."

"I don't wanna have a bastard, Johnser."

"Who said yer gonna have a bastard? No kid of mine is gonna be a bastard, right?"

94

"Yeh mean we're gettin married? Oh, Johnser, I knew yeh wouldn't let me down."

I didn't give him a chance to argue –

"Johnser, we'll have teh get married before the baby comes along."

He tried to say something but I pulled him towards me and stuck me tongue down his throat.

He left me home early that night. He said it was because he wanted me to tell me folks about the baby. I knew it was because he wanted to get rid of me so as he could go up to his mates and get pissed.

It took another week before I plucked up the courage to tell Ma and Da that I was pregnant. It wasn't as bad as I thought it would be. Once she got over the initial shock, Ma was grand. Da wanted to string Johnser up. But, once he heard that we were getting married, he calmed down. Ma had me up half the night planning the dress and the bridesmaids and the guest list. And she insisted that I hand in me notice at the salon –

"You'd never be able for all that standin in yer condition."

I didn't argue.

Marcus was hard-pressed to hide his fucking joy when I told him I was leaving. He told me that I didn't have to work any notice, I could leave straight away. Bastard. I thought he'd at least offer to keep me job open for a few months or maybe try to encourage me to finish me apprenticeship (I only had another year to go). But no, the fucker thought he'd never see the back of me.

I met Ma for lunch, as arranged. She was laden down with bridal magazines and we spent two hours going through them. After lunch we headed to the jewellers, we were going to buy me engagement ring.

Johnser had given me three hundred quid to spend on me sparkler. He said he didn't give a shite what kind of ring

95

I got as as long as I didn't expect him to go shopping for it. I didn't bother telling him that I'd rather go shopping with me ma, just in case he got a face on and took his money back.

Anyway, by the end of the day we'd organised the church, the hotel, the photographer and the dress. I flashed me shiny new three-stone twist all the way home on the bus.

Johnser couldn't believe how fast things moved. I took that as a compliment to me organisational skills. I knew that life with Johnser wasn't going to be easy but I also knew that we'd do all right together. I knew that we'd never be one of those couples who go all gooey in each other's arms. I knew he'd never send me bouquets of flowers for Valentine's Day. I doubted if I'd even get a card but none of this bothered me. There was more to life than flowers and presents and holding hands. There was money, and I knew he'd always give me that. Besides, I wasn't into all that lovey-dovey shite either.

* * *

Johnser went along with all the plans. He moaned like fuck but that was nothing new. Then one night me da showed up.

I knew from listening to me da talking that he wasn't very fond of Johnser. But Jasus, the hatred that Johnser had for him was something else. From that night on Johnser was convinced that he'd been set up. As far as he was concerned the pregnancy was something me and me da had planned between us, there was no convincing him that it hadn't been like that.

And it hadn't been, well, not really. OK, so Johnser wasn't the father of me child. But I was fucked if I was going to marry Marcus. Anyway, Johnser had had his fun and now it was time to pay. But, it still wasn't the set-up he was saying it was.

At first I couldn't understand why Johnser was so upset when he found out that Blue was me da. But after a lot of ear-wigging on Ma and Da's little chats-cum-slagging-matches I soon found out.

It seemed that Johnser had become the Brush's right-hand-man. And that meant, that when the Brush decided to retire, Johnser would become number one. And, if Johnser was married to me, well, it would be only right for him to make me da number two. I still couldn't understand what all the fuss was about. But, I swear to God, that wasn't the reason I wanted to marry Johnser. There were a number of reasons why I wanted to marry Johnser, the most important one being that I didn't want to be labelled an unmarried mother.

* * *

The hen-night was great craic. Ma and all me aunties got locked and they grabbed any young fella who dared to come near our table. Jasus, the poor fellas were afraid of their shite of them. They dressed me up as a baby and pushed me up and down the pub in a shopping trolley. The manager was doing his nut but, every time he came near us to complain, one of me aunties grabbed him by the balls.

Then the police arrived. That fucker of a manager must have reported us. I nearly died when the young copper grabbed me by the arm –

"Tara Coyle, I'm arresting you for making a public nuisance of yourself . . . "

I couldn't fucking believe I was going to be arrested on me hen night –

97

"But, guard, we're only havin a bit of a laugh. We didn't mea . . . "

He didn't let me finish –

"I'm sorry Tara, but, anything you say will be taken down and used against you."

Auntie Maude shouted –

"Yeah, yer trousers."

They all broke their shite laughing but, I didn't think it was funny. I was the one being arrested –

"Maud, will yeh shurrup."

I turned to the copper and tried to explain. He threw his notebook on the table, took off his hat and pulled open his jacket. The gang were all singing the stripper music –

"Da da da . . . de da da da . . . "

He ripped off his shirt. I covered me face –

"Yez bleedin wagons, I'm scarlet . . . "

His trousers were off and he was pushing his leopardskin pouch into me face. There was a crowd around us now and they were all shouting –

"Get them off yeh, yeh ride . . . show us yer baton."
Auntie Maud made a grab for his pouch.

"Ahh, me micky," he screamed.

"Com'er an let Betty kiss it better for yeh."

He was hanging on to his balls for dear life. The women were all pulling at his G-string, it snapped and he ran like fuck.

We were pissing ourselves laughing.

"Here," Maud said, throwing me the G-string, "give them teh Johnser."

JACKIE

Chapter Twenty

Jasus, I never felt like I needed me friend more than I did at this minute.

No, not Ann. She was standing beside me. The friend I needed was the one sitting at home in the bottle labelled vodka. I looked longingly at the pub on the corner.

Just one, I thought. That's all I'd need, just enough to give me a bit of Dutch courage.

But I said nothing. I knew that if I as much as hinted to Ann about going to the pub, she'd throw a fit –

"Giv'us a smoke, Ann."

She rooted in her bag –

"Fuck it, I must've left them at home."

"There's a pub on the corner, I'll run down and get us some."

"I'll come with yeh."

I started to run –

"No, it's all right, I'll be quicker on me own."

As I pushed open the door of the pub, four heads turned to see who was coming in.

Jasus, I thought, you'd think they owned the fucking

99

place. The barman barely looked up. He was busy polishing his glasses. I walked up to the bar –

"Can I have a large vodka an orange please, an forty Rothmans." I was out of breath.

He continued polishing his glasses –

"Why are ye young people always in such a hurry?"

I wanted to tell him to mind his own business and just get the fucking drink but I held me tongue. He moved slowly towards the bottle of vodka hanging upside down on the far counter –

"I remember a man used teh come in here, wouldn't have been much older than yerself. And, he was always rushing around. Paddy, I think his name was. Yeah, Paddy Brown, that's what he was called." He held the glass up to the bottle. "Did yeh say large?"

"Yeah." I felt like fucking strangling him.

"Do you remember Paddy Brown, Jimmy?" he called to the aul fella sitting two stools away from where I was standing. The aul fella coughed, took a drag on his Woodbine and a swig of his pint before he answered –

"Deed I do. Sure wasn't I sittin on this very stool deh mornin he dropped dead on deh floor, not three feet away from me?"

"That's right, Jimmy. So you were. An' what did the ambulance man tell us? What did he say he'd died of?"

"A heart attack . . . brought on from all dah runnin round."

"That's right, Jimmy, a heart attack," the barman said nodding in agreement.

Jasus I thought, there'll be another fucking heart-attack victim on the bleedin floor if yeh don't hurry up with me drink.

"Did you want anythin with the vodka?"

I had wanted orange but Jasus, that could take all day

100

and I knew Ann would be coming through the door at any minute –

"No, just the cigarettes." I said handing him twenty quid. By the time he came back with me change I was finished me drink.

"Take care now, and slow down," he called after me as I raced out the door.

Ann was three steps from the pub –

"Jasus, Jackie. Where deh fuck did yeh get teh. I thought yeh were *makin* deh bleedin smokes?"

"Ah, there's a fuckin aul fella in there who'd talk the legs off a chair." I handed her a packet of cigarettes –

"Major?"

"Yeah, he'd no Rothmans."

* * *

I took a deep breath and walked into the funeral parlour.

"Mr Kiely's is a closed casket," Dracula informed us as he led the way to room number three.

There was a chill in the almost dark room. But I wasn't afraid. I turned to Ann –

"Can yeh give us a few minutes?"

Ann didn't argue, she was happy to get out. She hated anything to do with dead people and she was afraid of her shite in the dark.

I stood beside the coffin, rubbing me hand along the shiny wood –

"Howya luv? I'm sorry I wasn't here sooner, but, yeh know how it is. Are they lookin after yeh all right? I wanted teh come an see yeh in the mortuary but, they wouldn't let me." I held on to the brass handle, pretending it was his hand. "Why did yeh leave me, Johnser? Why?

What am I gonna do without yeh? Who's gonna look after me an the kids now?"

I was starting to cry –

"Look at me, Johnser, what am I like? I just can't stop whingin. I'm tryin teh be strong cause I know that's what yeh want but I can't. I just can't get me head round any of this. Yeh told me that yeh were finished with all that dealin an I believed yeh . . . " I wiped me eyes with the back of me hand. "Oh, Johnser. Why did someone want teh kill yeh? What did yeh do teh make someone hate yeh so much?"

I walked around the coffin, smoothing it with me hand, like I was trying to tidy it –

"I wanted teh give them yer favourite suit, the black one. But, Tara Coyle, bitch that she is, wouldn't let me. Yeh always looked lovely in that suit. It's a pity yeh didn't wear it more often, I always loved yeh in it. An I had yer brogues as well, I even polished them for yeh. They weren't as shiny as you'd have done them but I done me best."

I smiled – Johnser had always been fussy about his shoes.

"And, another thing. I know yeh were never very fond of Ann, but she's been great. I don't know what I'd have done without her. And the boys, they're been very brave, you'd be so proud of them." I had so much to tell him that everything was getting jumbled up. "And, yer not teh worry about the cost of the funeral, I'll sort something out. An don't worry about the priest either, I'll make sure he says as little as possible. And . . . Tara's acting up again, yeh know her? Always wantin teh be the centre of attention. She's sayin terrible things about us, Johnser. I know if yeh got yer hands on her, yeh'd brain her. But don't worry, she'll get her com'uppence. Yeh know what I always say – what goes round, comes round."

I could hear someone shouting in the hall but I paid no attention –

"Oh, by the way, Johnser. A fella called round the other night, he said he was from one of your clubs. He gave me six hundred quid – he said it was your cut from the door or something, I can't really remember but . . ."

I nearly jumped out of me skin when the door to room number three crashed open. Ann was being pushed backwards into the room and Tara Coyle was screaming at the top of her lungs –

"Get that fuckin bitch outta here, deh yeh hear me? Get her fuckin out."

TARA

Chapter Twenty-One

The day of me wedding finally arrived.

Ma had me up at six even though the hairdresser wasn't coming until eight. Ma was one of those people who believed that a good breakfast was the most important thing in the world. I swear, if I came down the stairs with me head under me arm, she'd insist on feeding me before she brought me to the hospital. But I couldn't eat a thing, I was so excited. I mean to say I was going to be the centre of attention for a whole day!

Ma had arranged for Marcus to do our hair. I'd tried to talk her out of having him but she wouldn't listen. As far as she was concerned, he was the best there was. And I didn't want to put up too much of an argument, just in case she got suspicious.

Anyway, Marcus arrived, he was all business. Ordering everyone around and having a panic-attack every time a curl fell down. I was having me headdress arranged and, I swear the bastard got great pleasure sticking hundreds of them fucking hairpins into me scalp.

But, credit where credit is due, by nine o'clock he had us all looking great. Especially me.

By ten o'clock the house was jammers. Da insisted that all the neighbours come in and toast his daughter's future. They didn't have to be asked twice, Jasus, they'd do anything for a free drink.

The house was like a brewery. He'd even bought two kegs of Guinness. The aul fellas buzzed around the kegs like flies around shite. Jasus, you'd swear they'd never seen a pint being pulled before. Auntie Maud was sitting in a corner knocking back the Bacardi and every time she looked at me she'd start whinging –

"Oh, Tara, I can't believe yer gettin married. It seems like only yesterday that yeh were gettin christened."

"Jasus, Auntie Maud, will yeh ever stop. Ye'll have me whingin in a minute."

Marcus jumped up –

"Tiara, you must not cry, think of your make-up."

"Relax, Marcus. I'm not gonna ruin me make-up."

I didn't want to put on me wedding dress cause I was having such a good time. I knew that when I put on me dress the party would be over and the day would move on, until eventually that was over too. And I wouldn't be the centre of attention any more.

* * *

The baby jumped and I grabbed me stomach –

"Oh, Jasus, that hurt!"

Auntie Maud screamed –

"Quick, quick, it's the babby, it's comin."

"It's not fuckin comin, Auntie Maud, it's only kickin. All the noise must've woke her up."

"What deh yeh mean, her?" Da asked. "It's gonna be a boy, it's gotta be."

"Not a chance. The bump's all teh deh front so that means it's gonna be a girl," Auntie Maud informed him.

Every aul one in the room joined in the discussion about the "bump". They seemed to have forgotten that today was about me, not the lump in me stomach. It suddenly dawned on me that for the rest of me life I was going to have to share the spotlight with someone else and I didn't want that. From that moment on, I hated the bump.

* * *

As I finished dressing there was a knock on the bedroom door –

"Who is it?" Ma shouted from under me dress, where she was trying to sort out all the under-skirts.

"It izz me, Marcus, I've come to zee dee finished product."

When Ma was satisfied with me skirts she opened the door –

"Marcus, will yeh check the headdress? Make sure it hasn't come loose. I'm just goin teh get me bag an then we'll go down."

He stood looking at me for a minute, then he whispered –

"Tiara, you look so, how you say, magnifick . . . "

I wanted to tell him to fuck off and speak properly but I couldn't, cause me bridesmaids were in the room. He started fiddling with me hair –

"You will look after my masterpiece, yez? There will be no tearz?"

"No tearz," I promised, smiling at him. He took me hand in his and whispered in a thick Dublin accent –

"Here's a little somethin teh calm yeh down . . . "

He'd dropped three little pills into me hand –

106

"But I'm pregnant . . . "

"They won't do the babby any harm."

Then he was gone. I looked at the pills in me hand and decided that he was right, I did need something to calm me down. I swallowed one of the pills and within minutes I felt better, much better.

Da was proud as punch when he walked me out the front door and down the garden towards the waiting car. The neighbours were out in force waiting to get a look at the bride. I could hear their gasps as I walked by –

"Isn't she lovely?"

"She's the spit of her ma."

"Isn't the frock only gorgeous?"

"Jasus, she's very pregnant."

The kids were all jumping up and down, millions of the snotty little fuckers shouting at me da –

"Hey, mister. What bout deh gruchie?"

They were standing between us and the car. Jasus, it was like a bleeding protest. No gruchie, no car. As long as none of the snotty little fuckers touched me I didn't really mind. But, if one of them put as much as a finger on me dress, I'd kill him.

Da took out a bag of coins and threw them onto the road. The kids were gone from the car in seconds flat. Jasus, they were like savages, nearly taking the hands off each other for the sake of a penny.

As we drove to the church, Da told me about the job they had planned for that day. He said it was going to be the biggest job he'd ever done. He told me that it wouldn't spoil the wedding cause they'd be back in plenty of time to have a great night. But he needn't have worried, I didn't mind. Being the daughter of a full-time criminal was like being married to a doctor. They often got called away in the middle of family occasions too. You just had to get used to it. Besides, we all liked the standard of living these professions gave us so there was no point moaning about the hours.

The wedding service lasted no length of time. Fair play to the priest, he kept the whole thing short and sweet. When we finished the wedding breakfast, Da and Johnser and a few more of the men went missing but, nobody took any notice, they just carried on having a good time. Before we knew it, they were all back and the party got into full swing.

There were a lot of serious-looking conversations going on between me da, Johnser and Brush. Obviously, things hadn't gone as smoothly as they would have liked. But, I didn't ask any questions. If I needed to know, I'd be told. That's the way things worked. Anyway, I didn't really care what was going on, this was me big day and I was going to enjoy it.

Johnser danced one dance with me and that was only because he had to. The minute the dance was over he made a bee-line for the bar where he stayed for the rest of the night. Granny Coyle kept telling me that I shouldn't be drinking cause it was bad for the baby but what did she know? Anyway she needn't have worried, cause no matter how much vodka I drank, it had no effect. I just couldn't get drunk. I was in the toilet when I remembered the pills Marcus had given me, I still had two left. I popped one, and suddenly I was flying high, as high as a kite.

* * *

I couldn't believe it when Ma told me it was time for me to get changed into me going-away outfit. I was having a great time and I didn't want to leave all the craic. But, she insisted –

108

"Now, Tara, I know yer enjoyin yerself, but yeh have teh leave now. Yeh know that the bride can't stay till the end of her own weddin. Anyway, I'm not havin Granny Coyle moanin teh me about yeh breakin tradition."

"OK, OK, I'm goin. Never let it be said that I broke a million-year-old tradition."

I'd only been back at the reception about five minutes when the police arrived. Jasus, they were taking a bit of a chance upsetting a crowd of over one hundred and fifty people. Me uncles were all cursing and shouting at them –

"Yez fuckin bolloxs are yez enjoyin this?"

"Ah, for fuck sake, lads, not today. Com'on, show a bit of respect."

"Jasus, if we'd known yez wanted teh com teh deh weddin we would've invited yez. There was no need teh gate-crash."

The police didn't say a word. They just grabbed Johnser, Da and a few more of the guests and led them away.

Me and Ma started crying in the hope that one of the policemen might take pity on us and let our men go. Needless to say, they didn't. They were well used to our little act by now. Uncle Albert, who had nothing to do with the fight, decided to swing a dig at the guard who was holding me da's arm half-way up his back and got himself arrested.

Me and Ma spent the night together, in the bridal suite.

The next morning Johnser was released and we left for our honeymoon.

* * *

Bermuda was great. The sun, the sea, the sand and the . . . waiters.

109

Johnser, the fucking eejit, fried himself on the first day. Well, it had nothing to do with me, it was his own fault. If he hadn't been in such a rush to get down to the pool and ogle all the topless women, I might have seen what cream he was taking. But no, typical Irishman that he was, the thought of a bare diddy made him stupid. Jasus, you'd swear he'd never seen a tit in his life, the way his head swivelled round every time a woman walked past. And yet, the minute I took me top off, he hit the fucking roof. He said it was because I was pregnant but, I think it was cause he didn't like other fellas looking at his mot's diddies.

Johnser was laid up for nearly a week. I don't know whether he thought I should sit in and mind him, I never asked. As far as I was concerned, there'd be plenty of time for sitting in when we got home.

I made friends with a crowd of English people, they were great craic. We went on some serious drinking sessions together. And when the drinking was finished, there was always Carlos. Beautiful dark-skinned Carlos.

He'd spend hours running his hands through me blonde hair, telling me how beautiful I was. The fact that I was well pregnant didn't seem to bother him in the least.

Carlos had a continuous supply of hash. Not the muck you got on the streets of Dublin – no, this was the real thing. One blow and you were floating, two and you were seeing little pink elephants, a full joint and you were on the elephant's back, heading for the moon.

One night after we'd smoked the biggest joint I'd ever seen, Carlos brought me down to the beach. All along the beach couples lay in different states of undress but I hardly noticed them.

Carlos was talking softly and the sound of his voice was having a hypnotic effect on me. When we reached the harbour he helped me into a little boat and for the first time in me life, I made love. I'd never realised there was difference between sex and making love until then.

I went back to Johnser, knowing I'd made the biggest mistake of me life. I'd jumped at what I thought was the best instead of waiting for someone who'd make me really happy.

Saying goodbye to Carlos was the hardest thing I'd ever had to do. He wanted me to stay but how could I? I was Irish, I was pregnant and above all, I was married. Married, now that was a laugh. We hadn't even consummated our marriage. Johnser had spent the first night of our marriage in a police cell, the first week of our honeymoon in bed with sunstroke, and the second week as drunk as a skunk.

When we arrived back at Dublin airport, we were whisked through security as if we were film stars. I loved the attention, I loved the way people were looking at us, wondering who we were.

Unfortunatly, there wasn't a roller or a limo waiting for us – there was a black Maria.

The honeymoon, as if I needed to be told, was well and truly over.

JACKIE

Chapter Twenty-Two

She was screaming like a fish-wife as she pushed her way past Ann –

"Get deh fuck outta here, Jackie Clarke. You've no bleedin right teh be sneakin round in here."

"I've every fuckin right teh be here, I'm deh one he lived with, I'm deh one who loved him."

"Yeh loved him? So fuckin what? I'm deh one he married, I'm Mrs Kiely, his widow. And, all deh fuckin love in deh world won't change that."

She was right and I knew it. I hadn't a leg to stand on. It wouldn't have mattered if we'd lived together for fifty years, she was the one he'd married, she was the one with all the rights. She was his widow.

I cursed meself for having let this happen. Why oh why hadn't Johnser tried for an annulment? God, knows, we'd talked about it often enough. But, typical me, I'd always put it off. Now, as I faced Tara Coyle across Johnser's coffin I knew there was only one thing left to do. I was going to have to beg.

"Listen teh me, Tara, please? I know what yer sayin is true. But, please let me mourn him too. Yeh know how much he meant teh me, how much I loved him, all I want now is teh bury him. I just want deh world teh know that me and Johnser were a couple. I know yeh never liked me but, I don't care about all that, that's all in deh past. All I'm askin is that yeh please, please, let me be a part of Johnser's funeral?"

She looked at me as though I'd just asked her to part with her life savings –

"You've got some fuckin cheek, askin me for favours. All this shite about how much he meant teh yeh, how happy yous were together is all in yer fuckin head. Cause, from what Johnser told me, he couldn't fuckin stand yeh."

I was in shock, I couldn't believe what I was hearing.

But, she didn't seem to notice, she was on a roll –

"Oh yeah, Johnser told me all about yeh. How yeh were always pesterin him. Even when he was in jail, yeh wouldn't leave him alone. He told me how yeh tried teh turn him against me by makin up all sorts of lies about what I was doin while he was inside. He told me how much he hated you an yer two snivelling bastards. Yeh see, Johnser was only usin yeh, just like he did all them years ago in Ballyer."

I wanted to scream at her to stop but the words wouldn't come out –

"Yeh see, Jackie, this is deh way it was. Johnser always needed teh have an alibi, just in case a job he was on went wrong and deh police came callin. He had teh be able teh say he was somewhere else at deh time, an that somewhere was with you. So yeh see, Jackie Clarke, that's all yeh were teh Johnser, an alibi. I mean, yeh don't honestly think that he fancied yeh? Cause, if yeh did you're a bigger fool than I thought yeh were."

"Yer a lyin little cunt, Tara Coyle. I wouldn't believe deh Lord's prayer outta yer mouth."

"I couldn't give two shites what yeh believe. As far as I'm concerned, yeh can go fuck yerself. Now get deh fuck outta here before I have yeh thrown out. Go and look for someone else's husband teh pester, cause mine's dead, he's no use teh yeh any more. Oh, and another thing, don't show up at deh funeral, cause if yeh do, I'll have yeh fuckin dragged kicking an screamin outta deh church."

The door opened and the ugliest looking fucker I'd ever seen came in.

"You OK, Tara?" He pointed a nail-bitten finger at me, "Is this bitch hasslin yeh?"

"No, Stan. She's just goin, aren't yeh, Jackie?"

He laughed into me face –

"So, yer Jackie Clarke? Jasus, Tara, yeh weren't fuckin jokin when yeh said she was a weapon, were yeh?"

As I walked towards the open door, he grabbed me by the arm –

"Ye'll stay away from deh fuckin funeral if yeh know what's good for yeh. Understood?"

I pulled away and walked out. There was nothing more I could say. I knew she wouldn't change her mind.

TARA

Chapter Twenty-Three

So me and Johnser never consummated out marriage. The minute we came home from the honeymoon he was arrested and then sent to prison. You can dress it up any way you want, swear on all the bibles in the world, that he was innocent but, at the end of the day, he was in jail. And there was nothing anyone could do about it. Johnser wasn't with me when I had the baby. He was on remand and they wouldn't let him out. I didn't think it would bother me, but it did.

I'd had a few scares during the pregnancy, swollen ankles, high blood pressure and on two occasions, slight bleeding. But, nothing prepared me for the night I went into labour.

Ma and Da had me head wrecked. They were always fussing, making sure that every little pain and ache was checked out. I swear, the gynaecologist saw me more often than he saw his wife. Anyway, one night I persuaded Ma and Da to go out for a few hours. So once she was satisfied that I had enough pillows behind me (six), me feet up, a flask of tea and a tray of tuna and sardine sandwiches within reach, they left. I'd always hated fish, but from the minute I became pregnant I ate nothing but tuna and sardines.

Ma said that they'd only be for an hour or so. She made me promise to stay on the couch and ring her if anything happened. She needn't have bothered with all her pampering cause I was up and down to the toilet so often I hadn't time to enjoy me comfort.

I was on me way down from the toilet for the twentieth time when I got the most unmerciful cramp in the bottom of me stomach. It was so unexpected that it took me breath away. I sat on the stairs until the pain eased, then I made me way back to the sitting-room. I'd only just sat down when the next one came.

I rang the pub but the phone was engaged. I'll give it another ten minutes, I thought, and if I still can't get through, I'll ring for an ambulance. I walked up and down the room but it was no good, the pain was getting worse. I rang the pub again but it was still engaged –

"Fuck, fuck, fuck. Get off deh bleedin phone!" I screamed at the receiver. I looked out the window hoping to see Ma and Da coming down the road when I seen the next-door neighbour standing at his gate. I made me way to the front door puffing and panting like a marathon runner –

"Martin, quick, help. Deh babby's comin."

Shelia, his wife, came running in –

"Com'on Tara, it's all right. Martin has the car ready, we'll be in deh hospital in no time."

She was great. She got me into the back seat and ordered him to drive like the clappers.

I was in terrible pain but the sour-faced nurse wouldn't give me anything until the doctor examined me –

116

"For Jasus, sake, I'll be fuckin dead by then."

Eventually, the doctor arrived and gave the go-ahead for me to be given some gas.

As I lay with me legs caught up in stirrups and every cat, dog and devil pulling and poking at me, I cursed Johnser from a height. I knew it didn't make sense to be cursing him, he wasn't even the father. But it felt great to be able to curse like a trooper and have no one complain. One of the nurses tried to get me to relax, she was holding me hand and telling me –

"It won't be too long now."

I had real long nails and, when I squeezed her hand, me nails dug into her. At first she tried to be polite but, eventually the pain became too much for her, cause she let out a roar –

"Tara, let go. Your nails are digging into me."

She pulled her hand away and I could see the little red slits I'd made with me nails.

After what seemed like days the baby finally arrived. I was knackered. I must have lost about three stone in sweat. I remember thinking about all the film stars I'd ever seen having babies, they'd never had as much as one bead of sweat on their perfectly made-up faces. "Wagons," I thought, as I drifted off to sleep.

I woke to the sound of someone singing –

"Ali, bali, ali bali bee, sittin on yer granny's knee . . . " I groaned –

"Ma, will yeh shurrup. I'm tryin teh sleep."

"Oh, Tara, she's only gorgeous. Absolutely perfect."

I pulled meself up in the bed –

"Where's Da?"

"Ah, yeh know yer da, he's not able for hospitals."

"Yeah, right."

I didn't believe her. I knew the reason he wasn't here was because I'd had a girl. Him and Johnser had both wanted a boy, nothing else would do. Jasus, you'd think I had a choice.

That night all me aunties came to visit me. They'd left the uncles in the nearest boozer –

"Yeh don't want that lot up here takin up space," Auntie Maud told me. But she was wrong. Cause I did want them all up, I wanted everyone to know what I'd been through. I wanted to be told how great I was. But, it didn't seem to matter what I wanted.

They were all gooing and gaaing over the baby, showing off the presents they'd bought for *her*. Why was she the one getting all the presents? Did they not realise that I was the one who'd done all the work? I was the one who'd carried her around for nine months, the one she'd kept awake all night with her kicking. I'd even lost me lovely figure, because of her.

And now, as I lay here, half-dead and looking like something the cat dragged in, the only thing *they* wanted to know was whether or not I was going to breast-feed. Well, the answer was no. I wasn't going to have that little monster sucking the life out of me.

The next day as I lay in bed feeling more depressed than I'd ever been in me life, the door to the ward opened. I didn't know if it was a man or a woman who came in, cause they were hidden behind the biggest bouquet I'd ever seen. When they got to me bed, the flowers spoke –

"How izz my favourite mama?"

"Marcus!"

I couldn't believe how happy I was to see him. He gave

me the flowers and a huge box of chocolates. It was great to be the one getting all the attention and presents. I was thrilled with meself. I told Marcus how depressed I was and asked him if he had any more of them tabs he'd given me on the morning of the wedding. He had. But, he told me, I'd have to pay for them. I gave him thirty quid. He gave me a little brown bag.

Ma was great, she done everything for me. Even the night feeds. And, Da wasn't too bad either. He seemed to be coming around to the idea of his grandchild being a girl. The only thing that annoyed me was them going on about having her christened. For fuck sake, I hadn't even thought of a bloody name for her yet. That was another one of Ma's favourite nags –

"That child has teh have a name. We can't keep callin her babby."

So, in order to shut her up, I told her that I'd name her after the next female singer who came on the radio. Needless to say, she wasn't too happy –

"That's no way teh name a babby. Yer supposed teh call her after someone yeh like or, a fambily member."

"Well, I'm not namin her after Maud, if that's what yeh think."

The next female singer who came on the radio was Na Na Mouskouri. I waited for the next one, Tina Turner.

I had no great love for religion, none of me family had. When I was a kid Ma used to insist on me going to Mass. When I asked her why I had to go to Mass when her and Da never went, she always said the same thing –

"Just do what I say, not what I do."

From time to time, I'd come home from school full of religious notions. Usually after a visit from a missionary.

119

One day I'd want to be a nun, the next I'd be joining the missions. Da always made a laugh of me, especially when I insisted on saying grace before meals. We'd sit around the table with our heads bowed, holding hands and he'd shout "Grace!"

And start eating. Ma would laugh, I'd cry and that would be the end of religion in our house.

Anyway, they insisted on a christening, so we had one. One big piss-up, that's all it was. We had the party in the local boozer where we ate, drank and sang to our hearts' content. We didn't even bring Tina home to bed, we just hid her basket in between all the coats.

* * *

From time to time, I visited Johnser in prison. I hated it, he always had a big puss on him. I'd go to a lot of bother doing meself up to the nines in the hope of cheering him up. But of course he wouldn't be cheered. No, not Johnser. As far as he was concerned I was only prick-teasing the screws.

He was an ungrateful pig. He didn't care that I spent a small fortune on taxis getting to this fucking place. Nor that I had to queue for an hour, in the cold, with all the aul ones wanting to know me business. And, when they did decide to open the gates, they'd want to search me –

"Search me arse!"

A quick feel of a tit, that was all they wanted. And the gas thing about it all was, I probably wouldn't have minded all the hassle I had to go to, if Moany-Drawers had shown the slightest bit of interest in me. But, he didn't. All he ever wanted to know was –

"What jobs has Brush got on?"

Not a word about me or the child. Not once did he ask how I was getting on. He never asked me about money, about friends, about what I done, whether I went out. He just didn't care.

So, when the weather got bad, I didn't bother going up at all. Well, I was fucked if I was going to go all that way, in the freezing cold, just to look at his moany puss.

Besides, I was seeing someone else now.

I didn't go out looking for another fella, it just happened.

It was Da's birthday, and Ma decided to throw a party. One of the guests was "Stan the Man".

I'd often heard me da talking about Stan.

From what I'd heard, he was the reason Johnser was in jail. He was the one who'd killed the old couple the night they'd robbed the pictures. Jasus, he was as ugly as sin, built like a wall but twice as thick. Every time he finished a can of beer, he crushed the can in one hand. He thought he was the gear. I thought he was simple. He really lost the run of himself when he asked me to dance. Imagine, me, dancing with the likes of him? When I said no, I didn't want to dance, he got annoyed –

"Why? Am I not good enough for yeh?"

I ignored him, he grabbed me arm –

"Hey, you. I asked yeh a question."

I pulled away –

"Fuck off, yeh bollox."

Uncle Albert was beside me –

"Everything OK, Tara?"

Stan grabbed him and pushed him against the wall –

"Fuck off, an mind yer own business."

Brush's hand was on his shoulder –

"Com'on Stan, let him go."

He did. Brush apologised to Uncle Albert. Then making his excuses, he left. Taking Stan and the rest of his gang with him. Da grovelled all the way to the gate. When he came back in, he turned on me –

"For fuck sake, Tara. Yeh could've danced with him, yeh know what he's like."

"No, I couldn't. He's an ugly pig."

"Yeah, but he's a fuckin strong pig."

STAN

Chapter Twenty-Four

Who the fuck did Tara Coyle think she was, acting like she didn't remember me? Well, she could say what she liked cause, I fucking remembered her. Jasus, she was a wild thing, always was. I remember the first time I saw her, she was only about fifteen but, even at that age she was gorgeous. That was until she opened her mouth. Jasus, she had a gob on her like a fishmonger's daughter.

I was driving down the road in a robbed car when I saw her coming towards me, I drove straight at her, stopping at the last minute. She went fucking mad –

"Wat deh yeh think yer playin at, yeh fuckin wanker?"

I tried to be cool. I leaned over the passenger seat and opened the door –

"Hop in, I'll give yeh a ride."

"Would yeh ever go an fuck yerself, yeh pimply-faced bastard."

She walked off. I drove after her with the door still open –

"Ah, com'on, Tara. It's only a bit of craic."

She stopped and leaned into the car. Jasus, she had a great pair of tits –

"Well, seein as yeh want a bit of craic, why don't yeh go home an use yer mirror as a dart board an get rid of them fuckin carabuncles on yer face!"

"Fuck off, yeh smart cunt," I shouted as I sped off down the road.

If anyone else had said that, I'd have slapped their fucking head off. But, I fancied her. So, I didn't. It wasn't my fault I had spots, I just had greasy skin. I tried everthing to get rid of them but nothing worked. I even stopped using soap cause Ma said it was full of chemicals but it made no difference.

I didn't have any friends either, I didn't need them. All that hanging around corners acting tough wasn't for me, it was kids' stuff. No, I preferred to be on me own, do me own thing. As for big bad Johnser Kiely, well, fuck him, and all his shite about never robbing from your own people. Who did he think he was? Fucking Robin Hood? As far as I was concerned, robbing was robbing. It made no difference to me if I robbed from a rich fucker in Howth or a poor fucker in Ballyer, they were all fair game.

I could never understand what was so cool about robbing a Saab in Sandymount when it was just as easy to rob a Ford Anglia in Pearse House. I mean to say, they all ended up the same way. As soon as we got fed up driving the fuck out of them, we rammed them into a wall, then burned them out.

Besides, I always robbed a car in the hope of making a few bob. That's why I stayed local. There was more chance of finding a tool-bag in the boot of a banger from Pearse House than there was in a Saab from Sandymount. All you'd find in a Saab was a poxy briefcase and, who'd want that? I always got a good price for a set of tools.

And, sometimes when Lady Luck was in a really good mood, I'd get power tools. Now they were worth a bob or two.

It was the same with houses. Them posh gaffs were too much hassle, they all had alarm systems and big fucking dogs. And, because they spent so much money building their bleeding houses, they'd fuck-all left to buy any robbable furniture.

Now, council houses, they were a different kettle of fish. They all had electricity meters, that meant cash in even the poorest homes. And not an alarm system in sight. They were a doddle to get into. All the windows had big fucking latches on them, all I needed was a hand drill, a clothes hanger and I was in.

I remember the first time I robbed a house I was bricking it. I swear to Jasus, I was nearly shitting meself at the sound of me own heartbeat. And who could blame me? After all, I didn't know who lived there. What would I do if someone heard a noise and woke up? Or worse still, what if someone had been asleep on the couch and jumped me as I struggled through the window? But, I needn't have worried, no one ever woke up. With the result, I became braver and braver. I started carrying a hammer. And believe me, I would have used it if necessary.

I used to wander around people's houses as if I lived there. Going from room to room, looking in drawers, opening presses. I even became brave enough to go into bedrooms and root around on bedside lockers for wallets or purses or whatever they might have left there. And, if I was hungry, I'd think nothing of making meself something to eat.

I always done something to let them know I'd been there. Like putting a pair of knickers over the teapot or, writing, "Mrs Roach is a ride" on the bathroom wall. Or else I'd just rob something worthless that I knew they'd miss. I remember one time I robbed a wig, a man's wig. Jasus, I got a great laugh out of that. I could just imagine the poor fucker waking up the next morning, penniless and baldy.

* * *

I'd grown up a lot since then. I was twenty-three years old, six foot four, and built like a shit tank.

I was no longer interested in petty crime for petty money. No, I wanted to taste the big time. And when you're built like me and have a temper like a rabid dog, people soon get to know your name.

I became a debt collector. I was very good at me job but it bored the fuck out of me. Everyone paid up on time. Now, I ask you, where's the fun in that? I thought I was going to spend me time beating the crap out of fellas because they wouldn't pay there bills but, I was wrong. The whole fucking world seemed to have turned into a God-fearing pay-on-time brigade.

Then one day I met Johnser Kiely.

He had a big job on and needed some muscle. I didn't like him very much but fuck it, work was work.

* * *

The job went wrong. Tough shit. That wasn't my fault. OK, so I was a bit rough on the aul lad but, how was I supposed to know he'd croak it? After all, I'd been hired as the muscle so I was just doing me job. Anyway, if Johnser Kiely had cased the joint properly, I wouldn't have had to deal

126

with anyone. And I let him know it. I told him I wouldn't be taking the rap for his fuck-up. And if the police questioned me, I'd tell them whatever I had to to save me own skin.

The Brush came to see me. He gave me an envelope full of cash and told me to get offside for a while. I took the ferry to Liverpool to visit me Uncle Pat.

* * *

Jasus, you should have seen the size of the gaff me uncle Pat had. I thought I was in Buckingham fucking Palace. The downstairs jacks was bigger than our sitting-room. He said that all the bedrooms were *On Sweat* I thought that meant they all had heaters in them but, I was wrong. They all had their own jacks and shower.

The basement (as he called it) had been turned into a leisure centre. There was a huge swimming pool, a sauna and loads of exercise equipment. And, when you got bored with that, you could play snooker on the full-sized table and listen to the Wurlitzer Jukebox.

And as for the garden, it was bleeding massive. He even had his own forest with a river running through it. Uncle Pat had it all. Including a sex-on-legs-wife. Jasus, she was a fucking beaut. I swear, if I'd been given half a chance, I'd have rode her senseless.

Pat seen me looking at her and laughed –

"Yeh like yer pussy, don't yeh, Stan?"

I was fucking mortified at being caught gawking at his mot but he didn't seem to care –

"Don't be fooled, Stan – pussy like that is only interested in one thing . . . MONEY. Do yeh honestly think she'd be here if I didn't have all this? Not a chance."

127

We stood and watched as she dived into the pool.

After eating the biggest dinner I'd ever had, me and Uncle Pat went to play snooker –

"Yeh know, Stan, this could all be yours."

"Yeh mean yer gonna leave it teh me in yer will?"

He laughed –

"No Stan, that's not what I had in mind. I mean yeh could have yer own place like this in Dublin."

"Yeah, right. All I'd have teh do is rob a few fuckin banks."

"Don't be stupid, Stan. Do yeh think I got all this from robbin banks? Banks are for mugs. Jasus, Stan, banks have cameras in every fuckin corner nowadays."

He was starting to annoy me. If he was going to make a big mystery out of telling me how to get rich, he needn't fucking bother –

"No offence, Pat, but I've no idea what yer on about."

"I need someone I can trust, in Dublin."

"Trust with what?"

"Exports."

"Exports?"

"Yeah, I export goods to Dublin. And, I need someone over there to distribute the goods and collect the cash."

"There's millions of companies can do that for yeh. I'm not bein smart, Pat, but pen-pushin's never been me strong point."

He leaned towards me –

"Who said anythin about pen-pushin? I just need a fambily member I can trust."

"For what? What are yeh so worried bout? W'dah fuck are yeh sendin over, gold?"

"In a manner of speaking, yes. I feel Dublin is ready for a little powdered gold."

"What . . . ?"

"DRUGS," he roared.

"But, there's fuck-all money in hash. Yeh need tons of that fuckin stuff before yeh make a shillin."

"I'm not talkin bout hash, yeh gobshite. I'm talkin bout heroin."

"Heroin? There's no market for heroin in Ireland."

"That's cause, up till now, it's been too expensive. I intend teh flood the market. Heroin for a fiver, now who could refuse that? And, when they try it once, they'll be runnin back for more."

"I don't know. It all sounds a bit risky teh me."

"The only ones at risk are the dealers. We're the suppliers. We bring deh gear in, sell it in lots of twenty grand, collect deh money and fuck the risk."

"The police'll easy cop twenty grands' worth of gear comin in."

He reached into his pocket, took out a small package and threw it on the table –

"That's twenty grands' worth."

"Fuck me . . . "

"I send over trucks carrying boxes of small electrical appliances, one box per truck will be marked . . . yeh know the rest . . . "

* * *

And so me life began. I came back to Ireland with a list of contacts and enough money to rent a warehouse. I hired people to look after the legitimate end of the electrical business. All I had to do was make sure I picked up the marked box.

In no time at all I was up and running and getting the respect I deserved.

Six months ago, Blue would never have invited me to his party, I wouldn't have been important enough. But, that was all in the past. Now I was invited everywhere, met all the gorgeous birds, gorgeous birds like Tara.

OK, so she wasn't interested in me at the minute, but I could wait. Once she learned how much money I had, she'd be eating out of me hand.

JACKIE

Chapter Twenty-Five

I didn't give a fuck about Tara Coyle's threats. I wasn't going to miss Johnser's funeral. And the boys were coming with me. After all, Johnser was Jonathan's father. OK, so we wouldn't get to travel in the first mourning car like proper family but at least we'd be there.

Meanwhile I had other things to worry about. I had to try and sort things out with Ma and Da. The kids needed their grandparents and I needed a baby-sitter for when I went back to work. Work, Jasus, I hated the thoughts of going back to that kip. But, I knew I'd have to go back sooner or later. I was so lost in thought that I nearly jumped out of me skin when the sitting-room door opened –

"Christ, Jonathan, yeh nearly frightened the life out of me. What's wrong? What are yeh doin up?"

"I can't sleep."

I sat looking at him, studying him, like I hadn't seen him in years. He looked so like Johnser, it was hard to believe that other people didn't notice the resemblance. He was a tall sturdy child. It was a good thing he enjoyed all kinds of sports, cause, if he hadn't he'd be the size of a house. He had an appetite like a horse, he never stopped eating for a minute.

Pancake Tuesday was a nightmare. I'd no sooner have one one off the pan than he'd have it eaten, I used to go mad. Not because he ate the pancake but, because I was crap at making them and hated standing over the pan for hours with nothing to show for all me hard work.

I remember one time I made the batter the night before so as to get a head start. But sure I needn't have bothered. The kids were in the kitchen before I had time to blink. It was as though they'd heard the batter hitting the pan. I swear to Jasus, they were unbelievable. Any other morning I'd have to drag them out of bed – they hated getting up for school. Jonathan would spend ten minutes begging me to let him stay in bed for another five minutes and, when he ended up late for school, it was all my fault.

* * *

Jonathan coughed, bringing me back to the present –

"It's very late, Jonathan, ye'll have teh go back teh bed."

He didn't answer. I held out me arms –

"Come on, luv, tell me what's wrong?"

He fell into me arms and I hugged him tight. It was the first time in ages we'd been this close. He was at that awkward age where he was too old to cry or hug his ma but too young to understand his emotions.

He'd become very broody the past few months, wanting to do everything himself. He knew all there was to know about life. He was defensive and secretive about everything and, if I dared to walk into his bedroom without knocking, well, there was blue murder. And as for washing himself? That was another battlefield. If I wasn't up by six am, I

132

hadn't a hope of getting into the bathroom before he left for school. He was worse than having ten girls.

I'd seen one of the young ones he palled with writing *"Kurt Cobain is a ride"* on the bus-shelter one day and, when I told him about it, he accused me of hating his friends. The only thing I hated was the thought of losing him. I couldn't bear to think of him not needing me, of growing up and becoming a man.

But, that all seemed very far away now as he sat cuddled up to me on the couch –

"Ma . . . I miss Johnser."

I held him tight –

"Me too."

He lay against me and I could feel his body shake with crying. As I tried to think of something to say that would make him feel better, I noticed me vodka sitting just out of reach on the coffee table –

"Fuck off, Jackie," I told meself, "Jonathan is more important than your drink."

I took Jonathan's face in me hands, forcing him to look at me –

"Johnser was very proud of you and Edward. Yous meant the world teh him, he was always talkin about yous."

He sniffled –

"Really?"

"Yeah, Jonathan, really."

He straightened up and took a deep shivery breath –

"I wish Johnser was me da."

Me brain screamed at me to tell him the truth but I couldn't –

"Johnser would've liked that too."

I ruffled his hair –

"Now, com'on sleepy-head, time for bed."

He smiled as I kissed him goodnight.

* * *

Ann sat on the bed watching me struggling with me earrings –

"Do yeh think it's wise, goin teh his funeral?"

I ignored her and continued with me earrings. They were claddaghs Johnser had given me for me birthday. She went on –

"Tell me teh mind me own business but, yeh know what she's like. She'll be waitin for yeh, an when that one gets goin, there's no stoppin her."

"For the last time, Ann, I'm goin teh Johnser's funeral and no one's gonna stop me. I don't give two fucks what kinda scene Tara Coyle makes."

"Jasus, Jackie, for once in yer life would yeh think of someone other than yerself?"

Ann had a tongue like a whip but at least she was honest. She was a real friend, who told you what you needed to hear not what you wanted to hear. But that didn't stop me wanting to scream at her to mind her own fucking business. I didn't say anything, I just sat glaring at her in the mirror. Silence usually knocked Ann off her soap-box but not today –

"Jackie, yeh can look at me any way yeh like and I still won't change me mind about yeh goin teh his funeral. She told yeh she didn't wan . . . "

"Ann, yeh might as well save yer breath, I'm goin . . . an that's that."

"OK, but, don't bring deh kids."

"They have teh go . . . "

"Why? Jackie, Johnser wasn't their father."

I started to cry and she lowered her voice –

"I'm sorry, Jackie, I'm not tryin teh be a bitch but yeh know what I'm sayin makes sense. Funerals are not for kids."

Reluctantly I agreed. Ann smiled her I-know-I'm-right smile and squeezed me arm.

"I'll just go to the toilet before I go," I told her as I headed for the bathroom.

I locked the bathroom door, opened me make-up bag and took out me naggin of vodka. Jasus, whoever invented the naggin was right up there with the inventors of the bra and the tampax, as far as I was concerned. I took three large mouthfuls, I'd gotten quite used to the taste of straight vodka, it didn't make me gag anymore. Its effect was almost immediate. I flushed the toilet and ran down the stairs. I was ready to do battle.

TARA

Chapter Twenty-Six

While Johnser was inside, I was well looked after, every whim was catered for, money, clothes, food, the lot. Apart from the fact that I now had a baby, it was just like the old days. Like being a schoolgirl again.

* * *

I hated school.

All that learning and cooking and sewing. I mean to say, I didn't need to know what two hundred and eighty multiplied by sixty was. Why should I?

I remember one day Sister Agnes giving me a riddle –

"If you had twenty-five apples and I gave you five more, what would you have?"

As she stood over me, waiting for me pearls of wisdom to surface, I said –

"I'd have a dose of the shits, Sister."

And it was the truth, cause apples didn't agree with me. Even the toffee-apples we got at the seaside gave me cramps. I remember I used to cry into me ma's face until she bought me one. I'd have barely swallowed the last bite when I'd fart. Except it wouldn't be a fart. Me ma would go mad and drag me off to the nearest toilet where she'd have to throw me knickers away. And even though we'd only just arrived, we'd have to go home cause me ma wouldn't let me go around without me frillies. And me da'd moan all the way home, because of the traffic.

I couldn't see the point in learning to cook either. Da said we had a full-time cook already. Whenever anyone visited us he'd boast about Mr fucking Macari. That always got a laugh from his mates, so did Ma's response –

"Well, I hope Mrs Macari is open for business too, cause yeh won't be gettin near me tonight. Yeh smart bastard."

I had a da who gave me everything I wanted. I was always first with the new toys. Money was no object when it came to his "little girl". Whatever the little angel Tara wanted, the little angel got. And not from Santy, fuck Santy, who needs a randy grey-haired aul fella in a red suit when you had a da like mine.

I remember one year I ran into the grotto, delighted with meself, after wasting half the day queueing. I booted over to Santy and jumped onto his lap.

Well, Jasus, talk about disappointment. First he gasped, then muttered –

"Fat little bitch." Under his breath.

The cheek of him, it was only puppy-fat.

Then he seen me ma and fucked me to one side saying –

"Well, hello there . . . " An he tried to grab her onto his lap.

"And what would you like from Santa?" he asked as she giggled like a teenager.

137

"A pram an a dolly that cries an . . . " I said, but he was too busy flirting with me ma to hear. I didn't care.

While he was preoccupied with me ma, I was helping meself to a few parcels from the sack marked "Girls".

I heard he got the sack a few days later. The dirty bastard.

I had the first bridal doll on our estate, all the girls wanted to help me dress her but I wouldn't let them. And when they got a doll, I got a doll and a pram. When they got a pram, I got a doll, a pram and a cot. I had the first roller skates, the newest bike, the latest clothes. Ma was the same. We had Axminister carpets when everyone else had bare floors or lino. Ma had dresses that you only seen on telly or in fashion magazines. And she had every colour wig you could imagine. She was Twiggy with a bit more meat, that's what da said and then he'd pinch her bum, and she'd give him a clatter.

She used to wear blue eyeshadow with sparkly stuff in it, and she'd loads of bangles and hats. And when the style changed, she just bagged the lot and gave it to the knackers. For weeks after you'd see them walking around like romany gypsies, tripping themselves up in their wedgie shoes and maxi dresses.

And when I said I wanted a horse, Da went straight down to the Smithfield Market and bought the loveliest piebald you ever seen. He was a beaut. The man who was selling him told us he was a thoroughbred and a direct descendant of a famous grand national winner. Da was over the moon, the man seemed happy too, although he said it broke his heart to have to sell such a prized possession. They spat on their hands and shook on the deal. Da hitched the horse to the rear bumper of the car and drove the ten miles home. He kept saying it was a

138

great horse OK, cause we were driving at thirty miles an hour and the horse was keeping pace. When we got to our estate it was like a scene from Rocky, with all the kids running along behind the car. They were laughing and singing –

"Road runner, if he catches you, you're through."

Da thought that was a great name. And he was as proud as punch when he opened the door and led the horse in. No one else on our road had such an unusual pet.

Da said that the froth around the horse's mouth was a good sign and, when the poor thing shit all over the hall carpet, he said that was for luck. Jasus, that horse could drink. It drank five buckets of water that night and then lay down to sleep. It was a grand aul thing and I loved taking it out for a ride around the estate. It looked the gear, wearing the little red woollen slippers me ma made for it. The only thing about it was, every time it seen Da's car it peed with fright. About a week after we bought the horse, it jumped the back fence and legged it. We used to see it up at the dump where all the wild horses roamed but every time we came near him, he ran off. All the other wild horses ate the arses out of the rubbish bins but Road Runner never came anywhere near our estate again.

Anything that Da couldn't give Ma, she got elsewhere. She always goaded him about being second best. About being Brush's gofer. He hated that, it really got to him but she wouldn't let up. She told him she'd married the wrong man and that if she'd married Brush, she'd have been happier.

I remember one time she read about some big shop in London having a sale and wanted the money to go over for the weekend. Da wouldn't give it to her. All hell broke loose. She flung china and glass like they were going out of fashion and poor Da hid behind the leather couch he'd only just bought for her. He was trying to make her understand that he just hadn't got the cash –

"In a month or two, luv, I promise."

"Don't tell me a month or two, in a month or two the sale will be over."

It went on and on, until Da finally ran for the front door and out. Seconds before his pitch and putt trophy hit it.

The next day I mitched from school and it started pelting rain so I went home. Usually I'd hang around Lynch's Lane. It was great because everyone who mitched went there. The Brothers from the local school walked up and down hitting the bushes and shouting –

"Come out, yeh little feckers."

But they soon got fed up and once this happened we could play all day without being hassled. Once we did get caught but that was just because one of the fellas got bitten by a rat and when his hand swelled up, we thought he was going to die, so we had to get help.

Anyway, that day I went home and let meself in.

I heard me ma moaning as if she was in terrible pain. Jasus, I thought, isn't it lucky I came home. She sounded terrible, all oohs and aahs. She must have been trying to move the bed cause I could hear the headboard clattering against the wall. I booted up the stairs –

"Don't worry, Ma, I'll help yeh."

I pushed open the door and there was Uncle Brush lying on top of me ma. She seemed to be trying to give him a jockey-back and he was like John Wayne, slapping her bum.

"Tara, what the hell are you doin here?"

She was trying to get up but Uncle Brush didn't want to let her go.

Mammy had no clothes on. I started crying.

Ma got up, pulled on her dressing-gown and pulled me out of the room –

"Tara it's OK. It's OK."

Uncle Brush gave me five pound. He said he knew that I'd be good at keeping a secret. But, he needn't have worried, I wasn't going to tell me da anything about today, cause I didn't want to think about what I'd seen me ma and Uncle Brush doing. I didn't really understand what I'd seen, I just knew it was wrong. It made me feel nervous and sick inside.

Da came home that night, delighted with himself. He told us that Uncle Brush had given him two tickets for London and loads of money to spend.

* * *

Everyone was very appreciative of what Johnser had done. The way he'd taken the rap for them all, never ratting anyone else up. He was Brush's Big Man now. Even Da seemed to admire him. But, as they say, nothing lasts forever and eventually everything got back to normal.

It didn't take long for them to forget that they were supposed to be looking after the Poor-Little-Wife while Johnser was doing their time. The money that had been showered on me at the start of Johnser's sentence was no longer free-flowing.

Well, fuck them, fuck them all. I was still living at home with Ma and Da so I didn't need their money. Ma was great with Tina and Da always made sure I had a few bob.

141

But, despite all their help, it was hard work looking after a baby.

She was one of those babies who only needed about two hours' sleep a day. And, when she wasn't sleeping, she was whinging, for food. Thanks be to Jasus, I hadn't breast-fed her, she'd have sucked me dry. I swear to God, that child broke me heart.

I wouldn't mind but, I didn't even like babies. I'd see other girls gooing and gaaing at every pram they saw, not me. No fucking way. I think it was the smell of them that I didn't like, they either smelt of talc or shite. And could Tina shite? I never seen anything like it. I'd hardly have the babygro buttoned before she'd start again. And then Ma would start –

"That child's hungry."

And if I said I'd only just fed her, she'd pick her up and sniff her nappy saying in a stupid voice –

"I think little missie has a dirty bumbum, yes, she has, hasn't she?"

Then Little Miss Shitty-Arse would gurgle and spit up stale milk. I'd have to change the clothes I'd only put on her an hour before.

It was a never-ending cycle of ear infections, teething, nappy rash and whinging.

Tina's looks were another problem.

I'd see people with babies and they'd look so proud when told that the baby had their eyes, or its daddy's ears, or granny's smile. Nobody ever said that about Tina. She looked nothing like me or Johnser. She didn't have Ma's eyes or Da's nose. No, Tina looked like a miniature Marcus. Marcus, as he should have looked, a few copper curls around the edge of his head and freckles. Millions and millions of freckles.

Ma insisted on bringing her out in her pram. We'd no sooner have the pram out the door and they'd be over. Every aul one in Palmerstown would be hanging over the pram. And sour-faced aul fucks, who didn't smile from one end of the year till the next, would go all gooey –

"Ah, gizza looka deh babby?"

And before I had a chance to say – "No, I'm only after gettin her asleep," – they'd have the blankets off and Tina awake and bawling.

They'd be ready with their –

"Ah, she's deh image . . . "

And stop mid-sentence the minute they saw her. Then they'd cover her up quickly, like they were trying to hide the fact that she didn't look like any of us.

It was all too much for me to cope with, I was sick to death of everyone. I needed something to perk me up, something to help me sleep. I couldn't eat, not because I didn't want to but because I had to get rid of the spare tyre Tina had left behind. Pressure, pressure, pressure.

One night while I was out having a drink with Marcus he dropped a bombshell.

Marcus still gave me the little Happy Pills but he was starting to moan about sharing his supply –

"I'm a hairdresser, not a bleedin drug-dealer. Those tabs are for me own personal use, yeh'll have teh find yer own supplier."

"An' where deh fuck will I find a supplier?"

He nodded towards a fella sitting at the bar –

"Him over there. He supplies me."

I knew the fella he was talking about, he was one of Brush's men –

"I can't ask him for drugs. He's a friend of me da's."

"Well, he's the only one I know."

I was sitting looking into me drink, wondering what I was going to do without me Happy Pills when someone tapped me on the shoulder –

"Howya, sexy? Can I get yeh a drink?" I turned around to see Stan the Man smiling down at me.

STAN

Chapter Twenty-Seven

Word gets around.

People think they're so smart, they think no one knows their secrets. But, Dublin's a small place, with loads of dealers and only a few suppliers. And everyone wants to keep on the good side of a supplier. So when the word got out that I fancied Tara Coyle, people started telling me things. Things they thought I might like to know, things like –

"Tara has a little habit."

Tabs weren't me scene, no money in them. But, Uncle Pat said that once we cut the supply of hash and tabs on the streets, offered coke and heroin at a decent price, we'd have the whole market sewn up. And he was right.

At first most people refused heroin but, when they seen there was nothing else on offer, they changed their minds. They decided to take us up on our cut-price offer of a little White Gold. And, hey presto! Within a week, they were hooked. Once that gear got into their veins, they'd have sold their grannies for another fix.

The streets were alive with customers. I was shifting

twenty grands' worth every couple of days. I was working on ten per cent commission, and pretty soon I had a fancy car just like Uncle Pat had promised. I had a fancy place to live, and now I was standing next to the woman I fancied. And I knew that pretty soon, I'd have her too.

OK, so she'd told me to shove me drink up me arse, but I knew she didn't mean it.

JACKIE

Chapter Twenty-Eight

Jasus, I was like a fucking spy hiding at the side of the church, pulling on me cigarette like a good thing. But, I wanted to stay out of the way. I didn't want another row with Tara.

I'd wait here until they'd all gone in. Then I'd sneak in and stand at the back of the church.

The churchyard was packed. Every square inch of ground was taken up with people. All the fellas wore suits and ties. You'd know they weren't used to wearing ties cause of the way they kept pulling at their collars. They looked like they were choking to death.

I stamped out me cigarette and lit another one. I'd begun chain-smoking a few weeks ago, it was something I'd have to curb but not today.

"Gimme one of them, luv."

I spun round –

"Jasus, Mr Kiely, yer nearly after given me a heart attack."

I held out the packet and he took a cigarette. He lit it, took a long pull, coughed and said –

"I'm glad teh finally meet yeh, Jackie."

"I didn't know yeh knew me."

"I didn't, I just guessed it was you. After all, everyone else is gathered at the front of the church."

I looked down at the ground, scraped me shoe across a disgarded butt and watched the tobacco blow away.

"Johnser thought a lot bout yeh," he said, putting his hand on me shoulder.

"It's nice of yeh teh say that."

"I didn't say it teh be nice, luv. I said it cause it's true."

As the crowd began moving into the church Mr Kiely turned to me –

"We'd better get movin, luv."

I hesitated –

"Com'on, girl, I know how yer feelin but it's time teh pay our last respects."

"It's not that . . . Mr Kiely, it's . . . just that . . . Tara doesn't want me here. She said . . . "

"Don't make me curse in God's yard, Jackie. Yer goin in there teh pay yer respects teh me son. An that's an end to it."

I smiled nervously as he led me towards the church door.

Johnser's brothers stood waiting to escort their father into the church. They looked older than I remembered but, having said that, it was years since I'd seen them. We'd only got as far as the porch when we heard the screech of brakes. Tara had arrived.

As she struggled to get out of the limo, she reminded me of Jackie O, with her black hat and dark glasses. The fella who'd threatened me in the funeral parlour was with her. When she seen me, she went mental –

"Get that fuckin bitch outta here!"

Her minder ran towards me but Mr Kiely blocked his way –

"Outta me way, old man," he hissed, grabbing Johnser's da by the shoulder.

Before he knew what was happening, he was on his back, Johnser's brothers standing over him.

"That bitch has no right teh be here," he told them as he struggled to his feet.

"It's none of yer business who attends me son's funeral."

"But, it's my business, and I don't want her here," Tara informed him coldly.

"Well, that's too bad, cause I do and so would Johnser. Yeh do remember Johnser, don't yeh?"

I knew by her face that she was livid. She was nearly crying with temper.

"Com'on, Stan, I'll deal with that wagon later," she barked at her minder as she barged past me into the church.

As we took our seats, Gloria Gaynor's "I will survive" strained its way out of the organ. I couldn't fucking believe she'd chosen that as a tribute to Johnser. I sat with Johnser's family and cried non-stop throughout the service. (To this day, I can't remember a word the priest said.) When it was all over and we were once again standing outside the church, I moved away from the family and lit a cigarette.

"Howya, Jackie?"

I turned around, smiled and threw me arms around Slash –

"Oh, Slash," I whispered, holding him tight.

He wasn't alone. Tiny, Baldy and Froggy were standing just a few feet away –

"Howya, Jackie?" they mumbled awkwardly.

We travelled together in Slash's car to Glasnevin Cemetery. At first the conversation was all about Johnser and how he'd died. But, then we got talking about the old days, and the craic we used to have.

Suddenly I realised I was doing something I hadn't done in a long long time – I was laughing. I laughed so much, I got a stitch in me side –

"Oh, stop will yehs? I can't breathe," I begged as the tears rolled down me face – "What will people think if they see us laughing like this?"

There was silence for a few minutes, then I remembered Fat Larry –

"How come Fat Larry wasn't at the church? What's he up teh these days?"

Slash shot Baldy a knowing look.

I panicked –

"What? What's wrong with him?"

We were at the cemetery –

"Well? Com'on, tell me what happened teh him?"

Slash stopped the car –

"I'll tell yeh later, OK?"

I couldn't understand why they were being so secretive about Fat Larry but I hadn't time to think about him now. The hearse had arrived and they were taking the coffin out. Why were they taking the coffin out here? Sure the graveyard was another half-mile up the road. I spotted Johnser's sister and made me way over to her –

"Rita, what's goin on? Why are they takin him out here?"

"Yeh mean yeh don't know?"

"Know what?"

"She's havin him cremated."

Cremated. I couldn't believe it. The only thing that had kept me going was knowing that I'd be able to visit his grave. That when things got on top of me, I'd be able to come up and see him, tell him me problems, talk to him.

But, now that bitch Tara Coyle had taken even that away from me.

I sat in the little church and watched Johnser's coffin disappear through the curtains. I knew now that he was gone from me, forever.

* * *

Jasus, I needed a drink.

I directed Slash to the nearest pub (I'd noticed it on the way in) and knocked back a double vodka.

"Beats drinkin down deh naller, eh?" Baldy joked.

We were sitting at the bar and I ordered another double and knocked that back too.

"Hey, Jackie, slow down a bit," Froggy told me, picking up his first pint.

"Fuck off, Froggy. It's me own money I'm spendin."

"Jasus, I was only sayin . . . "

"Yeah, well don't only say. OK?"

Slash jumped up –

"Hey, I've got an idea, why don't we head down deh naller?"

"What?"

"Let's get a few cans and head down? It'll be like deh old days."

"Are yous fuckin mad, or what?"

"No, I'm serious. Are yehs on for it?"

And so we went back to the naller.

We bought a bottle of vodka and a tray of cans, jumped into the car and headed down to *our* bridge.

It was just like old times. Froggy set a fire and we all sat around drinking and talking. We talked about how our lives had changed since the last time we'd been here.

Froggy worked as a porter in a hotel. He said it was crap but, a job was a job. He'd married a girl from Bluebell, (I didn't know her). Anyway, she'd left him years ago and he hadn't heard from her since. Baldy wasn't working but he was married with six kids. Tiny and Slash hadn't married. Tiny still lived at home with his ma. Slash had his own place and his own business, something to do with computers. He said it was doing really well.

I was embarressed when it came to me, cause I'd done nothing with me life. Everything I'd tried had turned to dust. But, I didn't tell them that. Instead, I panned them off with the dreary aul housewife excuse and brought the conversation back around to Fat Larry. There was silence –

"Com'on lads, what's the big secret? Why won't yehs tell us what happened teh him?"

Eventually, Slash spoke –

"Fat Larry's dead."

I laughed nervously –

"Yer jokin, right?"

I knew by the silence that he wasn't –

"How did he die? When? Where?"

"He got in with a bad crowd. When we all moved on, he didn't. He still hung round here, drinkin with anyone an everyone. Then drugs came along an he got into that too.

"He had a big habit, two hundred quid a day, so he started robbin handbags, cept, like yeh know, Fatso couldn't run teh save his life so he was fucked. Got sent down, it was only a short stretch but, when he got out his habit was worse. He was runnin a bill with a dealer, and eventually deh dealer called in his debt. Fat Larry couldn't pay so they beat him up, broke both his legs.

"Poor fucker, couldn't take it. He'd no way of making the money teh feed his habit or pay his dealer. Frankie Fitz, was his name. Anyway, Johnser got involved. He told Frankie that if he didn't leave Fat Larry alone he'd have him to deal with. As far as I know they came teh blows over it. But, it made no odds, Fat Larry couldn't hack it. Yeh know yerself, he was a soft bastard. He was found hanged a few months ago."

I couldn't believe what I'd just heard. Jasus, poor Larry. I felt so guilty about the way we'd all treated him. The way we'd always slagged him about his weight. Maybe if we'd been better mates, or stayed in touch, or something, he'd have been OK –

"Where did he . . . yeh know . . . die?"

Tiny coughed nervously –

"Up there," he croaked, pointing at the bridge.

A shiver ran down me spine, making the hairs on the back of me neck stand on end.

"He hung himself outta deh bridge, poor fucker, wasn't found till deh next mornin."

Me whole body shook. I felt so angry. Angry about what had happened to Larry, angry about Johnser, angry about life –

"Christ Almighty, Slash, why didn't yeh tell me all this before we came up here? Are yeh fuckin simple or what?"

"I'm sorry, Jackie, I didn't think. I only wanted teh remember the good times, yeh know how it is?"

We headed back to the car, leaving anything that we hadn't drank behind us. Jasus, that was a real sign of the times. Back in our younger days we'd never have left a can unfinished.

* * *

I was the last to be left home. As I went to get out of the car, Slash grabbed me arm –

153

"Jackie, I'm really sorry bout today. What I did was stupid."

"Forget it, Slash. I didn't mean teh go off on one like that. It's just that I got such a shock, an I'm ragin with meself for not knowin he was dead. I'm surprised I never seen his name in the paper."

And that did surprise me, cause I always read the deaths. It was one of me habits that drove Johnser mad.

"Yeah, that's cause they used his proper name, Ignatius . . . "

"Ignatius? I never knew that was his name. Come teh think of it, I don't even know his surname."

"Ignatius Ruhbottom. It's not the kinda name yeh shout about, is it?" We laughed.

I got out of the car –

"It's been really great seein yeh again, Slash."

"Yeah, you too, Jackie."

I smiled.

"No, really Jackie, I mean it. I've thought about yeh a lot, yeh know I've always kinda . . . "

I stopped him –

"Not now, Slash. Please?"

"OK, but yeh know, maybe sometime . . . "

I nodded, leaned over and gave him a peck on the cheek –

"See yeh, Slash."

As I ran towards the house, he shouted something about me not having his number. I didn't turn around.

I already had everything I wanted. I had me boys, me memories, and me little friend. That was all I needed to get me through the days ahead, there was no room for Slash in me life.

Slash! For fuck sake, I didn't even know his name.

TARA

Chapter Twenty-Nine

Living at home had its advantages when it came to having someone to help me with Tina, but when it came to having a social life it was a different story.

Jasus, I felt like a bleeding prisoner, and me ma was like a fucking screw –

"Where do yeh think yer goin?"

"What time do yeh call this?"

"That babby never sees yeh."

"Would yeh not feed the babby yerself?"

"Why don't yeh take her for a walk?"

Jasus, it never ended.

And, as soon as she'd finished Da would start –

"What deh yeh need more money for?"

"Christ, yeh can't possibly need more clothes?"

"Ah, Jasus, not more nappies!"

"Can she not eat ordinary food instead of all them cans?"

Hassle, hassle, hassle. Twenty-four hours a fucking day. On the odd occasion when I did get out on me own, I was under orders about the time I was to be home at. And, if I was late, well, life just wasn't worth living. Me ma'd do nothing but moan for the whole of the next day.

Jasus, it was enough to drive me up the fucking wall. I needed me little supply of Happy Pills more than ever. And of course, the more you need something, the harder it is to get. Marcus's dealer couldn't get anything, neither could any of the others he knew.

* * *

I confided me problem to Leanne one night when we were out having a drink.

I knew the crowd she hung out with took all kinds of drugs. So, if anyone could get me Happy Pills it would be one of them.

Leanne thought I was mad –

"Jasus, Tara, I can't believe yeh want me teh get yeh drugs!"

"For fuck sake, Leanne, it's only a few tablets."

"They're *drugs*, Tara."

"Well, you go and spend a few fuckin days with that whinge-bag babby of mine, an we'll see how yeh react."

Eventually, she agreed to ask one of her friends. But, she came back empty-handed, not a tab in sight.

Simon, another one of her friends, came sidling over to us. He was a great dresser and really gorgeous-looking, but he knew it. I couldn't stand the smarmy fucker.

Anyway, he told us that he had some coke if we wanted to try it. Leanne was mad about him so she agreed to come back to his apartment with us.

Everything in the apartment was black. The walls, the ceiling, even the furniture.

Fuck sake, I thought I'd died and gone to hell.

The only thing to break all the black was a lamp that changed into thousands of different colours. It was like a giant kaleidoscope. He went to his tape deck and put on Pink Floyd's *Dark Side of the Moon*. As the intro started he smirked at us –

"'Fanfare for a High'. Very apt, eh?"

He sat down and measured out six small white lines of coke onto the glass top of the coffee table. Then he took out a gold-coloured straw-like tube from his top pocket. He covered one nostril, then putting the straw up the other, he snorted noisily along one of the white lines. When he'd finished, he blinked, let out a long satisfied sigh and handed the straw to me.

I put the opposite end of the straw to me nose (I wasn't going to use the same end as him) and attempted to do what he'd just done. I snorted, the powder hit me nose at such a pace that it tiddled me. I could feel a sneeze coming on but there was nothing I could do about it. I sent the remaining lines flying away on a breeze.

It didn't take Simon long to come out of his dreamy state –

"Bitch, fucking stupid bitch. You're going to pay for that."

I couldn't answer, I was sneezing so much.

Leanne panicked –

"She's sorry, Simon, honest. Here don't worry, I'll clean it up for yeh."

She took out a tissue and started wiping the coke off the bare floorboards.

"STOP! Stop, just leave it!" He screamed at her.

"Ah no, honest Simon. Sure I don't mind, I'm always cleanin up at home. I don't mind a bit."

He turned to me –

"You stupid cunt. Do you know how much that lot cost me? Have you any idea?"

I'd stopped sneezing –

"For fuck sake, keep yer hair on, we'll give yeh a few bob towards it."

"Just get out. GO! Get fucking out."

As we left he was crawling around the floor with the straw stuck up his nose. Sniffing and crying at the same time.

We walked down the street without saying a word. I couldn't believe I'd just wasted all that lovely coke. What was I going to do? I needed something to make me feel calm. There was no way I could go home and face a whinging baby without something to relax me.

We were passing by a kebab shop when someone shouted –

"Yo, Tara."

I looked around. It was Stan the Man –

"Not now, Stan, I'm not in deh mood," I said without stopping.

He caught up and walked backwards, facing us –

"So where are yous off teh now, girls?"

"We're lookin for some gear, deh yeh know where we'd get any?"

I could've killed Leanne. She didn't know when to keep her mouth shut. She was linking me arm and I gave her a sly dig in the ribs –

"Wha? Why'd yeh dig me, Tara?"

"I didn't dig yeh, yeh stupid cunt." I said pinching the arm off her.

"Well now, girls. I might be able teh help yous out there. It just so happens that I've got some really good heroin back at me pad."

"No thanks, yer alrigh," I told him.

"Well, I am surprised. It's not everyday someone turns down free heroin and clean needles."

"Jasus, I bleedin hate needles." Leanne shivered.

"Well, we can just chase deh dragon if yeh like?"

"Chase the what?" Leanne asked.

"Com'on, I'll show yous."

* * *

I have to say I was impressed by Stan's place.

When he told me he was living in an apartment down by the quays I thought he was just trying to impress me and that he really lived in Oliver Bond Flats. So you can imagine me surprise when I discovered it was one of them real posh pads down by Guinnesses that he was living in.

The heating must have been on high – the place felt like a sauna. I'd say this had more to do with him not being able to work the timer than it had to do with hospitality. A brown leather suite took up three of the walls in the massive sitting-room. And he had a stero system that wouldn't have looked out of place in a nightclub. The wall-to-wall gold curtains shimmered in the light of the eight bulb chandelier.

"Nice place," Leanne told him, looking around in awe.

Stan smiled with pride.

"Where'd yeh buy the curtains? Lawerance's Jewellers?"

We all laughed as he led the way into the kitchen and lit the gas cooker. He took out a well-scorched spoon, mixed the smallest amount of heroin with a drop of water and held it over the flame. As it boiled, he breathed in the vapours – we all did. I could feel me head starting to spin. Jasus, this was great, brilliant. It was so good it was frightening.

I walked into the other room and Stan followed me. Leanne was still in the kitchen attempting to boil up another fix. I sat down and Stan sat beside me. He put his hand on me knee and smiled –

159

"Yeh know yeh can move in here anytime yeh like, Tara?"

I gave him a dirty look –

"Yer fuckin jokin, aren't yeh?"

He was offended –

"No, I'm not fuckin jokin. I can give yeh a good life, you an yer kid."

"Stan, I don't know yeh, I know nothin about yeh, and anyway, I don't want teh know anythin about yeh."

He moved his hand further up me leg –

"Well, we can soon put that right."

"Would yeh ever, FUCK OFF!"

I jumped up –

"Com'on, Leanne, we're goin."

Leanne took a deep breath and followed me.

* * *

Two days later we were back at Stan's. He smiled as he let us in –

"I've been expectin yous."

A week later we tried the needle for the first time. It was unbelievable, nothing could be better than this. I was shooting up twice a day, and then it happened.

STAN

Chapter Thirty

I knew the minute they walked into me pad and chased the dragon, that they were putty in me hands.

And when a few days later I showed them how to shoot up (using some of me own gear) they were mine. Uncle Pat would have thrown a wobbler if he knew I was using the gear meself, but sure, what he didn't know, wouldn't hurt him. Anyway, as long as I was in control of me habit, it was OK.

About a week after they'd tried heroin for the first time, they were back on a daily basis. And I started thinking, that it was about time I got something back in return for all me kindness. After all, I'd just introduced them to the biggest thrill they were ever likely to get.

Tara, hadn't been very receptive to me advances but that was all about to change.

They came to see me, expecting another freebie. Well, they were in for a surprise, cause freebies were a thing of the past. I put me arm around Tara, she pushed me away –

"Will yeh fuck off, Stan, an get the gear out."

Leanne started dancing around the room –

"Yeah, Stan, me main man, let's . . . PARTY!"

"Yeah, let's party," I agreed.

I sat down on me leather settee and watched her dance. Suddenly, realising there was something up, she stopped dancing –

"Hey, Stan, what's deh story? Where's deh gear?"

"Just keep on dancin, Leanne, I want teh watch yer little tits jumpin up an down."

"Fuck off, yeh spotty pervert," she roared.

I jumped up, grabbed her by the throat and, before she knew it, had her pinned against the wall –

"Watcha call me?"

Tara, was trying to pull me back –

"Fuck off, Stan, leave her alone."

I swung me arm round, trying to push her away, but I connected with her face, sending her flying across the room. She smacked her head on the side of a chair –

"Jasus, Tara, I'm sorry. I didn't mean teh . . ."

She got up and ran at me. Kicking and clawing like a fucking mad thing. I let go of Leanne and grabbed Tara. She wrestled me to the floor, wriggling like a maggot. She was strong but not as strong as me. Eventually, she stopped wriggling. I smiled down at her –

"Take it easy, relax."

All the wrestling had done something for me. I felt horny. I bent to kiss her but she raised her head and just as I was about to make contact, she spat in me face and kneed me in the balls. I rolled off her. She jumped up and ran to Leanne.

"Bitch, fuckin bitch," I moaned, "yeh can go fuck yerself, if yeh think yer gettin any gear offa me now."

A look of horror crossed Leanne's face but Tara just turned on her heel and was gone.

I heard Leanne asking Tara what they were going to do now, but Tara didn't answer.

JACKIE

Chapter Thirty-One

I let meself into Ann's house. I had to be careful not to make noise. I mean, the last thing I wanted at this time of night, was a confrontation with Ann. I was raging with meself for having agreed to stay here but, what with her minding the boys and me supposed to be home at a respectable hour, it had seemed like a good idea at the time.

Anyway, I sneaked into the sitting-room, took off me shoes and poured meself a drink. I sat down and looked around the room. It was a nice cosy room, not as nice as mine. Well at least, not as nice as mine used to be. But, that was before that terrible night.

"Shut up, Jackie," I told meself sternly, "you're not goin down that road again. It's over."

I got up to pour meself another drink and noticed an envelope with me name on it, leaning against the clock. I opened it. It was full of twenty pound notes. I found a note, telling me that the money was from Johnser's bouncers. They told me how sorry they were about Johnser, and, how they hoped this few bob would help me in the months ahead. According to them, Tara and Stan had taken over the business and they were all going to lose their jobs. So, they wouldn't be able to give me any financial help in the future.

I counted the money, two thousand pounds. I'd have to be careful with it – after all, this was going to be me nest-egg. This was the last money Johnser was ever going to give me. From now on, I'd be on me own.

Jasus, I thought. I'll really have to make an effort to go back to work. After all, I had two kids to rear and a mortgage to pay. God, why hadn't we got the mortgage in both our names? At least that way, it would have been paid in full on Johnser's death. I'm not for one minute saying that I wanted to benefit from Johnser's murder but it would have helped. For the first time in weeks I became positive Johnser was gone and he wouldn't be coming back. But, life had to go on. I vowed there and then that tomorrow would begin the rest of me life.

* * *

I looked at the clock: 6.45 am. It was too late to go to bed. So, I decided to have a shower, change me clothes and set about making breakfast. The smell of frying slowly brought the house to life. Ann was the first to arrive, dragging her feet and tightening the belt on her dressing-gown –

"Are yeh alrigh, Jackie?"

I grinned at her –

"Sit down, Ann, brekkie's on the way."

"I didn't hear yeh come in last night. Who were yeh drinkin with?"

I looked her in the eye and lied –

"Ann, I'm sorry I was late last night, but I wasn't out drinkin. I was with Johnser's sister, Rita. We were both very upset after the funeral so she asked me if I wanted teh go

164

back teh her house for a few hours. We just sat talkin, and before I knew it, it was three o'clock."

"Ah, Jackie, I'm sorry. I shouldn't have said that, it's just that every . . . "

"It's alrigh, Ann, really. I don't blame yeh for thinkin the worse. But, that's all in the past. Now, sit down and eat yer brekkie."

"Jasus, Jackie, I couldn't eat at this time of the mornin. A coffee'll do me fine."

I ignored her, and placed a full fry on the table –

"Get that inteh yeh."

She pushed it away –

"I swear, Jackie, I couldn't . . . "

"Well I could." Tommy sat down beside her – "Jasus, this is great, Jackie, you'll be kept."

"Well, if it's all the same teh you, Tommy, I think I'd rather go home," I told him laughingly.

Ann smiled at me –

"God, Jackie, I think that talk yeh had with Rita really did yeh good."

Jonathan and Edward were next into the kitchen –

"Ma, what's wrong?"

I laughed out loud –

"Nothin's wrong. I just wanted teh cook breakfast, if yehs don't mind."

God, I felt so guilty. The kids had got so used to me sitting around all day doing nothing that even making a breakfast seemed like a big deal.

I put two more full plates on the table –

"Right, yous two, eat up cause we have teh get movin. We've loads teh do today."

When the washing-up was done I made me exit. I hugged Ann as though I was never going to see her again –

165

"Jasus, Jackie, steady on, yer only goin two doors away."

I had tears in me eyes –

"I know, Ann, but you've been so good teh me."

"Will yeh ever stop, Jackie. You'd have done the same for me."

I thought about all the excuses I'd made to get rid of her whenever Johnser had come home early. The way I used her for company when he wasn't around. I wondered if I'd have taken her and her kids in if it had been Tommy who'd died? I can't honestly say that I would.

I pushed a hundred quid into her hand, I know it wasn't nearly enough, but I had to be careful with the few pounds I had. She pushed the money back at me –

"Fuck off, Jackie."

I insisted –

"Please, Ann, take it? It's the least I can do."

"No way, Jackie, I mean it, yer insultin me."

Reluctantly, I put the money back in me pocket. I made a mental note to buy her something nice, something special, just for her. Maybe some of that perfume I'd seen her looking at. She'd never buy it herself, she was like me, always watching her few bob. She wouldn't spend thirty pounds on anything for herself. As far as she was concerned, thirty pound would buy a lot of clothes for the kids, when you knew where to shop.

The boys were in great form, laughing and joking with each other, in a way I hadn't seen for ages. It gave me a good feeling.

I walked into the sitting-room, it was freezing. I knew this was because the fire hadn't been lit for a few days, and had nothing to do with Johnser dying in the room. But, still, it set me thinking.

I decided I was going to re-decorate the room. I was

going to buy a new settee, and new wallpaper, and maybe even a new carpet. I called the kids –

"Jonathan, Edward, get yer coats we're goin shoppin." They answered in unison –

"Ah, Ma."

I laughed. I knew now, that I had me old boys back. I never thought I'd be happy to hear them moaning, but I was –

"Don't 'ah, Ma' me. We have teh go shoppin, sure there's nothin in the house."

"Well, can we go teh Nana's while you do it?"

"NO."

Me answer was harsher than I'd intended. I tried to redeem meself by promising a trip to McDonalds, but the moment was lost.

I took some of the money I'd been given and hid the rest in a box I kept in the freezer. I used to keep it in the tea caddy but Johnser had told me that was the first place a robber would look so, I changed to the freezer.

We made our way along all the furniture shops, looking at all the latest designs and colours, but I couldn't bring meself to spend the kind of money they were asking. In the end, I bought a second-hand couch for eighty quid. The only problem was, it wouldn't match me two armchairs so I'd have to buy a throw-over rug for it. I picked up a lovely carpet for forty-five quid. I couldn't believe they were calling a ten-by-twelve carpet a remnant. But they could call it what they liked, as long as it meant more money in my pocket. The wallpaper was another bargain. I got six rolls for twenty quid. According to the girl in the shop, the design was discontinued so they were selling it off cheap. But, if I'd bought the exact same paper a month ago, well, it would have cost me eight ninety-nine a roll. I was delighted with meself, I loved getting a bargain.

We done the food shopping. I let the boys have a bag of minibars each, and I even bought a tub of expensive ice cream as a special treat. We had our tea in McDonalds, and got a taxi home.

We lit a big fire, and cuddled up together on the couch. We were in the middle of watching *The X-Files* when Edward fell asleep. I didn't bother putting him up to bed cause I didn't want to disturb Jonathan's enjoyment of his favourite programme. I think he was having his first major crush, on Scully. He went real quiet when she was on the screen, hanging on to her every word, and laughing at all her stupid jokes. I knew all too well how it felt. For me, it had been Paul Michael Glazier. As far as I'd been concerned, he was it. I'd wanted to be sixteen instead of twelve. Cause, if I'd been sixteen I'd have been allowed go to a film premier. He would have spotted me in the crowd and whisked me away for a life amongst the stars. We'd appear in loads of films together, we'd be the Fred and Ginger of the seventies. I dreamt about him almost every night – we'd be sitting together on his porch, in our matching cardigans and perms.

I don't know when I stopped loving him. It was probably when I found out he was married with kids. Jasus, when I think about it now, I feel like a right fucking eejit. But, at least he'd been good-looking. As far as I was concerned, that Scully one hadn't got a look in the world. I knew better than to voice me opinion to Jonathan, I'd no intention of falling out with him over some woman he'd never even meet, let alone marry.

* * *

When the programme was over, he ran ahead of me up the

168

stairs, I carried Edward up and tucked him into bed. The minute his head hit the pillow, he was awake –

"I have teh go deh toilet."

He ran barefoot into the bathroom, I heard the lid crashing down –

"Edward, be careful with that lid."

A broken toilet was the last thing I needed. With the prices those plumbers charged, you'd swear they were doing open heart surgery on the loo.

Back in bed, I tucked him in, kissed them both goodnight and made me way downstairs. I'd only just walked back into the sitting-room when there was a knock on the door. Thinking it was Ann, I opened the door wide, a big smile on me face. I was dying to tell her about all the things I'd bought –

"Come in, An . . . "

I stopped short when I seen who was on the door-step –

"Well, Jackie, aren't you going to invite me in?"

TARA

Chapter Thirty-Two

Leanne was wrecking me head. She was asking the same question over and over again –

"Where are we gonna get our gear now, Tara?"

I grabbed her by the arm, and swung her around to face me –

"Read me fuckin lips, Leanne. I don't bleedin know where we're gonna get our gear. So, don't keep goin on bout it. It's not my fault that bollox tried teh kiss me . . ."

"I'm not fuckin sayin it was yer fault, Tara. But, it wouldn't have killed yeh teh give him a kiss."

"Would yeh ever cop on, Leanne? He didn't only want a fuckin kiss. He wanted a ride."

"Yeah, well OK. But, it probably wouldn't have been too bad."

"Would yeh ever fuck off, Leanne?"

We walked on in silence. Jasus, I really needed a fix but I only had a tenner –

"How much have yeh got on yeh?"

Leanne looked in her bag –

"Fifteen quid, and a bit of loose change."

"Ah, for fuck sake, Leanne!"

"Wha? It's not my fault I don't get paid till tomorra."

* * *

Jasus, I was in bits. I was breaking into cold sweats. I knew there was a dealer living nearby (I'd met him at Stan's place). I also knew he'd probably want more than twenty-five quid for two hits. But, fuck it, it was worth a go. We went up to his flat, the place was scruffy. Some of the windows were broken and boarded up with cardboard. Someone had carved *Scum Out* across the front door. I knocked on the door, and after what seemed like an eternity "Woody" the dealer, staggered out. He was trying hard to focus –

"Hey, girls, what's deh story?"

"Woody, me aul mate, remember me? Tara?"

"Tara? Yeah, sure Tara, baby. Long time no see. Com'on in we're partyin."

The room was dark and stank of stale sweat and urine. There were bodies everywhere, all at different stages of being stoned. Two fellas were flaked out on the floor, they still had their sleeves rolled up. They looked like they were dead (probably were). There was a girl flapping around the room, chasing an imaginary butterfly. And there were another three sitting huddled around the heating-spoon.

Woody tried to sit down casually but he ended up flat on his back. It was as if someone had lowered the floor while he was answering the door –

"Hey, guys, here's Tara and eh, eh, hey, I forget yer friend's name?"

"Leanne."

"Yeah, right, Leanne."

No one took a blind bit of notice of us. They were more

171

interested in their fix. One of the "Indians" was putting a strap around his friend's arm and tapping for a vein. "Bingo!" He whispered as he plunged the needle into the friend's arm. The look of pain on the junkie's face soon turned to ecstacy as the brown liquid hit the spot. Then, using the same needle, he injected himself.

A month ago, I would have been physically sick at the sight of a needle going into a vein but not now. Now all I wanted was to skip the queue and get meself jacked up.

When the rest of the party guests had been looked after, Woody began cooking up our fix –

"Well, now girls, show me deh colour of yer money?"

I handed him the twenty-five quid. He looked at me like I had two heads –

"Fuck sake, Tara, are yeh takin deh mickey or what?"

"Ah, Woody, please? That's all we've got. Com'on just this once, do us a favour?"

He looked us up and down –

"OK, Tara. But, it's just this once. An if this ever gets out . . . I'll fuckin kill deh both of yous . . . understood?"

We didn't say anything, just nodded.

He was filling the syringe –

"Have yeh no clean needles, Woody?"

"Don't start gettin fussy with me, Tara. For twenty-five quid yer fuckin lucky teh be gettin anythin at all. Now, who's first?"

I nudged Leanne –

"Leanne, you go first."

She didn't need to be told twice. She rolled up her sleeve and, pulling the strap tight, tapped on her vein. He injected half the stuff into her, then took the needle out –

"Yeh ready, Tara?"

I protested –

172

"For fuck sake, Woody. Is that all we're gettin?"

"Tara, this is good gear. It's worth fifty quid a go."

I rolled up me sleeve and he did his business. When he'd injected all the heroin into me vein, he filled the syringe with me blood, and shot it back into me arm –

"That's a little trick of deh trade, Tara, makes sure yeh get every last drop of the gear inteh yeh."

* * *

The first thing I thought about when I woke up the next morning was a fix. Tina was crying but I didn't give a shite. Ma came in –

"Tara, are yeh gone deaf?"

She took Tina, and left the room. I could hear her gooing and gaaing as she made her way downstairs –

"Com'on, chicken. Nana'll feed yeh."

"Oh, isn't Nana fuckin great," I mimicked.

As soon as I was sure she'd started the feeding, I jumped out of bed and legged it into her room. Da was still in bed but I knew from his snores that he was sound asleep. I found Ma's handbag and opened it, no purse.

"Well, fuck yeh, Ma," I thought.

I looked around. Da's trousers were hanging on the back of a chair. I went through his pockets, three twenty-pound notes. I took two.

Ma was shouting up the stairs –

"Tara, get up outta that bed, now. An get yer father up too. Tara, deh yeh hear me?"

I didn't answer. Da stopped snoring, he turned over.

"Da, are yeh right? Ma says yer teh get up."

When I went into the kitchen, Tina was on her second bowl of Readybrek. She was getting to be a right little

173

pudding. Ma said it was puppy fat, not that it bothered me, I didn't care what size she was. I made meself a black coffee and a slice of dry toast –

"That looks disgusting," Ma told me, making a face.

"Well, it's me who's eatin it, not you. So don't be annoyin me," I snapped back.

Da came into the kitchen, fiddling in his pockets and looking puzzled –

"What's wrong with yeh?" Ma asked as she poured his tea.

"I could've sworn I had sixty quid when I came home last night but, now I only have twenty."

"Yeh probably spent it on drink."

"Naw, I wasn't drinkin last night, I was workin. An I'm sure I didn't lose it cause I . . . "

"Well, I didn't fuckin rob it!" she roared, before he'd finished his sentence.

"I never fuckin said yeh did."

And so it began. More and more money went missing from the house. I pawned every bit of jewellery I had but it wasn't enough. Leanne lost her job with Marcus cause he'd caught her with her hand in the till.

Then just when I thought I was going to go mad, Stan reappeared.

"Hello, Tara," he smiled. Swinging a little bag of pure undiluted joy in me face.

STAN

Chapter Thirty-Three

Uncle Pat was happy, very very happy.

We were cleaning up. I was supplying heroin to almost every junkie in Dublin, our gear was the best. I was supplying three of the biggest dealers in the country, and they were happy enough with the set-up. I only ever dealt with the top men and always for cash.

OK, so they weren't making as big a profit as when they brought the gear in themselves but they weren't taking the risks either.

* * *

Frankie Fitz was one of the top men I dealt with. I liked Frankie. He was one of those men who had a knack for sorting things out, even when he was in prison.

Nothing ever happened on the north side of Dublin without his say-so.

The south side was ruled by Brush. Good aul Brush, Jasus, he was legend. An old man with a big reputation, that was him. And, if you only seen him, you'd never believe he was anything other than a lovely little granda.

Jasus, he even wore a granda's cardigan with pockets, for his snooker chalk and Woodbines. And, everytime he took out a cigarette, he'd tell the same old story. About how his missus didn't like him smoking. For fuck sake, I'm sure his missus would rather have him smoking than murdering people. If only she knew. Granpa Brush was one of the most vicious, heartless bastards in Dublin.

I knew Brush didn't like me very much, he blamed me for Johnser Kiely going to prison. But, fuck it, what did I care? I didn't give two shites who liked me, they could all go fuck themselves, as far as I was concerned.

I also knew that Brush hated drugs, hated having to deal with low-lifes, like me. But, he was clever enough to know that, like it or not, drugs were the way forward.

Drugs gave you power. As long as you weren't taking the gear yourself, you'd nothing to worry about.

* * *

I know I often took a bit of gear meself but that was nothing. I only wanted to see what all the fuss was about. You know yourself what it's like? You see a bar of chocolate being advertised on the telly and, the next time you're in a shop, you buy *that* bar of chocolate. Just to see what all the fuss is about. It's the same with everything. I remember when Paul McCartney brought out that record "Mull of Kintyre" and it got to number one in the charts. Well, like a big eejit I went out and bought it, I wouldn't mind but I hadn't even heard the fucking song. Anyway, when I got home and played it, I nearly went mad, it was the biggest load of shite I'd ever heard. I remember I fucked it against the wall and it smashed.

And, it was the same with the drugs. I only tried them so as I could find out what all the fuss was about. I wasn't a

176

junkie, I wasn't like them other fucking eejits, I could give up any time I wanted.

I remember the first time I ever injected, Jasus, that first trip was something else.

I was making a delivery to Frankie Fitz, and he asked me to join him for a drink. I didn't like to refuse, after all, he was a good customer. Anyway, we were on our second pint when he took out his works –

"Jasus, Frankie, I didn't realise yeh were inteh deh gear?"

"Don't be ridiculous, Stan, this is only a social habit. No different from having a pint. Would you like to try some?"

"Well, I don't know . . . what I mean is . . . I've never injected before."

"Really? Ah, well, not to worry. Maybe some other time, eh?"

"Ah, sure fuck it, I might as well try it now as later."

Frankie handed me a works and I done what I'd seen hundreds of junkies doing a million times.

The heroin shot through me system like a nuclear missile. It rushed around me body like a warm stream, flowing through me veins, warming me to the bone. Jasus, I thought, this is fuckin great. It felt like a giant orgasm, like every part of me body was orgasming at the same time. Me eyes were closed but I could still see everything that was going on around me, I could even see beyond the room, and out into the big wonderful world. I opened me eyes and looked at Frankie, he was a great mate, the best. He wasn't the man I'd seen kicking a pregnant junkie to the ground cause she'd left him short of a fiver. No, he was the most caring wonderful human being I'd ever met.

I never got that feeling again. I chased it, but I never quite caught up. I felt like I was in a maze, thinking that every time I turned a corner I'd find me way out but I never did.

* * *

I'd started putting a little bit less into the parcels I was selling. Nothing noticable, just enough for a few personal turn-ons. Besides, I had to make sure and have a little something for Tara, just in case she decided to drop in. As far as I was concerned, the way to a woman's heart was through her veins.

I knew the dealer who was supplying Tara. He was a wanker and the gear he sold was pure shite. When the gear left my hands, it was the best money could buy. But, by the time it hit the streets, it had been mixed so much it was more baking-powder than heroin.

I knew Tara would've noticed the difference.

I walked into the pub one night and found her sitting shivering in a corner –

"Well well, Tara, this is a surprise."

"Cut deh crap, Stan, I'm not in deh mood."

"It's not crap, Tara, honest. I really am glad teh see yeh. I wanted teh tell yeh that, I'm sorry bout deh other night."

She didn't answer. I held the little parcel in front of her –

"Wanna com back teh my place?"

Leanne was putting on her coat. I grabbed her arm –

"Sorry, Leanne, yer not invited. Three's a crowd."

"Don't worry, Leanne, I'll bring yeh back a fix," Tara assured her. Jasus, she was like a mother promising to bring sweets back from the shop.

When we got back to me pad, Tara took out twenty quid. "It's not yer money I'm after, Tara, it's you," I told her as I headed to the kitchen to get the gear.

Once she'd had her fix, she lay back on the couch, a satisfied smile on her face. I climbed on top of her –

"Yeh know I've always fancied yeh, Tara?

I pulled up her skirt, she didn't protest –

"I reckon me an you could be real good together."

I had her knickers off –

"Yeh know, if yeh wanted it, this could all be yours?"

I was in, I was moving up and down. Her eyes were distant and her smile was fixed but, fuck it, a ride was a ride. And the fact that it was Tara Coyle made it all the better.

JACKIE

Chapter Thirty-Four

"What the fuck are you doin here?" I croaked.

I couldn't believe the cheek of him, showing up here after all this time.

"At the minute I'm getting soaked," he said, with a smile, "aren't you going to invite me in?"

I hesitated for a minute, then stood aside and let him pass.

He walked into the sitting-room, and looked all around him –

"Nice place, Jackie. I'm impressed," he complimented me, rubbing his hands in front of the open fire.

I stood looking at him, who the fuck did he think he was? Coming in here and acting like an old friend who'd just dropped in for a chat. I didn't give a shite whether he was impressed or not, this was my home, not his.

"What are yeh doin here, Jeffrey?" I almost spat the words at him.

He spun round. He looked hurt by me tone –

"Any chance of a cup of tea, Jackie?" He asked, ignoring me question.

I wasn't going to be put off that easy –

"I asked yeh a question and, if I don't get an answer in the next ten seconds, yeh can get deh fuck outta here."

"Please, Jackie, there's no need for bad language. I didn't realise I needed to make an appointment to see me own wife."

"Of course yeh didn't, Jeffrey. Yous wife-beating bullies, think yer entitled teh turn up whenever yous please."

I walked over to the table and picked up me glass –

"Tut tut, Jackie, drinking alone? Now that's a bad habit."

"Yeah, an so's kickin deh shite outta women."

He turned away from me, and looked into the fire –

"That's all in the past, Jackie, I've changed."

"Haven't we all?"

He turned around and looked me straight in the eye –

"Really, I have changed. I got help."

"Yeah, well yeh fuckin needed it."

He moved towards me –

"And, I haven't gambled in nearly a year."

"Well now, Jeffrey, correct me if I'm wrong, but, I seem teh remember yeh given up gamblin before."

"That was different, Jackie. You know what I mea . . . "

"Yeah, too fuckin right, Jeffrey. I know exactly what yeh mean."

He lowered his head in that little-boy-lost way I knew so well. The bastard –

"Ah, what's wrong, with poor little Jeffrey? Is he sulkin cause big bad Jackie won't believe a word outta his mouth?" I asked.

He glared at me but, I didn't care, I was on a roll –

"Well, let me tell yeh somethin, Jeffrey. Yeh can sulk as much as yeh fuckin like, it won't bother me. Yeh miserable piece of shite. When we lived tegether yeh treated me like dirt. And, if I so much as said boo, yeh kicked the livin daylights outta me. So, don't come here expectin me teh believ . . . "

He cut across me –

"I know, Jackie. I know how you must feel, but please, try to understand . . . I was under a lot of pressure . . . "

I was back –

"And I wasn't? Don't forget, I was the one sittin at home all day, while you were out gamblin. I was the one who worried about havin enough food for the kids. Yeh do remember the kids, Jeffrey? Two boys . . . "

"Stop, Jackie, please. I'm sor . . . sor . . . sorry."

He started crying.

"Don't," I shouted, moving towards him, "yer snivellin won't fuckin work with me."

He fell to his knees, sobbing –

"Oh, Jackie, please believe me, I'm begging you. I really am sorry."

I hit him. I felt so angry I wanted to kill him. I punched him because he was crying, I slapped him because he was apologising, and I kicked him because of all the things he'd done to me. But, most of all, I hit him because he'd come back into me life.

When the anger finally left me, I flopped down into me armchair. Vodka bottle and glass in hand –

"Now, Jeffrey, let's start again. What deh fuck are yeh doin here? Why have yeh come crawlin outta deh woodwork after all this time? Jasus, how long has it been since yeh bothered with us? Let me think? Oh yeah, I remember. You'd spent yer redundancy, had the house repossessed, sold the furniture, lost the business, yeh even sold the fuckin lawn mower. Then, a few more beatins, I tell me ma what a bollox yeh are and, hey presto! Yer gone."

He was sitting on the floor. He coughed, trying to compose himself –

"My mother's dead."

Well, well, I thought. So the battle-axe had finally kicked the bucket. The woman who'd blamed me for all Jeffrey's

182

weakness was dead. So, what did he expect me to do, cry? I wanted to tell him that I didn't give a shite, but I couldn't. I knew how much it hurt to lose someone you loved –

"I'm sorry yer ma's dead, Jeffrey. And I'm not being smart but, what has her dying got teh do with me?"

He started crying, again –

"It's . . . it's just that now she's gone . . . I've no one . . . I've nothing left . . . "

"Jasus, Jeffrey, I find that hard teh believe. I mean, it's not as though yer ma was spendthrift, she was always very careful with her few bob."

"She was. But, she didn't expect to get sick so she hadn't any medical insurance. I wasn't able to look after her. So, I had to put her in a private nursing home, it broke my heart but, I had no choice, I had to do what was best for her. Anyway, by the time God was good enough to take her, it was too late. She'd been sick for two years. During that time I had to re-mortgage the house and sell everything we owned in order to make ends meet. And, now that she's gone . . . I have nothing."

"Like I say, Jeffrey, I'm sorry yer ma's dead. But, what can I do?"

He was kneeling at me feet –

"I know it's a lot to ask, Jackie. But, if you let me stay here, just until I got back on me fe . . . "

I jumped up –

"Noway, no-fuckin-way, Jeffrey. What deh yeh take me for?"

"No, Jackie, it's not what you think. Just hear me out, please?" He looked into me face, his eyes pleading. I let him continue –

"I know I treated you badly. Christ, Jackie, you've no idea how many nights I've lain in bed thinking of how, if I ever got the chance, I'd make it up to you."

I poured meself another drink.

"Can I have a drop of that?"

I handed him the bottle and told him where to find a glass. He poured himself a large vodka and sat down on the couch –

"I've got a new job, I start Monday week. It's a great job, with great perks. Not only do I get a company car, I also get company accomodation, in London."

"London!" I nearly choaked on the word.

"Yes, London. I'm really looking forward to it, I just know it's going to work out. It's the chance I've been waiting for all my life. I fly out the Saturday after next. All I'm asking of you, Jackie, is that you let me stay here for a few days? Then, if you want, I'll be out of your life forever?"

"What do yeh mean, if I want?"

"What I mean, Jackie, is that I want to try again."

Ignoring me look of amazement, he continued –

"What we had was special, it wa . . . "

"No!" I was on me feet again – "What we had was a sham. We shouldn't ever have gone out together, never mind got married. I was on the rebound from . . . " I stopped mid-sentence.

"From Johnser? Is that who you were going to say?"

I was taken aback, I hadn't realised he knew –

"How did yeh know about Johnser?"

"I didn't. Well, what I mean is, I wasn't sure, until now. I read about the murder in the paper but, I didn't think it was the same Jackie Clarke. I must say, I'm surprised, I wouldn't have thought you were one for living dangerously."

"I'm not."

I sat down –

"OK, Jeffrey, yeh can stay for a few days . . . on the sofa."

He started to thank me but, I stopped him –

"Don't bother thankin me, Jeffrey. Cause come Saturday, yer out. No excuses."

TARA

Chapter Thirty-Five

I couldn't believe I'd done it. I just couldn't believe that me, Tara Coyle, was now living with Stan the Man.

After all the things I'd said about him, all the names I'd called him, all the times I'd told him how ugly he was. I then go and move, lock stock and Tina, into his pad. Jasus, I hated him, he was such a doormat. I mean to say, he knew how I felt about him, he knew I'd no respect for him. So, why was he prepared to take me and Tina on?

I wasn't too happy with the set-up meself. But, I had me reasons for going along with his plans. Stan had money. And money meant a lot to me. I'd never had any intention of spending me life with some pauper, noway. All that stuff about money not being important as long as you had love was all me arse.

I'd no intention of being grey and wrinkled at forty, from worrying over bills and kids' clothes. No siree, that wasn't the life I had in mind for me. I wanted someone who'd provide me with the good things in life, someone who wasn't afraid to spend his money. And that someone was Stan.

185

* * *

Stan was the biggest drug supplier in Ireland, he was Top Dog. He lived in a real posh apartment (he called it a pad but, that was him trying to be hip). He drove a great car and, despite his looks, wore great clothes. Then there was me, I wanted for nothing, he bought me endless amounts of clothes, shoes, jewellery, he even bought me perfume, Christian Dior no less.

And, as well as all his money, there was another little thing he had in his favour . . . an endless supply of heroin.

* * *

Ma was very upset when I told her we were moving out. Well, what I mean is, when she'd finished ranting and raving because I hadn't been home for a few days (three to be exact), she got upset.

Jasus, the way she went on, you'd swear I made a habit of staying out all night. And I didn't. This was the first time I'd done it since Tina'd been born. I just couldn't understand the way her brain worked. I mean to say, I was old enough to vote, old enough to be married, old enough to have a kid but, as far as Ma was concerned, I still wasn't old enough to stay out all night.

She said it had nothing to do with any of that, the reason she was annoyed was because I hadn't phoned, and she'd been worried sick, thought I was lying dead somewhere, etc, etc.

But I knew that if I'd phoned she'd have given me an ear-bashing. She'd have gone on and on about how selfish and irresponsible I was. So, what was the point in ringing? I was never one for meeting trouble half way.

186

You might as well be hung for a sheep as a lamb was my motto.

But, having said all that, the real reason I hadn't phoned was because I'd been too out of it to see the phone, never mind dial her number.

Anyway, once she got over me going AWOL, I dropped me bombshell. I told her I was moving in with Stan. Ma started crying. Da started shouting –

"Ye'll move in with that bollox over me dead body."

I didn't say anything. I knew there was no point arguing with them, it was better to let them rant and rave, get it out of their systems. Eventually they'd calm down and I'd get me own way. I was right.

About two hours after I'd told them me plans, Ma was helping me pack, and Da was asking for directions to Stan's place. He drove us over to the apartment and, even helped me move Tina's things into the boxroom.

* * *

It was great. Stan had some really good gear. I couldn't get enough of it, and he couldn't get enough of me. I always talked him into shooting up before sex, cause, once he was stoned, he couldn't get a horn. And, after about ten minutes of fumbling, he'd flake out. Then, just when I thought life was really on the up, I got the biggest shock of me life . . . I was pregnant again.

I was devastated. What was I going to do with another baby? For fuck sake, most days I was so stoned I was barely able to look after Tina, never mind look after a new baby.

When I told Stan about the pregnancy, he was over the moon. Needless to say, he wanted a son, someone to follow in his footsteps, someone to take over his empire. He told me that we'd have to go off the gear and I promised that I would. But, we both agreed that there was no point starting a new routine on the weekend, we'd wait till Monday.

* * *

The baby arrived premature and bawling. I don't really remember too much about the birth.

I'd shot up early that morning and then conked out. Next thing I knew, I was lying in the labour ward with a nurse standing over me, pointing at the marks on me arms.

A doctor came in and gave me a lecture on the dangers of drugs, but Stan soon shut him up. Stan was great like that, he knew how to deal with these little shites. He told him we were paying good money for his skills as a doctor, not as a fucking lecturer. That soon got rid of him.

Because of all the fuss they were making about drugs, I expected a visit from a social worker but it never came. I left hospital a few days later with me new baby daughter, Sally.

Stan insisted that I wasn't to shoot up in front of his daughter. I agreed. But, most nights while I fed her, I took a little something for meself.

STAN

Chapter Thirty-Six

Uncle Pat was upset, I'd missed a payment.

The last parcel he'd delivered hadn't been sold, I'd kept it for personal use. So, I'd no money for him.

It wasn't my fault that I'd no money, things were just a bit tight at the moment, that's all. I mean to say, I'd a lot of outgoings now. What with me new family and everything. I tried explaining this to Pat but, he wasn't interested. As far as he was concerned, I was making two grand per delivery, that should have been more than enough to live on.

I got a week's grace by telling him that one of me main dealers was out of town and I wouldn't get paid till he got back. I wasn't sure if he believed me or not, but, fuck it, it was the best I could do.

I decided that the only way I was going to be able to pay him what was owing was to do a little bit of mixing. So, when I received me next four parcels, I mixed a little bread soda, and hey presto! I had five parcels. I got paid and sent him his money. But, I knew he still wasn't happy, the trust was gone. And, as well as having to deal with him, I also had to deal with the suppliers. They were upset, the gear wasn't up to scratch, clients were complaining, they didn't like being short-changed. Jasus, this was getting a bit close for comfort. These weren't the kind of people you cheated on. But, I convinced meself, this wouldn't happen again, it was a once-off.

* * *

Just when I'd got things sorted out, and life was moving along nicely again, Frankie Fitz dropped a clanger –

"Johnser Kiely is back on the streets."

According to him, Kiely was madder than ever, prison had done nothing to quieten him down. And, knowing Johnser Kiely as I did, I knew he'd be out to get revenge on all those who'd been involved in him going down. I also knew that I'd be top of his list. Cause, as well as having a hand in him doing time, I was now shacked up with his wife.

The last thing I needed was Johnser Kiely on me back, so I decided to go and see him.

* * *

Johnser Kiely had changed, he was much bigger than I'd remembered. All the weight-training he'd done in prison had paid off.

He didn't even look up from his pint when I sat down beside him. He'd obviously seen me in the mirror, behind the bar, when I walked in. In our game, you never sat with your back to a door, unless there was a mirror in front of you. I ordered two pints and turned to him –

"Johnser."

He didn't answer. He put his hand over his half-empty glass and told the barman –

"I'm alrigh, I don't wanna pint."

Well fuck you, I thought, I didn't really wanna buy yeh a drink, anyway.

The barman put me pint on the counter and, as I counted out the money I glanced at Johnser –

"So yer out."

"Jasus, Stan, yer sharp."

He was still a fucking smart-arse, always trying to make people feel stupid. I'd a good mind to knock his fucking head off, but that wasn't what I was here for –

"So, no hard feelins then?"

He emptied his glass and stood up –

"Oh, I've plenty a hard feelins, Stan. Plenty of scores teh settle, an' yeh know it. But, don't yeh go worryin yerself . . . just yet. I've bigger fish than you teh fry. Besides . . . "

He straightened his jacket, folded his newspaper, and putting it into his pocket, said –

"I hear yer shacked up with Tara, that's punishment enough for now."

Before I had a chance to say anything, he turned and walked out.

As I watched him leave the pub, I said to meself –

"One of these days, Kiely, one of these fuckin days."

But, not today. Today I was just happy to let bygones be bygones.

I was beginning to sweat. Jasus, I needed a fix . . . quick. I ordered another pint and was heading to the jacks when the pub door opened, I glanced over –

"Uncle Pat! I'll be with yeh in a minute, I'm just goin teh deh jacks."

Jasus, I thought, as I got me fix ready, what the fuck is Pat doing here? No doubt, I'd find out soon enough.

"I'll have to be quick," I told meself, holding me lighter under the tinfoil. It was taking forever to boil –

"Bubble yeh bastard, bubble!" I was saying to the tinfoil, when the door burst open. Before I had a chance to react, Uncle Pat had me up against the wall –

"What deh fuck deh yeh think yer doin? Yeh fuckin gobshite!"

I watched as me foil hit the floor –

"I was only testin deh gear, Pat. Yeh know, makin sure it was up teh scratch."

He wasn't alone. He'd two big fuckers with him. He turned to them –

"Yeh hear that, lads? Stanley here is doing a bit of quality control."

I was nervous. I was sweating again, shaking –

"Yeah, that's right, Pat. I was doin a bit of quality control."

The next thing I knew was me head hitting the wall. Then he ran me towards the sink, and smashed me face into the mirror. I couldn't see him but I could hear him –

"Yeh little prick, I should fuckin kill yeh. I should cut yer fuckin balls off an shove 'em up yer arse."

I lay on the floor, blood pouring from me head.

"If yeh weren't me nephew, I'd leave yeh fuckin dead. Yer finished with me, deh yeh hear me? Finished. I don't ever wanna set eyes on yeh again. Yeh useless piece of shite."

He kicked me again.

The door slammed. I struggled to me feet, and out into the pub. The place went silent for about two minutes, then, as suddenly as it had stopped, the conversation started up again. Two bouncers grabbed me, rushed me towards the back door, and fucked me out into an alleyway. The owner came running out –

"That fucker's after wreckin me jacks. There's blood an fuckin glass everywhere."

The bouncers searched me pockets –

"There's about two hundred quid here, Boss."

The owner of the pub grabbed the money. Then, throwing a tenner into me face, he said –

"Ye'll need that for deh hospital."

JACKIE

Chapter Thirty-Seven

I nearly jumped out of me skin when I walked into the kitchen the next morning. I hadn't expected anyone to be there, the place was so quiet.

So you can imagine me surprise when I seen Jeffrey and the boys sitting at the table having breakfast. The only difference between them and a normal family was the silence. No one was saying a word.

Jeffrey got up and switched on the kettle –

"Coffee, no sugar, right?"

I don't know why but I asked for tea with two sugars. I hated tea with sugar but I hated the thought of Jeffrey thinking that he knew anything about me even more.

He handed me the cup and I sipped at the tea. It turned me stomach. I put the cup down and turned to the boys –

"How come yous two are up so early?"

"I woke them at seven forty-five," Jeffrey answered for them.

Jonathan jumped up and grabbed his bag –

"I'm goin teh school."

Edward followed him –

"Me too."

Jeffrey glanced at the clock, it was only eight thirty –

"They're enthusiastic, aren't they?"

"No, not really."

"Well, they certainly leave early enough."

"I'd say that has more teh do with you bein here than their love of school."

The front door slammed, Jeffrey sighed –

"Maybe you could have a word with them?"

"Why?"

"Because I'd like to get to know them."

"But, why?"

"Because, Jackie, I'm their father."

"And?"

"And, boys need a father figure, a role model."

"Well, they've done alrigh so far. Besides, if I want them to learn about wife abuse and gamblin I'll let them watch *The Bill*, OK?"

As I looked at him across the table, I wasn't sure whether it was hurt or anger I seen in his eyes.

"I've changed," he said through clenched teeth.

"So yeh say."

He stood up and grabbed the back of the chair –

"It's true. You've got to believe me, Jackie!"

"No, I don't. I don't have teh do anythin for you, Jeffrey."

He knelt down in front of me –

"Jackie, I want us to try again . . . I want you to give me another chance. I know I've been a fool, and I know you don't owe me anything. But, I'm asking you, begging you, to give us another go. Don't you remember what we had together?"

"We had nothin tegether, Jeffrey. All we done was live a lie."

"But, I love you, Jackie. And, I know I can make you love me again."

"No yeh can't, Jeffrey. Cause, I never loved yeh in the first place."

He looked at me in stunned silence, then buried his head in me lap and started to sob.

I tried to lift his head up but he resisted –

"Please, Jeffrey. Don't, don't cry."

He pulled away from me and got to his feet –

"Why did you marry me, Jackie?"

I lit a cigarette, picked up the cups and walked to the sink. I flicked the switch of the kettle –

"Tea or coffee?" I asked without turning around.

"Whatever."

I spooned coffee into both cups, and stood gazing out the window while I waited for the kettle to boil.

"You should try cutting down on those things."

His voice cut through me thoughts –

"What? Oh yeah, right."

It had taken me a few seconds to realise he was talking about cigarettes. I filled the cups –

"Here, milk yer own, I wanna get dressed."

I picked up me cigarettes and coffee and headed for the door.

"Jackie, you never answered my question."

"I know."

By the time I came back to the kitchen, he'd the dishes washed and the table set for breakfast –

"Thanks, Jeffrey but I can't eat that. It's too early for me."

"Ah, go on. Sure I made it specially."

I forced meself to eat a slice of toast –

"Oh, by the way, there's a spare key on the hall table, just in case yeh wanna go out."

He smiled –

"Thanks. Will you be going out yourself?"

I immediatly became defensive –

"Why? What's it got teh do with you?"

"Jasus, Jackie, I was only asking."

"I'm sorry, Jeffrey. It's just that I've been a bit touchy ever since . . . " I couldn't finish the sentence.

He touched me arm –

"It must have been horrible?"

"It was."

"Would you like to talk about it?"

"No, I can't. I've tried . . . but . . . the words seem teh freeze in me throat."

"Well, I'm here if you need me."

That's nice of him, I thought, as I looked at the clock –

"Jasus, look at deh time? I'd better get goin."

"Can I ask where?"

God, had I really become such a bitch? That people had to ask permission to ask a question?

"I have teh go and see me supervisor about goin back teh work. And, I'm not lookin forward teh it, I'd rather eat coal than go back teh that place."

"So, don't go."

"Yeah, chance'd be a fine thing. And, what deh yeh suggest I live on? Fresh air!"

Jeffrey looked surprised –

"Surely you've got a few bob tucked away? Don't his type always keep money for a rainy day?"

"His type? What deh yeh mean by his type, Jeffrey? Deh yeh mean robbers an drug dealers? Is that deh type yeh mean?"

"No, not at all, I meant someone who had his own business, that's all . . . honest."

I believed him. He reached for me hand, I didn't pull away. I lit another cigarette –

"Everything Johnser had went teh his wife. I got a few hundred pounds but that was it."

I took a long pull on me cigarette.

"Christ, Jackie, I never thought . . . here . . . I'll write you a ch . . ."

As he reached into his pocket, I grabbed his arm –

"NO!" I hadn't meant it to come out like that. "No, Jeffrey, honestly. It's a nice offer but . . . please . . . I'm alrigh, I still have a few bob. And, sure I'm goin back teh work in a few days, all I have teh do is let me supervisor know. Then, I'll arrange . . . me ma, teh baby-sit."

"Why do I get the impression that your mother baby-sitting is going to be a problem?"

"Ah, it's nothin really, we had a bit of a fallin out over Johnser's death, that's all . . ."

"Well, I'm going to be here next week, so if yeh like, I'll look after the boys for you? That should give you a bit of time to make your peace with your mother."

"Thanks, but no thanks. I'll be fine."

"Please, Jackie, you'd be doing me a favour. I'd really like to spend some time with the boys."

"I don't know . . ."

"Just think about it, Jackie, it makes sense. Since I'm going to be here, anyway."

I knew he was trying really hard to please me. I also knew that what he was saying made perfect sense. And, as well as making sense, it meant that I wouldn't have to deal with Ma and Da for at least another week –

"OK, then. But only if deh boys agree."

He jumped up and kissed me, then realising what he'd done, he started to apologise. I laughed, some things never change.

TARA

Chapter Thirty-Eight

Everything was going wrong.

Stan came home looking like something out of a horror film, blood everywhere. He was rambling on about his uncle Pat, and how everything was ruined.

I think Sally had an earache cause she'd been bawling like a fucking banshee all day. Tina was moaning about a pain in her belly. On top of all this, I needed a fix, and Stan was telling me we'd no gear. His uncle Pat had taken it all back.

"Well, go an buy some GEAR! Yeh big fat fucker."

He grabbed me by the hair and swung me round the room –

"An what'll l use for fuckin money?"

He turned out his pockets, nothing. A cold shiver ran down me back, the thought of having to do without a fix frightened the shite out of me. And, the thought of a drug-free life with Stan didn't bear thinking about.

I rooted around in me bag and found twenty quid. The kids needed something to eat and there was fuck all food in the flat. But, fuck it, I'd worry about that tomorrow.

I left the flat without a word. Mr Band-Aid could mind

the kids for a change. I'd have to hurry, the dealer I was going to see, Scabby, didn't answer his door after midnight. The bells of Christchurch had started to ring just as I reached the end of his street. Me legs were shaking and I was sweating but, I think that had more to do with me not having run this fast since I'd grown tits than it had to do with withdrawal symptoms.

I kept me finger on the bell. I knew he was in, he was always in. Eventually, a light came on in the hall and the door opened an inch –

"For fuck sake, Tara, wat are yeh doin here?"

I held out me money –

"I need a fix. Twenty quid's worth."

"Put deh fuckin money away," he hissed pulling me into the hall.

"Wha . . . ?"

He nodded towards a parked car. There were two men sitting inside – "Wa'deh yeh think them two are . . . lovers?"

"Yeh wouldn't know in this day an' age, Scabby."

"Don't get fuckin smart, Tara. It's been a long day."

When I got back home Stan heated the spoon and we shared the gear. Jasus, it was crap, pure fucking shite. But, at this stage, I'd have taken anything. I lay back on the bed and life didn't seem so bad anymore. But, even so, I was determined I wasn't staying with Stan, not now. Not when he had no gear and no money.

So, I decided it was time to pay Johnser a visit. Needless to say, because I was looking for Johnser, he was nowhere to be found.

I went up to me ma's. Me da was sure to know something. I brought the kids with me, Ma loved having the kids around. She always had loads of goodies for them. The minute we'd get in the door, she'd start feeding them chocolate and crisps. Chocolate didn't agree with Sally, it ran the guts out of her. But, at least it kept her quiet for a while.

Anyway, the minute Ma opened the door, I knew there was something wrong. She made a fuss of the kids but, it wasn't her usual fuss. I walked into the kitchen, Da was sitting staring into oblivion –

"Jasus, deh faces on yous two, who's dead?"

Ma looked at Da, he looked away, she started crying –

"The Brush's been arrested."

"Yeah, but he'll be out in a few hours, right?"

Da stood up –

"Naw, not this time. He's been set up good an proper. He'll be goin down for a long stretch."

Tina came into the kitchen and stood looking at the fridge. Ma wiped her eyes and went over to her –

"Ah, would yeh looka deh poor child? She must be starvin. Com'on, me little pet, let's see what Nana has for yeh." She opened the fridge and took out a large bar of chocolate –

"Ma don't give them any more chocolate, yet."

She put the chocolate back and took out two yogurts. She gave one to Tina. Sally started whinging.

"Ah, don't be cryin, me little Lana. Look what Nana has for yeh." Ma opened the yogurt and offered it to her. But Sally wouldn't take it – she'd already seen the chocolate. As Ma went to get her a spoon, Sally flung the yogurt across the room.

I let out a roar –

"Sally! Yeh bold little bitch."

Da grabbed her and started shaking her –

"Yeh little fucker."

"Da, stop it!" I shouted at him.

"Christy!" Ma's voice cut through the air. Da plonked Sally down on a chair –

"That young one needs teh be taught manners."

I sat Sally on me lap. She was sobbing uncontrollably. I glared at Da –

"Yer a mad fuckin pig."

Ma took Sally off me and patted her back –

"There, there, me little luv. Granda's a grumpy aul man."

She turned to Da –

"Go an get yerself a paper or somethin."

He grabbed his coat and stormed out of the kitchen. I told Ma I'd no cigs –

"An get cigs while yer at it," she roared after him.

While Ma settled Sally down, I cleaned up the mess the yogurt had made. Once peace had been restored, Ma turned to me –

"Is money so tight that yeh can't even afford a smoke?"

I hated it when Ma used that tone of voice. It usually meant, don't bother lying to me, cause I know there's something wrong –

"Stan's lost his job with his uncle."

"Ah no. Why?"

"Don't ask. Anyway, Ma, I don't wanna be with him any more. I wanna get back with Johnser."

"Johnser Kiely! Now there's a blast from deh past."

"He's still me husband, Ma."

"Yeah, I suppose he is."

"But, deh thing is, I can't find him anywhere. I was wonderin if me da might know somethin?"

"Jasus, Tara, yeh know me an yer da don't talk about things like that."

We hadn't heard Da come back in –

"Talk bout things like what?"

"She's lookin for Johnser Kiely, have yeh seen him?"

"No, I haven't. But I'll ask round."

* * *

Ma and Da started calling to the flat on a regular basis. They'd arrive laden down with food, cigs and clothes for the kids. I used to feel real embarrassed when they came cause we'd hardly any furniture in the place. It looked more like a squat than a penthouse apartment.

We'd either sold or pawned everything we had. The furniture, the telly, the video, me jewellery. We'd even pawned the fucking iron.

Stan was always going on about how he was going to start up again, cut his uncle out. But, it never happened. And as if it wasn't bad enough having to live with an ugly pig, I was now living with a paranoid, poor, ugly pig. Because of his lack of drugs, he'd become convinced that people were following him, spying on him, laughing at him, the list was fucking endless.

Then just when I thought he couldn't become any more paranoid than he already was, Ma and Da arrived with the news about Brush.

I opened the door and Ma burst into tears –

"Oh, Tara, poor Brush is after gettin twenty years . . . "

"Wha . . . he couldn't have." I looked at Da, he nodded.

"Jasus, he'll never be able for prison life . . . he'll die in there," I said to no one in particular.

I didn't really care what happened to Brush, I hated him. I know what I'd seen him and Ma doing all them years ago, was as much her fault as his. But, I didn't like to think about it like that. I found it easier to blame Brush.

Stan went mental, he was pacing up and down like a caged lion. Da was feeling sorry for himself (as usual) –

"What'll I do without him? I'll lose me job an eve . . . "

Ma was making a speedy recovery –

"No yeh won't, cause yer gonna take over. You know all his contacts. So, it'll be business as usual."

"I might know all his contacts, but, what about deh dosh? I haven't got deh kinda money it takes teh run that sorta business?"

Ma turned to Stan –

"Stan, ye'll have teh talk teh yer uncle, sort things out. Maybe he'll give yeh a bit of credit, eh?"

I couldn't believe what I was hearing, they were all fucking eejits –

"Are yous all gone mad, or what? Stan can't go near his uncle, he'd fuckin kill him!"

Stan stopped pacing –

"It's all that bollox Johnser Kiely's fault."

Jasus, I thought, he's gone fuckin gaga.

"An how deh fuck deyeh work that out, Stanley?"

He was sweating, he was starting to shake.

He grabbed me da –

"Think bout it, Blue. Who else'd have deh bottle teh set Brush up? No one hated Brush as much as Johnser Kiely did. Sure he even told me himself deh last time I seen him. He told me he was gonna get revenge."

He looked at Da –

"Well, what yeh say, Blue?"

Da turned to me –

"Com'on, Tara, it's time you an me had a little chat with that husband of yers."

* * *

203

We brought Tina with us, on the off-chance that she might soften him a bit. We needn't have bothered. Johnser was having none of it. Da was pathetic, begging him for a piece of the action. I wanted him to shut up. I figured that if I could just get a few minutes alone with Johnser, I'd have talked him round. But, I didn't get a chance. What with Da begging, and Tina looking like a simpleton, with her thumb stuck in her mouth, the whole fucking visit was a waste of time.

Eventually, Johnser got a pain in his arse listening to Da whining and slammed the door in our face. We came away from the house with Da cursing, and Tina with her thumb still stuck in her gob.

Stan still wasn't convinced. As far as he was concerned, Johnser was the anti-Christ, and all our days were numbered.

But me, I'd just realised why I'd fallen for Johnser in the first place.

STAN

Chapter Thirty-Nine

Why couldn't they get it through their thick heads that Johnser Kiely was out to get them? For fuck sake, it was obvious that he'd been the brains behind Brush going down. Jasus, all they had to do was look around them, Johnser Kiely was running everything.

He had bouncers on the doors of every club in Dublin. Security firm, he called it. He was doing all the biggest bank jobs, and he was heading the biggest drugs ring in Ireland. Rumour had it that he was buying in forty grands' worth of gear a week. But, they still couldn't see it, they couldn't see that he was slowly, but surely, pushing everyone else out.

And, as for Blue, he wasn't worth a fuck either. I mean to say, if anyone knew what a revenge-freak Kiely was, it was him. But, he seemed to have forgotten that he'd played a big part in Johnser Kiely going down, that he was as much a target as anyone else. And, for some strange reason, best known to himself, he was convinced he'd nothing to fear from Kiely.

He'd no money, no job, but above all, he'd no respect. No one was afraid of Blue anymore, not with Brush out of

205

the way. This was another thing he seemed to have forgotten.

* * *

Ever since Uncle Pat had sacked me, no one wanted to have anything to do with me. I'd rubbed some important people up the wrong way, and now I was paying the price. I'd no money, I'd sold everything I had, me lovely stereo, me leather chairs, me Nintendo, everything. And, I knew that it wouldn't be long before I'd have to sell me car and the apartment.

I'd gotten so used to having an endless supply of heroin, that I hadn't been aware of how addicted I'd become. But, now that it was gone, I realised how much I'd depended on it. And, paying for the gear was another problem. I mean, it's not as though I'd only me own habit to worry about, I'd Tara's as well.

It's amazing how much shite you'll pump into your body trying to recapture the feeling you got with your first hit. But, no matter what you do, You'll never get it again. I used to do drugs to feel good, now I needed at least a hundred quid's worth, just to feel normal.

Me whole life revolved around "getting a hit" I'd wake up in the morning feeling sick and shivery, I couldn't even face a cup of tea unless I'd had a fix. So, that meant I'd be out robbing at the crack of dawn. You see, there was no point in getting the gear the night before, cause, once you had gear in the house, you took it.

I remember one night I was on me way home from the dealers, and I seen a fella making a lodgement at a night safe. Just as he was about to drop his little bag into the safe, I grabbed it and ran like the clappers. When I was what felt like a hundred miles away, I stopped and opened the bag. I couldn't believe me luck. I'd expected to get a couple of hundred quid, instead I got four grand. I thought about going home but decided against it. I'd no intention of spending me little windfall on milk or bread or any of that other crap.

I bought a gansy load of gear and then I broke into a derelict shop on the quays. Jasus, I had a great aul time. I was as high as a kite for about a week, with not a care in the world. Then, one morning I woke up and it was all gone. All I was left with was eight pints of O-negative waiting for that familiar pin-prick, that was its next fix. And then there was me veins, they were another problem. They'd nearly all collapsed, the only ones that were any good were the ones in me big toes.

* * *

Like I say, I was a mess. I'd lost loads of weight so me clothes didn't fit me any more, and I'd scabs all over me arms and legs. Jasus, they itched like mad.

I knew I'd have to get meself sorted out but that was easier said than done. I'd tried to do "cold turkey" millions of times but it was too hard. The pain and the hallucinations were more than I could bear. Eventually, I'd have to give in.

"Tomorrow. I'll start tomorrow," I'd promise meself.

And me veins would laugh and say –

"Yeah, Stan, tomorrow."

Anyway, one day while I was out on the prowl (hoping to run into a stray handbag) I bumped into Frankie Fitz.

"Stanley," he greeted, "long time no see."

"Yeah, Frankie, you've been away."

He tapped his nose –

"A bit of a holiday . . . Yeh know yerself?"

207

His two henchmen laughed. He continued –

"I ran into an old friend of yours . . . on holiday."

"Yeah, who?"

"Johnser Kiely," he watched me for a reaction – "Yeah, he talked about you a lot. He was grateful to you for looking after his woman."

I tried to look casual but me Adam's apple was jumping up and down in me throat.

One of the henchmen decided to join in –

"Yeah, Stan, word is yeh were like a butcher teh her, always ready with a bitta white puddin."

I head-butted him, and before the others could react I had him in a headlock. That way I couldn't be attacked. Frankie laughed –

"Jasus, Stan, you never lost it. But hey, cool it, we're not lookin for trouble. In fact, I have a proposition for you."

I loosened me grip and his man pulled away gasping for air.

"So what's deh proposition?"

"This isn't the place to talk," he nodded towards a pub on the corner and we went in. I noticed an aul one struggling with her shopping bag.

Fuck yeh, Frankie, I thought, there goes me next fix. Me and Frankie sat at a table, the minders brought down the drinks, then went and sat at the bar. Frankie picked up his pint –

"*Sláinte.*"

I nodded. I didn't really want the pint of Guinness he'd bought me but I did want to hear what he had to say.

"I hear you have some interesting paintings, Stan?"

"Huh?"

"Paintings, you remember? The ones Johnser Kiely went down for. Rumour has it you still have them?"

"So?"

"So, I might have a buyer."

I couldn't believe me ears. *Hallelujah*, I thought. All me troubles were about to disappear. The papers had said the paintings were worth millions, but still, I had to be careful. I knew Frankie Fitz wasn't doing this for the good of his health –

"So, what's in it for you?"

He picked up his drink –

"You know me, Stan, I like to help me mates."

I stared at him, said nothing, just stared. And he knew I thought he was full of shite. He flipped a beer mat –

"Well, naturally there'll be a few bob in it for me, after all, I do have to cover me costs. Businessmen an all that . . ."

"So what kinda figures are we talkin bout?"

"I don't know yet, like I said . . . I might have a deal. There's nothing definite yet."

"Yeah, but yeh know yerself, they're worth a couple of mill . . . at least?"

He laughed. That annoyed me –

"What's so fuckin funny, Frankie?"

"You, Stan, you're funny. A couple of mill? Would you ever cop on. We'll be lucky to get sixty grand."

"Wha . . . are yeh fuckin mad? They're worth millions . . . I'm tellin yeh, fuckin millions."

"Keep your voice down," Frankie growled.

Heads were starting to turn in our direction.

"Listen, Stan, at the minute those paintings are worth fuck all. All they're doing is rotting away in some attic, and knowing you, you probably can't even fucking remember where. So if, and only if, you get thirty grand for them, you should consider yourself very fucking lucky."

"Whadeh yeh mean, thirty? Yeh said sixty a minute ago."

"Thirty each. We'll be equal partners, fifty-fifty. Deal?" He smiled and held out his hand.

"When do I get me money?"

"Patience, Stanley. You haven't shown me a single painting yet. I need proof that you still have them . . . and more importantly . . . that they're in good condition."

He snapped his fingers and one of his men was at his side.

"Envelope."

The "minder" handed him a bulging brown envelope. He threw it into me lap –

"But, as I already said Stan, I'm fond of you. So, I've put a little of what you like in there."

He stood up –

"I'll be in touch, OK?"

I nodded, fingering the envelope.

"And, when I do, make sure you have something to show me . . ."

I made me way to the toilet. I couldn't believe the way the day had turned out. A few hours ago, I'd had nothing. Now, I had the promise of thirty grand, and a little parcel of powdered gold in me pocket. Life was definitely on the up.

JACKIE

Chapter Forty

By the time I got to head office, I was a nervous wreck.
Because I'd spent so much time talking to Jeffrey, I'd ended
up late for me appointment with the supervisor. And, because
I'd kept her waiting for ten minutes, she left me sitting
outside her office for a half-hour. Wagon, I thought as I sat in
the hallway biting me nails, I could do without this pressure.

Anyway, when she finally decided I'd been punished
enough, she called me in.

"Jasus, Ger, I didn't realise . . . "

She looked up sharply –

"Hello, Jackie, take a seat."

"God, Ger, I didn't know you'd been promoted,
Congrat . . . "

"Thanks but that's not what we're here teh talk about."

"Yeah, sorry Ger."

"It's Ms Byrne now, Jackie."

Snotty fuckin cow, I thought.

The door opened and the man who owned the
company, Mr Crosby, came into the room –

"Well now, Jackie, this is a surprise. You've been away
for quite a while now, haven't you?"

"Yeah, I have."

Ger looked at me –

"And are yeh going to explain yer absence?"

I couldn't believe me ears –

"Explain me . . . what deh yeh mean?"

Mr Crosby spoke –

"Are you going to tell us where you've been?"

I looked at Ger –

"Yeh know where I've been!"

She avoided me eyes – "All I know is that I had one phone call from Ann Redmond. I've had no contact with you."

Me eyes were starting to sting but I wasn't going to let them see me crying – "My Johnser . . . yeh know . . . died?"

"And Johnser was . . . ?"

"Her common-law," whispered Ger.

"Well, Jackie, I'm sorry for your trouble. But, we do have a company policy to uphold. And, that policy clearly stipulates that employees are entitled to three days' leave on the death of a close relative. You've had ten."

"Eleven," Ger corrected.

"Did you not think it necessary to contact us, your employers, once in all that time? Did it never occur to you that maybe we might need to organise a replacement to cover your shift? That other people may have been inconvenienced by your absence?"

I couldn't think of anything to say, I just sat staring at him.

"Well, have you anything to say for yerself?"

"Like what?"

"Like, I'm sorry, Mr Crosby. Sorry for any inconvenience I may have caused by my lack of communication with my supervisor."

I coughed –

"Hmm . . . I'm sorry."

He looked at me coldly –

"Is that it? Is that the best you can do? It seems to me, from your attitude, Jackie, that you don't particulary want this job. And, to be quite honest, I'm not sure I want you . . . "

Ger jumped to me defence –

"Jackie's a good worker, Mr Crosby."

"I can appreciate that, Ms Byrne. But, what's the point in having good workers when they don't bother turning up to do good work?"

He turned away from us and stood looking out the window.

"Say yer sorry and it won't happen again," Ger mouthed at me.

I didn't want to apologise for going to Johnser's funeral. But, unfortunately, this poxy job was more important than me pride. I took a deep breath –

"Mr Crosby, I'm really sorry. I promise it won't happen again."

"Of that you can be assured, Ms Clarke."

He turned on his heel and stormed out of the office.

Up yer hole, yeh scabby bastard, I shouted in me head.

Ger fumbled through a pile of papers on her desk.

"Here," she said handing me a slip of paper.

I looked at it –

"Phibsboro!"

"Yeah, yer on the evenin shift. The coach'll pick yeh up at Inchicore at six pm. Tracy Coleman is the supervisor, she'll tell yeh what teh do."

"But, Phibsboro! For fuck sake, Ger."

"Look, Jackie, if you've a problem with the job you'd better talk teh Crosby."

"And fuck you too," I told her slamming the office door.

* * *

By the time I got home I was exhausted.

I let meself into the house, plugged in the kettle and burst into tears. I could do nothing right, nothing. Every fucking thing I done went arse-ways. Even taking time off work, for a fucking funeral, ended in bleeding disaster.

When I'd cried all the tears I had in me body, I went upstairs and splashed cold water on me face. Edward would be in from school soon, and I didn't want him seeing me like this. God knows, they'd had more than their fair share of tears over the last few weeks. I dried me face, combed me hair, had a quick look in the mirror – not too bad, I told meself as I headed for the stairs.

As I stood peeling potatos, I thought about Jeffrey's offer to mind the boys. "Please, God," I begged, "please let them agree." I really wasn't up to having a row over who looked after them while I was working.

Thankfully, Jeffrey didn't come home for dinner. That meant I'd have a chance to talk to the boys on their own. So, when we'd finished our dinner I told them to stay where they were for a few minutes cause I wanted to have a chat with them.

"Ah, ma, I wanna watch *Spiderman*," Edward protested. "It won't take long, I only want teh ask yous somethin."

"Watt?" they chorused.

I lit a cigarette. I was nervous. Jonathan had been very cool with me since he came home, I knew it was because of Jeffrey –

"Well, yeh know I was tellin yous that I was goin back teh work? Anyway Jeffrey has said that if yous wanted . . . he'd mind . . . "

"NO!" Jonathan shouted, jumping up from the table.

"Jonathan Adams! Don't you shout at me like that."

He looked down at his feet.

"Well? If yeh have somethin teh say, say it."

"I don't want him mindin us. I hate hi . . . "

"Me too," Edward chimed in.

Here we go, I thought, one for all an all for one.

"Don't yous talk about yer father like that."

"He's not me father," Jonathan mumbled. "Anyway, why can't I mind us? I'm old enough."

"Yeah, I want Jonathan teh mind me," Edward said standing beside his brother.

"Well, I don't. Jonathan isn't old enough teh be left in charge of a house at night."

"Why?" Another chorus.

"Because, save there was a fire? Or save one of yous had an accident? Or save there was a power cut? Or sa . . . "

"Well, why can't Nana and Granda mind us then?" Edward again.

"Cause they can't."

Edward loved spending time with his granda. Not only because he spoiled him rotten but also because he spent hours playing Monopoly with him. I remember once when I turned up to collect them and they were in the middle of a game, Da got out a notepad and wrote down all the details of the game. Who owned what streets, how many hotels and houses were on them, how much money each player had and so on. Jasus, I don't know where he got his patience. I fucking hated Monopoly, it bored me stiff. Besides, it was too close to real life.

All I ever got was, pay your income tax, go to jail, pay someone rent, pay doctor's fees. And, if by some miracle I did happen to have a few hotels, I'd get a bill for property tax. So, like I say, I hated Monopoly, it reminded me of me life.

* * *

215

After about two hours of arguing, promising, bullying, and eventually begging, the boys agreed to let Jeffrey mind them. I'd begged them to do it for me, as a favour. I'd promised them faithfully that it would only be for a week. And, that once the week was up, I'd organise with their nana and granda to take over. I knew that was going to be the hardest part of the bargain to keep, but fuck it, I had another week before I'd have to think about it.

I was just thinking about going to bed, when I heard Jeffrey letting himself in –

"Hello, Jackie. Everything all right?"

"Yeah, grand. You?"

"Fine," he answered taking off his jacket and hanging it over the arm of the chair.

"So, what have yeh been up teh?" I asked as he sat down. I wasn't really that interested in what he'd been doing, but I felt I had to say something.

"Oh, nothing much. I spent most of the day visiting the museums, and then I went for a meal. I didn't want to come back too early . . . you know . . . I wanted to give you time to talk to the boys." He was looking at me expectantly.

"I didn't know yeh were interested in museums," I said ignoring his look.

"Yes, well, some of them . . . so . . . did you talk to the boys?"

"Yeah."

"And?"

"And what?"

"And, what did they say?"

"They agreed."

"Oh, Jack . . . "

"For my sake. It had nothing to do with you, Jeffrey. So I don't think yeh should expect too much in the way of conversation, or cooperation, for that matter."

216

"We'll soon become friends again, Jackie. You'll see."

"I wouldn't be so sure of meself if I was you, Jeffrey," I told him coldly. I stood up – "Night, Jeffrey."

* * *

I left the house at four forty-five the next day. I know the coach wasn't due to pick me up till six but I wasn't sure of the buses and was terrified of being late.

When we arrived at the offices in Phibsboro, one of the girls I'd been talking to on the coach introduced me to the supervisor. She handed me a mop and bucket, and told me I was on toilet duty. I felt like hitting her, toilet duty was for new girls and trouble-makers. But I wasn't really in a position to argue. Anyway, I was probably better off being on me own tonight, first night back and all that.

I put me *Cleaning in Progress* sign outside the toilet and went in. I wiped the lid of me fourth toilet, then sat down and lit a smoke. Fuck them, I thought, I'm havin a break. I knew I'd another three floors to clean but I'd get them done in plenty of time. Some of the other cleaners were real slow, and I was fucked if I was going to help them, lazy cows. After all, I'd got the dirtiest job, and they hadn't exactly ran to help me.

They were a shower of fucking wagons, they hadn't so much as said hello to me on the coach, except that one girl. Helen, I think she said her name was.

I leaned back against the cistern and blew me smoke high into the air. I tried to make little smoke rings but I couldn't. Ah, fuck it, I thought, reaching into me smock pocket and pulling out me little bottle of vodka.

Even though I'd had an unofficial break I was still finished before most of them. And, despite what I'd said earlier, I ended up helping some of the lazy ones. I didn't have to help them, I could have sat on the coach, but, what was the point in that? The quicker the job was done, the quicker we all got home. When we were putting on our coats one of the wagons spoke to me. Curiosity must have gotten the better of her –

"So, yer deh one whose fella got shot?"

Before I had a chance to answer, another one joined in.

"Jasus, that musta been terrible for yeh?"

Within seconds they were all at it.

"Jasus, there must've been blood everywhere!"

"Watt kinda bastard would do deh likka dat?"

"My Danny says they're all gone mad on them drugs."

"Did deh police catch anyone?"

"Don't be fuckin stupid, sure he'll never be caught."

"Naw, sure deh police don't care bout deh likes of us."

Oh, it was *us* now, was it? I looked at them in amazement, did they honestly think that I was going to tell them anything? I wouldn't trust them to keep the time of day to themselves, never mind me most intimate secrets. Nosy cunts, I thought, but said nothing.

When I got off the coach, Ann was waiting for me –

"Jasus, Jackie, I'd just about given up on yeh."

* * *

The minute I seen Ann I panicked. Oh fuck, I thought, she knows about Jeffrey.

We walked in silence for a few minutes, then I said –

"Yeh never told me Ger Byrne was made a supervisor?"

"Yeah, an you never told me that Jeffrey was back."

"Ah, don't start, Ann. He's not back, his ma's dead, an he'd just stayin for a few days."

"Why?"

"Why what?"

"Don't start playin fuckin games with me, Jackie. If yeh

218

wanna go round with yer head in deh clouds, that's fine by me. But, don't treat me like a fuckin eejit, OK?"

"I'm not tryin teh treat anyone like a fuckin eejit, Ann."

"Well, what's he doin back."

"Lookit Ann, he's not back, alrigh? He's got a job in London, startin next week. I need someone teh look after the kids, he needs somewhere teh stay. Full stop. End of Story."

"An where have I heard that before, Jackie?"

"Ah, fuck off, Ann."

I stormed off down the street. Jasus, I thought, she's worse than me fuckin da.

I reached the bus stop just as the bus was pulling in. Jasus, wonders would never cease, I usually reached the bus stop just as the bus was pulling out. As I boarded the bus, I looked around, Ann was running down the road –

"Will yeh wait for a minute, mister, me friend's on her way?" I asked the busman.

"Two seconds," he barked, in the usual friendly busman way.

"Thanks," Ann gasped, sitting down beside me.

I sat looking out the window, Ann sat looking at her nails. Jasus, if she didn't say something soon, I'd go mad. I hated the silent treatment. She must have read me mind –

"Lookit, Jackie, I'm not pickin on yeh, I'm just worried about yeh. It's just that with all that's happened with Johnser . . . an everything . . . I don't wanna see yeh gettin hurt again."

"I know, Ann. An I'm sorry for been such a wagon. But, really, there's no problem with Jeffrey. Like I said, he's only gonna be stayin for a week . . . I swear. Now, tell me how Ger Byrne got deh supervisor's job?"

Ann sighed. I knew she was in a huff. She still wanted to talk about Jeffrey but I didn't. She knew better than to keep at it.

"Well, are yeh gonna tell us?" I asked again, ignoring her huff.

"The usual way, she slept with Crosby."

"Crosby! Jasus, he's a dog."

"Yeah, but, he's a rich dog. An her being deh fuckin eejit that she is, she thinks he's gonna leave his wife for her."

"An will he?"

"What deh you think?"

"I think he's stringin her along."

"Exactly."

We got off the bus and hurried down the road towards home. There was a gang of fellas standing at the corner but, they didn't even look at us. Jasus, I thought, that's a sure sign we're gettin old.

We got to my gate –

"Night, Jackie, see yeh tomorra," Ann said without stopping.

I knew now that I was definitely in her bad books.

I ran up me drive and let meself in, Jeffrey met me in the hall –

"Hello, Jackie, how was your first night back?"

"Don't ask, yeh don't wanna know." I told him pulling off me coat.

I went into the sitting-room and kicked off me shoes –

"Well, how did yeh get on with deh boys? Were they alrigh?"

"Yes, they were great, no bother at all. They went to bed about an hour ago."

At least something in this poxy day had turned out right, I thought miserably.

Jeffrey handed me a drink –

"Here, get that into you, It'll help you to unwind."

"Thanks, Jeffrey. God knows I need it.

TARA

Chapter Forty-One

Things were at an all-time low. We hadn't a ha'penny and we couldn't get gear anywhere. No one would deal with us, we owed money to everyone. Even the scabby little junk-heads who only sold shite wouldn't touch us. Jasus, we were pathetic.

Stan had started doing handbags and smash-and-grabs at traffic lights. But, it wasn't worth the bother, he never got more than about twenty quid. At least that's what he told me.

Anyway, one night he came home stoned out of his head. He was ranting and raving about some big job that was coming up, and how we were going to be on the pig's back in no time. I didn't believe him, he was talking shite. Everybody knows that junkies don't make plans for tomorrow, they live for today. Cause, if they don't get their fix today, there is no tomorrow.

He was a fucking gob-shite, a big fucking drug-addicted gob-shite.

The words drug-addict hit me like a slap in the face. It was the first time I'd ever used them about Stan. But, what frightened me most was the realisation that, if Stan was a drug-addict, then so was I.

I went into the bathroom and looked in the mirror. Jasus, I was a show. I didn't bother putting on make-up any more. Me face looked pale and blotchy. Me hair was like something you'd see in a bad porno film. It was black at the roots and yellow at the ends. I hadn't been to a hairdressers in months. I'd started buying them do-it-yourself home-colours. Cause they were cheaper than having it done professionally. And, as for me clothes, they were like rags, an aul pair of leggings and a sweat shirt that should have been thrown out ten years ago. I couldn't even remember the last time I'd bought something nice for meself, in fact, I couldn't even remember the last time I'd bought a new pair of knickers.

"Jasus, Tara," I whispered, "what's happened teh yeh? Where's yer pride gone?"

I sat on the side of the bath and cried me eyes out. When had this happened? How come nobody told me how bad I looked? Why hadn't I noticed?

I'll tell yeh why, said a little voice in me head, yeh were too busy plannin yer next fix to notice anything. I jumped up. Well, not any-fucking-more. That's it, I'm going off the gear.

All I needed to do now was get Johnser back. I knew I'd be able to beat the habit if he was there to help me.

* * *

When I eventually found Johnser, he was with her.

I'd heard he was seeing Jackie Clarke again, but I hadn't heard he was seeing her kids as well. I was furious. There he was stuffing her two bastards full of pizza and ice cream, while my kids were sitting at home, starving. The fucking cheek of him.

I wouldn't mind but the miserable pig had never even brought me to a chipper, never mind a fancy restaurant.

Well, I'd soon put an end to their party. I walked down to their table –

"Well, now, isn't this cosy?"

Johnser had me out of there, in seconds flat. When we got outside, we had a huge row.

I tried to tell him how I felt but, it came out all wrong. He wouldn't listen. I got annoyed and started roaring and shouting. In the end, he just walked away. I was heartbroken. I hadn't realised till now how much I wanted him. I really wanted us to try again. We'd never even had a chance together. All I wanted to do was talk to him, tell him how much I needed him (and I did). But, every time I opened me mouth the only words that came out were curses and abuse over money. It was so frustrating, instead of sounding like a desperate wife, I ended up sounding like a money-mad bitch.

There was nothing for me to do now but go home. I swore to meself that I wasn't going to give up. I'd try again, when he was in a better mood.

I made me way down Grafton Street like someone in a trance. I was so caught up in me thoughts (thoughts of where I was going to get money) that I walked straight into a woman, nearly knocking her flying –

"For God's sake, would you look where you're walking."

"Ah, fuck off," I told her, and carried on down the street. A hand grabbed me by the shoulder, and I jumped –

"Wha . . . ? Fuck yeh, Marcus, yeh gave me a fright."

I'd thought it was the aul one's husband, or something.

"So sorree, my little cherie . . . "

"Ah, don't bleedin start, Marcus, I'm not in deh humour."

"Ah, my little pet, you have zee problem . . . yez?"

"Yeah, that's right, Marcus, I've a big fuckin problem."

"Come, Tiara, come with Marcus, and we will talk."

He linked his arm through mine and bounced me towards a coffee shop.

He sat me in a quiet corner of the busy little coffee shop and made his way up to the counter –

"Two coffees please."

"Would yeh like cream?"

"I'd love some but I'm in a hurry. So, I'll just have the coffee . . . " He giggled like a schoolboy.

The aul one broke her shite laughing. Jasus, he was a fucking eejit. I'd love to pull your fucking wig off I thought spitefully, then we'd see who giggled.

He wiggled his leather-clad arse all the way back to our table, smiling and nodding at all the aul ones he passed on the way. Jasus, he was such a wanker.

"So, you have zee little problem, Tiara?" He said, picking up the milk jug.

"Marcus, will yeh ever fuck off. Remember it's me yer talkin teh, not one of yer blue-rinse groupies."

He fluttered his eyes at me.

"Marcus, I'm serious . . . I need help . . . I'm skint."

"What about yer hubby?"

I shook me head.

"Jasus, Tara, I'm sorry yer in trouble, I wish there was somethin I could do."

"There is . . . yeh could give me me job back."

The colour drained from his face.

"Christ, Marcus, don't look so fuckin terrified. I was a good stylist."

"It's nothin teh do with that, Tara, I know yeh were good but . . . I have new girls now . . . I can't just get rid of them."

"Why not? Yeh didn't have a problem gettin rid of me when I told yeh I was pregnant."

He looked away.

"Marcus, I'm desperate . . . I need the money."

"Jasus, Tara, I'm really sorry things aren't workin out for yeh but it's not my problem."

224

"Oh, well yeh see, Marcus, that's where yer wrong. Cause I think it is yer problem . . ."

"What are yeh on about? Oh, I see . . . yer gonna tell everyone that I'm bald . . . is that it?"

He grabbed me arm.

"Get yer fuckin paws offa me, yeh bollox. I don't give a shite about you or yer wig. But . . . I do . . . give a shite about me child havin a father . . ."

He spluttered his coffee down the front of his shirt –

"Wha . . . ?"

"You heard."

"Would yeh fuck off, Tara. We only ever done it once."

"Oh, and how many times does it take teh get pregnant?"

"Tara, I might be bald but, I'm not fuckin thick. Deh yeh honestly think yer gonna pin that kid on me . . . after all this time?"

"OK, Marcus, have it yer own way. Yeh can have a test done, then I'm gonna drag yeh through every court in Ireland till I get everythin yeh have."

He said nothing. I felt guilty, he'd been a good friend –

"Lookit, Marcus, I'm not tryin teh ruin yer life or . . ."

"Yeh could've fooled me."

"Yeah, well I'm not. I'm just desperate, that's all."

"Tara, I don't wanna play happy families with you an yer kid."

"The feelin's mutual."

"So, what deh yeh want, then? Child support?"

"What about a one-off payment, and a job?"

"How much?"

"Ten grand."

"Would yeh fuck off, I haven't got that kinda money."

"How much have yeh got?"

225

"I've a thousand pounds in the credit union, so I'd be able teh borrow three."

"Well, I suppose that'll have teh do."

"How do I know yeh won't come lookin for more?"

"Cause I'm tellin yeh I won't."

"OK then, Tara, I'll give yeh the money . . . but . . . I won't . . . "

"Marcus, don't start fuckin threatening me."

"I'm not fuckin threatening yeh, Tara. I'm just tellin yeh, that I won't be given yeh a job."

I knew by the look on his face there was no point arguing –

"When will yeh have deh money?"

"The weekend."

"Deh yeh know anyone who's lookin for a brilliant hairdresser?"

He didn't laugh. He thought for a few minutes, then wrote something on a tissue –

"This is the number of a friend of mine. He runs a beauty salon, for men. Mention me name, an he'll give yeh a job."

I took the number –

"Thanks Marcus, yer a real mate."

"Well, if I'm a mate, I'd hate teh see how yeh treat yer enemies. I'll have the money on Friday, call round to the salon, OK?" He stood up to go.

"Marcus . . . "

"What now?"

"Have yeh anything that might help me out, till then?"

"For fuck sake, Tara!"

He reached into his pocket, and then taking me by the hand, placed a little packet of Happy Pills in it –

"See yeh Friday."

STAN

Chapter Forty-Two

Frankie Fitz was hyper, he was marching up and down the warehouse shouting –

"That bastard is gonna die . . . deyeh hear me? He's gonna fuckin die."

No one answered him. I'd only just walked in, and I hadn't a clue who he was talking about –

"Who, Frankie? Who's gonna die?"

He looked at me with hate in his eyes –

"Johnser fuckin Kiely . . . that's who . . . he's got no fuckin respect."

He stood in front of me, pushing his torn jacket into me face –

"Look, look what he did teh me jacket!"

I looked at the jacket, then at him –

"Let me get this straight, Frankie. Johnser Kiely ripped yer jacket, an now yeh want him dead? Jasus, deh yeh not think yer overreactin a bit?"

Max laughed. Frankie was on him in a flash. He punched him in the stomach until he fell to his knees, then he kneed him in the face. Max fell backwards smashing his head on the concrete floor. He didn't move. I didn't know whether he was unconscious or dead, or whether he was lying still in the hope that Frankie would stop kicking him. Frankie stopped, the sweat was dripping off him. He turned to me again –

"It's not deh fuckin jacket . . . I don't give a shite about deh jacket . . . "

He grabbed his lapel, ripping it further –

"It's Johnser Kiely I'm fuckin worried about. He's fuckin everything up. Just cause he's stopped dealin, he thinks everyone else should do the same. He has bouncers on all the clubs, keepin deh pushers out. That's a lotta fuckin customers that I'm missin out on . . . "

"For fuck sake, Frankie, it's not deh end of deh bleedin world. Just cause John . . . "

"Oh, an yer a fuckin expert now, are yeh? Yeh don't think Johnser Kiely is anythin teh worry bout?"

"I'm not sayin yeh shouldn't worry bout him, but . . . "

"Good. Cause, from what I hear, he's still out teh get yous lot who put him inside. An, another thing, Stan, as long as Kiely's still around, yeh can forget our deal with the paintins."

He knew by the expression on me face that he'd hit a nerve, the bastard. He knew I needed money, knew I needed to offload them paintins –

"OK, so wha'are we gonna do?"

"I'm puttin out a contract on him."

I looked at him, a contract meant money. Money I could do with –

"Have yeh anyone in mind?"

"Why, Stan, are yeh interested?"

"I might be, if deh price is right."

"Well, thanks for the offer, Stan . . . but I already have someone for the job . . . someone who owes me a favour . . . "

"So, wha'deh yeh want me teh do?"

"Yeh know the story, Stan. I don't wanna take Kiely outta the picture only to have him replaced by some other fuckin gobshite, lookin for revenge. I need yer word that Tara Coyle won't make a fuss if . . . yeh know . . . ?"

"You've nothin teh worry bout, on that score, Frankie. She'll be as happy as a pig in shite teh see deh back of him. And, if somethin was teh happen him . . . well, she'd own the security business. After all, she is still his wife . . ."

"Yeah, Stan. The security business. Now, that's somethin you an me will have teh come teh an agreement over . . . "

As far as I was concerned, Johnser Kiely's death couldn't happen soon enough.

TARA

Chapter Forty-Three

At last me life seemed to be taking a turn for the best. I was really looking forward to me interview with Marcus's hairdresser friend.

The minute I got out of bed I took what was left of the tabs Marcus had given me. I knew they wouldn't keep me going all day but, at least they'd take away the longing for a while.

I had a shower, done me hair and make-up, and put on me shortest skirt and tightest jumper. I packed a bag with the tools of me trade. Me hairdryer with the defuser, a few combs, two scissors and a brush. When I was sure I wasn't forgetting anything, I took a last look at meself in the mirror. Satisfied, I left the flat.

I was a bit nervous about going back into hairdressing, it had been ten years since I'd held a scissors. But, I was sure that after the first two or three haircuts it would be like I'd never been away.

Herculus' Men's Salon was, according to Marcus, on Thomas Street. But, after walking the length and breath of Thomas Street, James Street, and any other fucking street that came in between, I still hadn't found it. And, everytime I rang the number he'd given me, it was engaged. So, I decided to ask one of the women selling fruit, if she knew where it was –

"Scuse me, missus, but could yeh tell us where Herculus' Salon, is?"

She gave me a dirty look and started fixing her apples and oranges –

"A lady like me wouldn't know anythin bout a place like that."

I hadn't a fucking clue what she was on about –

"I only asked yeh for directions, missus . . . "

A man appeared at her side, smiling from ear to ear –

"Is it Herculus' Club yer lookin for, luv?"

I smiled back –

"Yeah, that's probably it. I must've got deh name wrong."

"Well, that's it there. It has a buzzer with deh name on it," he told me, pointing towards a black door about three shops down from where we were standing.

"Thanks a lot, mister."

As I turned to leave the stall, he stopped me.

"So, are yeh gonna be startin work there, luv?"

"Yeah, I hope so."

"Well, I hope so, too. Tell Rayo that I might become a client meself if he starts takin on girls like you."

"I'll give him deh message. An, thanks again for yer help." I beamed at him, delighted with the compliment.

The black door was fucking manky-looking, and all the paint was flaking off. The buzzer was as bad, it was so dirty and faded that all I could make out was *Her lu*. Anyway, I buzzed and the door clicked open, I went in and felt me way up the mouldy-smelling dark stairs to the reception area. Jasus, I could see why the aul fella on the street was so happy about me starting work here. There was three ancient-looking fucking things sitting at the reception desk. They were wearing low-cut tops with miniskirts and fishnet stockings. For fuck sake, someone should tell them that fishnets and varicose veins just didn't go together. I didn't think much of the decor either the walls were plastered with pictures of half-naked women of every shape and size –

"I'm here teh see Rayo," I told the three aul ones sitting at the desk.

"Rayo . . . there's someone here teh see yeh," one of them roared at the door marked *Office*.

When Rayo appeared he done a double-take, and let out a low whistle. I hated the way he was looking me up and down but, I had to grin and bear it, I needed the job.

"Marcus said yeh might have some work for me?" I said with a pasted-on smile.

Jasus, he was horrible, a small, slimy-looking fucker with greasy black hair. The fucking head on him certainly wouldn't encourage too many people into the place, I thought as I watched him watching me. Eventually he spoke to me tits –

"We've always got work for girls like you. Have yeh any experience in this game?"

"Well, it's been a while since I last worked, but sure I suppose it's a bit like ridin a bike . . . ?"

He roared laughing –

"Jasus, that's one way of puttin it."

"So, can I see deh salon?"

"Salon?"

Jasus, I thought, he doesn't even know what a fuckin salon is.

I tried again –

"Yeah, deh salon . . . yeh know . . . deh place where yeh cut hair?"

232

He stared at me, like I'd two heads, then the penny seemed to drop. He looked over at the three grannies –

"She thinks this is a fuckin hairdresser's."

They all laughed. He turned back to me –

"What exactly did Marcus tell yeh bout this place?"

"Nothin . . . He just said it was a men's beauty parlour."

That caused him and the grannies to laugh even more –

"Good aul Marcus, he always did have a way with words."

They were laughing again. I was getting really fucking annoyed, I shouted at Rayo –

"Whadeh fuck's goin on here? What kinda kip is this, anyway?"

None of them were able to answer. I'd had enough –

"Ah, go an fuck yerself, yeh scabby cunt," I told him heading for the stairs.

I was halfway down when he called me –

"Hey, hey Blondie, hold on a minute, will yeh? let me explain?"

I stopped –

"Yeh have ten seconds."

"This isn't a beauty parlour . . . it's a massage parlour."

"A massage?"

"Yeah, yeh know, rub-a-dub-dub, an all . . . "

"I know what a fuckin massage parlour is," I hissed.

"Well then, what's deh problem?"

"Deh problem is that cunt Marcus Sinelli. Just wait till I get me hands on him."

"Yeh mean, Marcus didn't tell yeh?"

"No, he fuckin didn't."

I turned away from him, and continued down the stairs.

"Hold on, Blondie, yeh can still work here if yeh want. I mean teh say, a girl like you . . . an all that?"

"Well, a girl like me doesn't fuckin want teh work here."

"But, the money's good an . . . " He grabbed me arm and pulled up me sleeve, "I'd say yeh could do with a few bob."

I looked down at me scabby veins, he was right. The bastard.

"Com'on, I'll get Becky teh show yeh deh ropes."

I hesitated.

"Com'on, Blondie, someone like you could make a killing at this game. The customer pays me a tenner for a massage, any extras are up teh you."

* * *

He introduced me to Becky. She told me she was in her forties but she looked more like sixties to me. Anyway, at least she was friendly –

"Com'on luv, I'll introduce yeh teh Nigel, he's a regular. There's no kinky stuff with him, just a straightforward massage and a hand-shandy. And, if he's really flush, he might ask for topless but that's about it."

She led the way into a room. An old man who looked like he'd never missed a meal in his life was lying face down on a table. I looked at Becky –

"Becky, I'm sorry . . . I can't."

She closed the door –

"Course yeh can. All yeh have teh do is look an learn and follow what I think are deh most important rules. Don't use yer own name. Never kiss a client. Make sure they always wear a condom for sex, and always get deh money up front."

Before I had a chance to say anything she was at the table –

"Hello, Nigel, how are yeh feelin teday?"

"Ah, sure I'm grand, Becky."

234

"An how's deh arthritis?"

"It's playin me up a bit but sure I have me tablets for when it gets really bad."

I couldn't believe what I was seeing. Becky was slapping the back off him while he lay stark-fucking-naked on a bench. And, all the while they were chatting away like two neighbours over a garden fence, it was fucking madness. I was just about to make a run for it when Becky said –

"Nigel, this is Samantha, she's new. Yeh don't mind if she stays with me teday, do yeh? It's just that I'm trainin her in."

"No, not at all, Becky."

He turned his head to look at me –

"Howya, Samantha? It's nice teh meet yeh. Maybe I'll make an appointment with yeh for next week?"

Becky put on a hurt voice –

"Oh I see, Nigel. Yer throwin me over for a younger woman."

He laughed –

"Ah, yeh know me Becky, I like teh try deh new ones. But, sure don't I always come back teh yerself?"

She turned him over –

"That's right, Nigel. You an me is like an aul married pair, we know each other so well."

I can honestly say that, for the first time in me life, I was speechless. I couldn't understand how she was able to act so normal.

"So are yeh havin deh usual, Nigel?"

"Please, Becky."

I watched mesmerised, as she took his shrivelled-up mickey in her hand and started pulling at it.

"Samantha, will yeh get a tenner outta Nigel's pocket for me?"

235

It was a few seconds before I realised she was talking to me, that I was Samantha. I got the tenner without taking me eyes off them. As Becky pulled and dragged on his mickey, they continued to chat. They chatted about the weather and about how he'd had to wait twenty minutes for a bus that morning. They even talked about how he was going to spend his fucking afternoon. All of a sudden his breathing became heavy and he started moaning –

"Oooh, Becky, Becky . . ."

And it was all over.

Becky handed him a box of tissues then turned to me. I gave her the tenner and she headed for the door, calling over her shoulder as she went –

"Right, Nigel, I'll see yeh soon. Oh, an enjoy yerself this evenin."

Neither of them seen me picking up the bottle of tablets that had fallen out of his pocket.

"What now?" I asked when we were out of the room.

"Well, if yeh haven't got another customer waiting, yeh just sit around drinking tea or coffee. But, let me warn yeh, yeh won't get much time for sittin on deh weekends, they're usually hectic. Still, yeh can make yer own hours, so I suppose that's somethin."

"Right, Becky, OK. But, what's deh prices?"

"That's up teh yerself. But I charge ten quid for a wank, fifteen if I'm topless, twenty if I'm nude. Twenty-five if he wants teh touch me, and thirty-five for full sex. I don't do blow-jobs but you'd easily get thirty-five for them too."

Just as she'd finished rattling off her price list, the buzzer went. The client was a tall well-dressed businessman. He smiled as he handed greasy-head Rayo his tenner.

"I see you've got some new blood in the stable, I think I'll give her a go," he said without even looking at me.

236

Becky whispered –

"Giv'im a few minutes teh get his kit off."

When Becky gave me the nod I followed him into the room. He was lying on the bench, playing with himself –

"And you are?"

"Samantha."

"Well, Samantha, what are your prices like?"

I added an extra fiver onto all Becky's prices. He stopped me when I got to twenty quid for topless.

"That'll do."

He hadn't even bothered taking off his trousers, he'd just pulled them down. He searched in his pocket, found the twenty and threw it on the floor. When I bent down to pick it up he pushed his mickey towards me face –

"You might as well give me a blow-job while you're down there."

I stood up –

"If yeh put that bleedin thing near me face again, I'll bite it fuckin off."

He lay back and started whimpering –

"Oh, I'm sorry. I've been a very bad boy . . . miss . . . please don't hurt me."

I'd had enough, this wasn't for me. I grabbed his mickey –

"Hit yeh? I'll fuckin kill yeh, yeh little wanker. Now, unless yeh wanna be mickey-less for deh rest of yer life, you'd better empty out yer fuckin pockets . . . now."

I gave a little twist and he let out a roar. He dragged at his trousers, trying to get his hand into the pocket. He pulled out forty-five quid. I grabbed it and headed for the door.

"Cunt . . . you're a fucking cunt."

I turned back to him. He tried to protect his manhood but I grabbed it. I pulled it so hard that when I let go I had a handful of hair. He curled himself into a ball, whimpering like a baby.

I flew out the door, grabbed me bag, and was gone before anyone knew what had happened.

I had sixty-five quid, a bottle of tablets, and all I'd had to do was grab a handful of pubic hair.

"That wasn't a bad day's work, Tara," I told meself happily.

But, it wasn't over yet, I still had a bone to pick with Marcus.

JACKIE

Chapter Forty-Four

By the time I hit me fifth vodka, I'd told Jeffrey all about me first night back at work, and how much I'd hated it. He never once interrupted me. For the first time in his life, Jeffrey actually listened to what I had to say.

"How come yeh couldn't do this when we were married?" I asked him.

"Couldn't do what?"

"Listen teh me . . . let me have a job . . . let me have an opinion . . . let me be independent?"

"Because I couldn't . . . I was too proud."

"And yer not proud now, is that it?"

"Yes, something like that."

"So, what made yeh change?"

He looked down at his glass, he was still on his first drink –

"Lots of things."

"Such as?"

"Mother's illness for one thing. Before she got sick she'd always been there for me, a shoulder to cry on, my crutch. She was so proud of me, always happy to see me, never asking questions." He smiled and took a sip of his drink. "You know, when you and I split up and I went back to live with her . . . it was like I'd never been away. My bedroom was exactly the same as it had been the day I'd left to marry. Nothing had been touched, she hadn't even taken my posters off the wall. It was incredible . . . like a shrine. And, it made me feel great. Knowing that she still loved me, that I was still her blue-eyed-boy was all that mattered. And then . . . suddenly . . . she was gone. It seemed like, one minute she was making my dinner and ironing my underpants, the next, she was this skeleton that I was wishing dead."

He bowed his head, and I knew he was trying very hard not to break down –

"Anyway, her death made me face a few home truths. I suddenly realised that I'd have to stand on my own two feet. From now on I'd have to take responsibility for my own life. I no longer had someone to make excuses for my failures, or blame other people for my mistakes. For the first time in my life, I was forced to take a long hard look at myself and, I didn't like what I saw. I'd never done the decent thing by anybody in my whole life, all I was was a selfish egotistical mammy's boy. And that was nothing to be proud of. So, one night while I listened to Mother screaming in agony, because there was nothing more doctors could do for her, I made a pact with God. I swore to Him, that if He'd just take her out of her pain, I'd change my ways and become a better person. An hour later she died."

He raised his head and looked at me –

"Hey, Jackie, com'on don't cry. I didn't mean to upset you . . . "

I pulled him close, and kissed him.

"What was that for?" He looked confused.

"That was for bein so honest," I told him getting to me feet, "an now I think it's time I went teh bed."

He stood up –

"Jackie? Do you think . . . you know . . . you and me?"

I looked at him, he looked lost –

"I don't know, Jeffrey, it's too early teh say."

I'd just got into bed when I heard Jeffrey's footsteps on the stairs. I listened as he went into the bathroom, flushed the toilet, and made his way back down the stairs again. And as I lay in the dark, I couldn't help thinking what would have happened if he'd taken the few steps to me bedroom door?

TARA

Chapter Forty-Five

The Friday that Marcus gave me the promised three thousand pounds was one of the happiest of me life. Of course, I cursed him from a height for setting me up with the job in the massage parlour but, the sight of the brown envelope and the knowledge of what was inside helped to keep me temper at bay.

Da was waiting outside. I'd asked him to give me a lift cause I didn't like the idea of walking the streets of Dublin with so much cash in me bag. Needless to say, Da wanted to know why I was going to see Marcus so I told him I had to collect a reference and me certificates –

"Why? Are yeh thinkin of goin back teh work?"

"Yeah, maybe."

"So, have yeh given up on Johnser, then?"

"No, I fuckin haven't. That bastard's gonna be dragged through every court in Ireland."

"Jasus, Tara, deh yeh think that's wise? Yeh know what them courts do teh deh like of us."

"Yeah, well, I've no fuckin option."

"What if you an me go an see him, one more time?"

242

"Sure I don't even know where he lives."

"Well, I do." Da took a sharp left and drove into the car-park of a posh apartment block.

Our luck was in. When we got to the main door there was a man coming out, so we were able to get into the block without having to buzz Johnser and beg him to let us in. Anyway, we got to the fourth floor and knocked on number ten. Johnser's face dropped to the floor when he seen us –

"Whadeh fuck . . ."

We pushed past him, we were in. I couldn't believe the luxury he was living in. I walked around looking at furniture, picking up ornaments, I didn't know if they were valuable or not but they certainly looked it. Jasus, the place was like a fucking mansion.

Of course, Johnser wanted to know what we were doing there, what we were after now. So, I told him.

Now, you can imagine me surprise when, instead of him flinging me over the balcony, he handed me twenty-eight thousand pounds. At first I thought it was a joke, I thought the money was going to fucking explode or something. But, it didn't. He threw a notebook at me da, telling him it was a list of all the big drug dealers in Dublin. Then, just when I thought life couldn't get any better, he tossed the deeds of the apartment and the keys of his car onto the table. I pinched meself, convinced I was dreaming but I wasn't. Da was talking to Johnser –

"OK, so what's deh catch?"

But, there wasn't one. All Johnser wanted in return for his fortune was never to set eyes on me or mine, ever again. And for Da not to sell drugs in any of the clubs where he employed bouncers. Once Da agreed, Johnser grabbed his jacket and left.

I danced around the apartment, throwing bundles of money in the air and singing –

"*Money, money, money . . .* "

Da was as bad, he was singing –

"*Money makes deh world go round, deh world go round . . .* "

He was delighted with himself, delighted to be back in the big time. Ever since Brush went down he'd lost a lot of respect, but not any more. Now he'd show them all, show them that he didn't need Brush, he could stand on his own two feet. But, the best thing of all was that no one would know that Johnser had just given him the drugs trade. They'd all think that he'd forced big bad Johnser Kiely into retirement, something no one else had been able to do.

* * *

When I told Stan about me windfall, he couldn't believe it either. He wandered around Johnser's apartment like he was lord of the manor. Later on that evening we left the kids with Ma and went cruising in the BMW.

We bought five grands' worth of heroin off Frankie and partied for the whole weekend. It took us eight weeks to get through the money, eight glorious weeks spent in a constant state of bliss. Ten weeks after that, we'd sold the car and every bit of furniture in the apartment. We were down to our last two fixes when I got the news that Johnser was dead.

It really hit me hard. Sounds stupid I know but it was so unexpected that I just couldn't take it in. Johnser was only me own age, he wasn't sick, he didn't do drugs, he'd only just got his life in order, and now he was dead. I started bawling me eyes out. I looked at Stan, he was heating a spoon –

"For fuck sake, Stan! What are yeh doin?"

244

"Cookin dinner, what's it look like?"

"Johnser's dead . . . "

"So?"

"So, we need teh find out who fuckin killed him."

"Why?"

"Because he's me fuckin husband, an whoever killed him might come after us as well."

"Don't be fuckin stupid, Tara, they're not interested in deh like of us."

"An, how deh fuck deh yeh know that?"

"Jasus, Tara, are yeh fuckin thick or what? Johnser Kiely wasn't a popular man, he was always stepping on other peoples' toes. It was only a matter of time before . . . this happened."

I walked over to him –

"Stan . . . did yeh know . . . he was gonna be killed."

He didn't answer, just kept fiddling with his precious spoon.

"Stan, I asked yeh a question."

He still wouldn't answer me. I grabbed his arm and he spilled his fix.

He hit me –

"Yeh stupid fuckin cunt. Of course I knew, everybody fuckin knew, includin yer bleedin aul fella."

245

JACKIE

Chapter Forty-Six

The next few days were great. I had a real spring in me step and no matter what happened at work, it didn't bother me. Just knowing that Jeffrey would be waiting with a large vodka and a friendly ear at the end of the day was enough to keep me going.

I'd come home from work and he'd have everything done for me. The kids would be in bed, the lunches made and their uniforms all ready for the next day. It was great. All I had to do was sit and moan about how much I hated me job. He never interrupted, just listened quietly, nodding from time to time. The only time he moved away from me was to refill me glass, Jasus, he was so considerate, I didn't even have to get me own drink.

The boys seemed to be getting on well with him too. Although, I think that had more to do with the pound he gave them every morning than anything else. But, no matter, they were all getting on great and that was all I cared about. He brought us bowling once and to the pictures twice. He liked us to do things together, as a family, and I have to admit I liked that too. By the end of the week I was dreading the thought of him going. We were sitting together on the couch one night and I told him –

"I'm gonna miss yeh when yeh go."

"Really?"

"Yeah, really. It's been great havin someone teh moan to."

He laughed.

"No, seriously, Jeffrey. I will miss yeh. It's been great comin home to a cooked meal, happy kids and a hot bath. But, what I'll miss the most is havin someone teh talk to."

"I don't have to go, Jackie."

I hesitated for a minute –

"No, Jeffrey, you've got a new job . . . an everythin."

He sat up –

"Yes, Jackie, but sure I'll get a job here instead. The only reason I was going to London was because I didn't think there was anything here for me . . . but, now that I've found you and the boys again . . . well, you know. I won't have any problem getting a job in Dublin, sure they're always going on about the booming economy and everything . . . what do you say?"

I didn't know what to say. I was worried. One half of me wanted him to cancel his plans and stay like this forever, the other half was afraid that if he stayed, the old Jeffrey might raise his ugly head again.

He must have read me mind –

"Jackie, I know what you're thinking, but I promise you, you've nothing to worry about. I told you, I've changed and I meant it. You said yourself how nice it was having me around . . . and . . . you know how I feel about you?"

"I don't know Jeffrey, things are moving a bit fast for me. I mean . . . Johnser dying . . . you reappearing . . . "

"Yes, but, you do like having me here, don't you?"

"Yeah, Jeffrey, I do. But, liking isn't enough . . . "

"I know, Jackie, but if you just give it time . . . well, who knows?"

It felt like he was giving me an ultimatum –

"Jeffrey, I've really enjoyed havin yeh round but I can't agree to become a family again . . . just like that. It's too soon."

He sat looking at me for a minute, then he agreed –

"You're right, Jackie, maybe it is too soon. And I'm sorry for putting you in this position but I want you to know . . . that I won't give up. I'm going to go and establish myself in London, then I'll be back for you."

I smiled. It was nice to hear him talk like this, nice that he still cared about me and the boys and wanted us back. But, above all, it was nice that he was respecting me wishes, that he wasn't forcing the issue.

I leaned over and kissed him –

"So, what time's yer flight?"

"Flight? I'm not flying, I'm going by boat and coach."

"But, you told me you were flying out on Saturday!"

"I was, until I realised that the difference between flying and sailing would pay three nights accommodation in London."

"I thought yeh said you'd be gettin a flat with deh job?"

"I did, and I will. But that'll probably take a couple of weeks to sort out. And, I don't want to risk running out of money."

"I didn't realise yeh were short of money?"

"I'm not. I just have to be careful in case there's any delay with the accommodation. What with B&B's costing thirty-five quid a night it wouldn't be long before I'd end up in a hostel."

"Well, if yeh like . . . I can lend yeh a few bob . . . "

"No way, Jackie. I couldn't take your money."

"You're not takin me money, Jeffrey, I'm given yeh a

lend. Yeh can pay me back when yeh get yerself sorted." I went into the kitchen and took me money out of the freezer. I counted out three hundred pounds.

"Here Jeffrey," I said, handing him the money.

He looked at me in disbelief –

"I can't take that, Jackie."

"Yeh can, and yeh will. Like I say, it's only a lend."

He hugged me tight –

"Thanks, Jackie, you're one in a million, I don't deserve you."

The next morning while we were eating our breakfast Jeffrey told the boys that he'd be going to the bank to get his sterling sorted out, and he'd get them a savings box each.

"Do yeh have teh go teh London?" Edward asked.

"I'm afraid so, but it won't be for long. I'll be home before you know it, and we'll spend plenty of time together."

Their faces sank into their porridge –

"Hey, you two, less of that. I'm not going anywhere until Monday, and I don't want to be tripping over your faces till then."

No matter how hard I tried I just couldn't stop thinking about Jeffrey leaving. The idea of him going to England and forgetting about us was something I didn't want to think about. So, I decided to buy him a wallet and put a picture of meself and the boys inside. That way he'd always remember us. I also wanted him to know that I really did want us to try again . . . some day.

I got off the bus at the Central Bank and made me way down Temple Bar and across the Ha'penny Bridge. There was a leather shop on Liffey Street that I knew was reasonable. I know I wanted to buy Jeffrey a present but, I'd no intention of spending the week's wages (some of the shops would be asking) on a wallet. Anyway, I found what I was looking for, paid the girl fifteen quid and headed to the nearest coffee shop.

I got meself a coffee and a Twix bar and sat down. I took out the wallet, I thought it was lovely. It had loads of different-sized compartments, and in the front there was a plastic-covered pocket for photographs. I took the picture I'd chosen for the wallet out of me bag and set about fitting it in. I had to be careful not to cover any of our faces, I mean to say, what would be the point in giving him a picture to remember us by if he couldn't see our faces? I must have been concentrating very hard cause I didn't notice that someone was standing in front of me –

"Jackie? I thought it was you . . . I think I owe you an apology . . . I was very very wrong . . . "

TARA

Chapter Forty-Seven

The whole business of Johnser's death was really getting me down, and I'd nothing to help ease me depression.

We'd no gear but, worse than that, we'd no way of getting any. Stan was driving me mental, trying to convince me that Johnser had loads of property all around Dublin –

"He has teh have, Tara. Jasus, he couldn't have spent all deh money he earned. He musta invested it in somethin!"

"Stan! For deh last fuckin time, he hadn't any money. I'd know if he had."

"How deh fuck would you know what Johnser Kiely had?"

"I just would, right," I said defensively.

I hated the way everyone just assumed that I knew nothing about Johnser. OK, so I know we never really had much of a relationship, and I'm not saying he ever confided his innermost secrets to me, but I did know some things about him. And one of those things was that Johnser wasn't a liar. I knew without a shadow of a doubt that when he'd told me and me da he was giving us everything,

251

that's exactly what he'd done. But trying to convince Stan of this was something else –

"For fuck sake, Stan, would yeh ever cop on. Yeh know yerself how much this place is worth, and yeh also know that he bought it for cash. Now, correct me if I'm wrong, but that seems like a hell of a lotta money teh me. An' another thing, deh yeh really think he'd have been livin on some poxy council estate if he'd more places like this?"

"Yeah, well, OK. But he musta had a few insurance policies, or somethin . . . an' wha'bout his bouncer business? That must be worth a few bob."

"An' so what if it is?"

Stan's temper had never been his strong point, and now that he had no gear it was worse –

"I'm warnin yeh, Tara, don't get fuckin smart with me, right?"

I nodded, moving out of his reach. I'd been caught with the back of his hand too many times not to have learned me lesson.

"All I'm sayin is that whatever Kiely had is yours now, right? So, yeh better not do anythin teh fuck it up. I don't want that one he was livin with gettin her fuckin hands on what's rightfully ours."

"She won't."

I fucking hated the way he talked to me, like I was the simpleton, not him.

"Good. Now yeh better make it seem like you an him were still an item . . . an that she was deh other woman."

"I will. Just leave me alone . . . right?"

* * *

Jasus, being a bitch to Jackie Clarke wouldn't be hard. After all, it was her fault that things hadn't worked out

252

with me and Johnser. Every time I thought there might be a chance of patching things up, she appeared and ruined everything. So, I wasn't going to have a problem telling people how she'd destroyed me life.

I lied to everyone. The police, the papers, the radio and anyone else who wanted to listen. I was really enjoying playing the role of the grieving widow. I was getting loads of attention, it was great. I'd always wanted to be an actress. I remember when I was in school, the only part I ever got in the Christmas play was as an angel. And the one time when I did get to play Mary, it went wrong.

When we knocked on the door of the inn, and the innkeeper told us there was no room, I had to say –

"Joseph, it's cold."

But, Sister Treasa, who was in charge of the play, told me to put more emotion into me part. So, when it was my turn to talk again, I said with gusto –

"Jasus, Joseph, I'm bloody freezin."

I ended up back in me angel wings. I swear to God, them nuns wouldn't know talent if it jumped up and bit them.

So, like I say, playing the part of the grieving widow suited me down to the ground. I knew I always looked great in black, I even bought a little pillbox hat and a pair of dark glasses.

When Jackie Clarke showed up at the funeral I nearly went mad. I'd told her a hundred times she wasn't to come, but of course she didn't listen. She had to try and steal the limelight one last time. Hanging onto Johnser's father, acting like she was someone important when all she was, was his bit on the side. And now that he was gone, what had she got . . . a big fat nothing. She didn't even have a grave to visit, cause I'd had him cremated. Although, I have to admit, having Johnser cremated wasn't something

253

I'd done out of spite, it was more to do with me own hatred of graves, and a fear of being buried alive. But, I'm sure she didn't see it like that.

I kept Johnser's ashes in an urn on the mantelpiece, Stan thought this was great. He used to open it and tapping his cigarette in, he'd say –

"Jasus, Johnser, yer puttin on weight."

I thought it was funny the first few times he done it. But, after hearing it for the thousandth time, it lost its humour.

JACKIE

Chapter Forty-Eight

Mrs Adams sat down –

"What's wrong, Jackie? You look like you've seen a ghost."

I stared at her –

"You're dead . . ."

She looked confused –

"Pardon?"

Her confusion turned to pain –

"Is that what he told you?"

I couldn't speak, I just nodded.

"After you threw Jeffrey out he moved back home. I was delighted to have him back. You know how I felt about him?"

What she was really saying was, you know how I felt about you. She'd never liked me, I knew she thought that Jeffrey could've done better. As far as she was concerned, her precious son with his great job had married beneath himself.

She touched me hand, interrupting me thoughts –

"At first I blamed you, convinced myself that it was all your fault, that you were putting too much pressure on him. To me he was still my loveable little boy, the caring thoughtful Jeffrey I'd always known. Anyway, he'd been back home about a month, when I started noticing money going missing. Nothing much, just the odd fiver or tenner. But, as well as that, he was always borrowing from me. He always promised to pay it back but never got around to it. Then about four years ago I got sick and had to go into hospital. I signed everything over to Jeffrey, my widows' pension, my post office book, my bank account . . . everything."

This story was beginning to have a familiar ring to it and I wasn't sure I wanted to hear any more –

"Lookit, Mrs Adams . . . I don't reall . . . "

She interrupted me again –

"By the time I came out of hospital he'd cleaned out all my accounts, remortgaged the house and disappeared. I haven't seen him since."

I felt sorry for her, I could see the hurt in her eyes –

"What about deh police? Was there nothin they could do?"

"I couldn't get the police involved, Jeffrey might have gone to prison. I couldn't do that to me own flesh and blood."

I felt sick to me bones. I just couldn't believe what a fool I'd been. How could I have been so fucking stupid?

Mrs Adams was talking again –

"I know you'll think I'm an old fool, but I'm worried sick about him. I have nightmares about him ending up in a gutter . . . somewhere. If only he'd ring me and let me know he was OK . . . "

Jasus, I felt so sorry for her, I reached out and took her hand in mine –

"Mrs Adams, your son is fine . . . "

Her face lit up –

"You mean . . . you've seen him? Where? Is he all right?"

I squeezed her hand –

"Yeah, I have seen him, an he looks fine."

"But . . . why did he tell you I was dead? I don't understand."

I couldn't tell her. I mean, how could I? How could I sit here and tell her that her bastard of a son had told me she was dead in order to worm his way back into me life?

"Maybe I picked him up wrong . . . maybe, he just said you were sick . . . "

"Jackie, I may be old but I'm not stupid. I know the difference between dead and sick!"

"Well, Mrs Adams, I don't understand either. The only thing I can do is, if I see him again, I'll ask him to ring you."

* * *

I couldn't listen to any more, me head was in a spin. I made me escape by telling her I was due in work in an hour. And, with a promise to keep in touch, I left the coffee shop. I made me way to the bus stop in a fit of fury. I hated the thought of having to go to work but I knew if I took the night off I'd be sacked. So, I'd no choice other than to let me fury for that fucking con-man bubble away on the back-burner till I got home.

The only thing that got me through me night's work was planning me revenge. Me first plan was to run in and drag him out of the house by the hair. But then I thought about the boys, they'd been through enough already and I didn't want them being upset by another ugly scene. So I decided on plan two. I'd go home and act like there was

257

nothing wrong. I'd play along with his happy families and then, when the boys were in bed, I'd confront him.

When I opened the door the boys came running to meet me. I knew by their faces that there was something wrong. "Mammy, Mammy, he's gone . . . Jeffrey's gone."

I couldn't take it in –

"Gone? What deh yeh mean, gone?"

I couldn't understand a word they were saying, they were both talking at once –

"Hold it. Hold it, one at a time. Jonathan, tell me what happened?"

"I collected Edward after school, an we walked home together. But, when we got here there was no one in, so we played football in the back garden. After a while it started lashin rain, so I went down teh Ann's and got deh spare key."

He hesitated, eyeing me nervously.

"It's OK, go on, tell me what happened then?"

"Well, we watched telly, and then Edward was hungry so I made him beans an' toast. I made milkshakes as well but, when I was bringin them inteh deh sittin-room . . . I let one fall an it spilled all over me, an I had teh change me clothes . . . "

He looked at me, waiting for me to start giving out but I didn't. I seen the look of relief on his face. On a normal day I'd go mad if they spilled something on their uniforms, espcially since I'd have told them a million times to change out of them the minute they got in from school. But, this wasn't a normal day.

"Jonathan, forget about the milkshake an just tell me what happened?"

"When I went up teh me room teh change me clothes, I seen it was gone."

258

"What? What was gone?"

"Jeffrey's case . . . At first I thought that you'd moved it when yeh were cleanin but, then I looked in deh wardrobe where he hung his suits, an they were gone too."

"An his shoes were gone as well, Ma." Edward added.

A horrible thought crossed me mind. I ran to the kitchen, the boys ran after me –

"Ma, where are yeh goin . . . Maaa!"

I opened the freezer and pulled out me box . . . empty. I started pulling everything out, just in case I hadn't put the lid on properly and the money had fallen out. I pulled out the frozen carrots, the frozen peas, the chips that hadn't seen the light of day since Jeffrey's arrival (he always made real chips), the burgers and the sprouts that Edward wouldn't eat. I pulled and pulled, until there was nothing left on the shelf, but ice.

I fell to me knees, on top of the frozen peas, and cried –

"Yeh dirty fuckin bastard, Jeffrey Adams . . . yeh dirty fuckin . . ."

STAN

Chapter Forty-Nine

Life couldn't be better. We'd had a great couple of months, never having to worry where the next fix was coming from. And, then just when things were starting to dry up, Frankie Fitz finally got someone to put a bullet into Johnser Kiely. Tara was going to be worth a small fortune. After all, he'd been able to offload a thriving business, twenty-eight grand, a car and an apartment without batting an eyelid. So, in order to do that, he must have been loaded.

I think Tara was really upset by his death, well at first anyway. She was making all sorts of stupid statements about how she just wanted to forget about it, let things go, let his family have whatever was left. But I soon sorted that out. I explained to her that she didn't have any option, that she was entitled to everything he had and I was going to make sure that she got it. And, when I pointed out that her arch-rival, Jackie Clarke, would get everything if she, Tara, didn't get her arse in gear, that done the trick.

She played a blinder, acting out of her skin. She could turn on the waterworks at the drop of a hat and she had the media eating out of her hand in no time.

And, as soon as all the fuss died down, I contacted me uncle Pat again.

* * *

He told me he'd found a new supplier in Ireland, someone he said he could trust. But, after much begging and promising, he agreed to give me me own supply. He was only going to charge me fifteen grand per parcel but I'd have to make me own arrangements for getting it into Dublin. As usual he was insisting on money up front, but once again I got two weeks grace by telling him I was waiting on a payment from Johnser Kiely's death.

So, the only problem I had now was how to get the gear in. I soon realised that I only had one option, and that was Tara. I couldn't go meself, it was too risky, too much chance of getting caught. Them custom police were always stopping fellas like me. Just because you had a few scars on your face, they immediately branded you a criminal. As far as I was concerned that was discrimination. I mean to say, they never stopped them student types, oh no. Just cause they wore little roundy glasses and knitted scarves, that made them good citizens. I wouldn't mind but they brought in as much hash as anyone. Anyway, none of that really mattered. What mattered now was persuading Tara to go to England to collect me parcel.

At first she refused. There was no way she was going to risk being body-searched by some dyke in a uniform. But, when I told her how much money we'd make out of one little parcel, she began to waver –

"Yeah, but if we sell all deh gear, what'll we do for our own fix?"

"That's what I'm tryin teh tell yeh . . . we're gettin two

parcels. One for distrubution, the other, well . . . that goes teh me . . . an you."

She agreed. Money and heroin meant more to Tara than anything else on this earth.

This was going to be our big chance, the one we'd been waiting for. We were going to set up our own business. Now that Johnser was out of the way, we'd be able to flood the clubs with as much gear as we could get our hands on.

Johnser Kiely's death was turning into something of a godsend.

"Thanks, Johnser," I told him, tapping me ashes into his urn.

JACKIE

Chapter Fifty

I told the kids to go to bed.

"But, Ma, we're starvin," Edward protested.

"I don't care, just get teh bed."

Jonathan put his arm around Edward and led him up the stairs. I knew I shouldn't have shouted at them but, I just couldn't help it, I was so frustrated.

I picked up the frozen sprouts and flung them across the room, they hit the wall and the packet burst open. As I watched the freed sprouts rolling around the floor, I told them what a fool I'd been –

"I'm a stupid fuckin bitch . . . how deh fuck could I have let meself be taken in by that slimy bollox? I'm not worth a shite . . . I deserve everythin I fuckin get . . . "

I went into the sitting-room, opened me vodka and drank straight from the bottle. The vodka had the desired effect. It made me feel calm, helped me to think straight. I thought back over the last few nights, the lies, the attention, the way he'd listened to me moaning . . . pretending he was interested. Jasus Christ, he must be having a right laugh now. While I'd been pouring me heart out, thanking him for being so considerate all he was thinking about was how to get his dirty paws on me money. Jasus, I'd been so stupid. I should never have let him inside the door, I should've ran him the minute I seen him. But, I hadn't, I'd let me guard down. I'd invited him to stay with us, I let him get close to the kids again, let him get close to me again, Jasus . . . I'd nearly let him fucking sleep with me.

* * *

Jonathan's voice startled me –

"Ma, are yeh OK? Ma . . . "

I hadn't realised I'd been talking out loud –

"Wha . . . yeah, I'm fine."

"Ma, can I make Edward somethin teh eat? He's starvin."

I felt so guilty – once again I'd let them down –

"Jonathan, I'm sorry . . . I shouldn't have shouted at yous. Now, you get Edward an I'll make yous both somethin teh eat."

I went to get up, but I couldn't. I stumbled and fell. Jasus, I hadn't realised I was so drunk.

Jonathan helped me up –

"Ma, it's alrigh, I'll make us somethin. You stay there."

I woke up the next morning with the worse hangover I'd ever had. I must have dropped off soon after Jonathan left me, cause I was still on the couch. The house was very quiet, the boys mustn't be up yet. I stood up, me bones were stiff from me night on the couch. I opened the curtains, the daylight nearly fucking blinded me and brought a new level of pain to me head. I struggled into the kitchen and nearly jumped out of me skin when I seen the boys sitting at the table. I got a glass of water, took two tablets then turned to them and asked hoarsely –

"What did yehs have for yer breakfast?"

"Frosties."

"Good. I'm just gonna get washed an changed, then we're goin teh yer nana's."

They didn't answer. I left the kitchen and went upstairs. The bed called out to me, and I hadn't the willpower to resist –

"Just ten minutes." I told meself, lying down.

As I turned on me side I noticed the clock –

"Fuck . . . three o'clock," I shouted jumping out of the bed. I took a quick shower, got dressed, and with me hair still wet ran down the stairs. The boys were watching the telly –

"Get yer jackets, we're goin out."

They sat glued to the telly –

"Jonathan, Edward . . . NOW."

* * *

I wasn't looking forward to seeing Ma and Da but I'd no choice. I was skint, and all the crying in the world wasn't going to bring me money back. Edward was struggling with the zip on his jacket. I grabbed him –

"Here, show me."

As I zipped him up I had another thought –

"Now, when we get teh Nana's, I don't want yous mentionin Jeffrey . . . deh yehs hear me?"

Edward looked up at me –

"Why?"

"Cause I said so, that's why. An that goes for you to, Jonathan."

I spit on a tissue and rubbed it across Edward's face –

"When are yeh gonna learn teh wash yerself properly?"

When I reached Ma's gate, I felt very nervous. I wanted

to turn and run but, I couldn't. Edward was already knocking on the door.

"Edward!" Ma exclaimed, hugging him tight.

When me and Jonathen reached the door, Da was beside her.

He smiled –

"Hello boys, long time no see. Hey, Jonathan, what did you think of Arsenal, eh?"

"I don't know, Granda, I didn't hear any results."

"Well, com'on, an we'll look them up on the Ceefax."

They walked down the hall. Ma stayed where she was –

"Well, Jackie, this is a surprise . . . a nice surprise," she told me, looking really pleased.

TARA

Chapter Fifty-One

When Stan asked me to go across to Liverpool and collect his parcel, I nearly had a fit. There was no way I was going to risk getting stopped by the police with a gansy load of heroin in me bag. He kept telling me how easy it would be, how women never got stopped. I didn't believe him. Cause, if it was as easy as he said it was, how come there wasn't a queue of fucking women waiting for the ferry every day of the week?

But, after about a week of constant nagging and begging and promising, I gave in. I had to, he had me fucking head wrecked with his non-stop talk of new starts and great lifestyles and all that. I knew that if I didn't go to Liverpool, I'd be hearing about it for the rest of me life.

I was to collect two parcels, one for us, and the other for distribution. Stan reckoned we'd make enough money out of one to settle our account with his uncle. Then when the money came through from Johnser, we'd be able to buy as much gear as we liked, we'd be on the pig's back. It all made perfect sense. I knew meself that all dealers mixed their gear to at least three times its original amount. But, that still didn't stop me being nervous. And the minute Stan told me I'd be travelling on Friday the 13th, I just knew something was going to go wrong. I told him I didn't want to go on that date cause it was bad luck. But, he wasn't interested, he told me not to start all that superstitious nonsense, I'd already agreed to go, so I was going.

On the Wednesday of that week, I got word about Johnser's fortune. I had to go and see a solicitor. Stan couldn't come with me, he had other business to see to.

The solicitor was a grumpy aul fuck. He rattled on for nearly an hour with Mr Kiely this, Mr Kiely that. But, the bottom line was that Mr Kiely had fuck-all. Well, fuck-all worth talking about. He'd an 1988 Honda Civic, a Kawozaki 250, and a hundred and twenty-five pounds in a bank account. The only thing worth talking about was his contracts with the clubs.

Stan went fucking mad. He'd borrowed ten grand from Frankie on the strength of Johnser's legacy. This was the first I'd heard about it. Anyway, he wanted to know where the car and the bike were, I told him it would be a few weeks before I got them. So, he told me the sooner I got to England, the better.

Friday the 13th arrived. I got up early and cooked meself a fix. I'd decided to bring Tina with me. I was going to buy her a little haversack in Liverpool, and put the gear into it. No one in their right mind would want to search her, she was such a little whinge-bag. I put the name and address of the pub where I was to meet Uncle Pat into me bag and set off.

The boat was empty, except for a few truckers and a gang of fucking eejits going over for a match. They were singing "Ole, Ole, Ole," at the top of their voices, and one of them kept grabbing Tina and shouting "Keano". Tina didn't like shouting, she started crying. And, what with all the crisps she'd eaten, the rocking of the boat, and the crying, she ended up being sick for the rest of the journey.

I was fifteen minutes late for me appointment with Uncle Pat. It wasn't my fault, it was the fucker of a taximan who'd made me late. I think he must have come over on the same boat as me cause he hadn't a clue about Liverpool. When we eventually got to the pub, I jumped out, paid him the exact fare, and grabbing Tina by the hand, made me way into the pub. I'd never even seen a picture of Pat so I hadn't a clue who I was looking for. But I needn't have worried. The minute I walked in, he was over –

"Jasus Tara, Stan certainly knows how teh pick his women."

I flashed him a big smile. I could never resist a compliment –

"Howya, Pat? Stan said yeh had somethin for me?"

"Yes, I have. But, let's have a drink first, there'll be plenty of time for business later."

I had a great time with him, he flirted like mad. It was so long since someone had treated me like this, I was like a starved cat, lapping it up. And he made it very clear that he'd like to get me into bed.

"The next time yeh come over, ye'll have teh make it an overnight . . . an come on yer own," he told me, looking at Tina who was stuffing her face again.

"I might just do that," I told him flashing plenty of knicker as I crossed me legs.

He squeezed me knee. I knew he was getting horny. Jasus, I'd forgotten how much fun prick-teasing could be.

Eventually, like all good things, me visit came to an end. When Pat gave me the gear, I told him me plan for getting it into Ireland.

"Nice one, Tara. There's very few custom officers who'll search a kid's haversack."

"Specially when it's full of kids' puke-covered clothes," I told him laughingly.

The minute the boat set off, me nerves started jangling.

And by the time we docked, I was in such a state I could hardly stand. "Jasus, why did I agree to do this?" I kept asking meself, looking around, trying to find the group most likely to be stopped by the customs. I spotted two Rastafarians and four New-agers, I decided to follow them. I had to walk really close to them and I was convinced that their head-lice were hopping all over me. Jasus, they must have been lousy, they were reefing the heads off themselves. Still, a few fleas would be a small price to pay if they got me through safely. "Thank you, God." I prayed when they were all stopped. The two Rastas were brought into an office, and the other four were told to empty their bags. No one even looked at me and Tina. We'd just reached the exit door when I heard someone calling me. I quickened me step, nearly pulling Tina's arm out of its socket from the way I was dragging her.

I felt a hand on me shoulder –

"Excuse me, Ma'am . . . "

I turned slowly, and looked into the policeman's face. I tried to think of something to say but me mind went blank. He was staring at me. I was sure he could hear me heart beating. He spoke –

"I'm sorry Ma'am, I think you dropped this."

I looked down at his outstretched hand. A teddybear . . . I'd bought it for Sally. I took the teddy and walked away without a word of thanks.

I got outside and looked around for Stan. Jasus, you'd think he'd be here to meet me, it was the least he could've done but there was no sign of him. I got into a taxi and told the driver where I wanted to go. The taximan was full of chat but I wasn't listening. I sat back and took a deep breath. I enjoyed the rush of blood through me body. Jasus, it had been a nerve-wrecking experience but the rush of adrenalin I got when I walked out of the customs building almost made it worth while.

JACKIE

Chapter Fifty-Two

Ma brought me into the kitchen. I could hear me da and Jonathan slagging each other over the football results, God, how I wished I was a child again. Kids didn't have to deal with a crisis, they just blocked out the bad things that happened, and moved on to enjoy the good things in life. Something us adults couldn't do. We had to deal with our crises, we had to worry about paying the bills, putting food on the table, settling arguments, swallowing our pride. We couldn't just block out the things that hurt or upset us but we did have to keep them to ourselves.

Like when someone asked, "How are you?" You always answered, "Fine." You'd never dream of telling them the truth cause you knew they didn't really want to know. So when Ma said –

"How are you? How are things going?"

I answered in me usual way –

"Grand . . . everything's fine."

Thankfully, she knew me better than anyone else.

Ma put a pot of tea and a plate of chocolate biscuits on the table –

"Now, Jackie, I'll ask you again . . . how are you?"

I tried to hold back me tears but, I couldn't. The floodgates opened and a month's tears came pouring out. I was gulping like a child, trying to talk and breathe at the same time –

"Everythins gone wrong . . . it's terrible . . . Johnser's dead . . . Jeffrey's back . . . me money's all gone . . . me job . . . me baby-sitter . . . "

I went on and on. Ma said nothing, she just kept pouring me tea. Edward came running in. I hid me face and Ma rushed him back out with biscuits and drinks for him and Jonathan. I blew me nose and wiped me eyes, me throat was as dry as a desert. I picked up me cup, trying to compose meself –

"So, there yeh have it, me life's a total mess."

Ma tried to console me –

"No it's not, Jackie. You're just having a bad run, that's all . . . sure it happens to everyone."

"No, Ma, it's not just a bad run, it's always been like this, I've always had to struggle . . . an now," I began to cry again, "you an me da even hate me."

She looked shocked –

"No we don't!"

"Yes yous do. Daddy even said that I was no daughter of his . . . "

"Don't be silly, Jackie. Your daddy didn't mean that! He was upset at the time . . . that's all."

I knew I was only feeling sorry for meself but, I couldn't help it –

"Well, why did he run off inteh deh sittin-room when I came in?"

Ma was having none of it –

"Now, hold it right there, young lady. Would you like the boys to be sitting here listening to your problems, and seeing you crying like this? No, you wouldn't. You know

272

right well that the reason your daddy didn't come in here was because the boys would have followed him."

She was right, of course.

"And as for minding the boys while you're at work, you know that's not a problem. It never has been, and it never will."

As she finished speaking, Da walked in. He sat beside me –

"The boys wanted to watch *The Gladiators*, so I left them to it."

Ma looked at him –

"I'm just telling Jackie that we don't mind looking after the boys while she's at work."

Ma had a great way of looking at people when she spoke. It was a look that said, I'm not asking you, I'm telling you what I've already decided. It reminded me of when I'd lived at home, and a friend (she didn't like) would call for me, and she'd say –

"I don't think she wants to go out, do you Jackie?" Or, "Didn't you tell me you were going to have a bath?"

And I'd know by *the* look that I wasn't to disagree.

* * *

Ma asked me would I like to stay for the weekend but, I said no, I'd rather get home and get things sorted. But, the boys could stay if they liked. Needless to say they were delighted, and so was I. A couple of days' spoiling would do them the world of good. She told me to give Da their schoolbags and uniforms when he left me home, so they could go to school from her house on Monday. I told her I hadn't had time to wash their uniforms but, she told me not to worry she'd do them.

The house felt very lonely but I was glad of the space. It

was after ten when I got home, so I didn't bother lighting a fire, there was no point wasting a bucket of coal for one person. Besides I hadn't cleaned it out that morning, and I wasn't in the humour for doing it now. It was the job I hated most in the world. Johnser had always been talking about getting central heating put in, but, with one thing and another, we'd never bothered. I wished now that we had. Anyway, it was late so I decided to go to bed. I filled me hot-water bottle, got me vodka and a glass, and made me way upstairs.

I know hot-water bottles are old-fashioned, but the bedroom was freezing so I needed something. I didn't like electric blankets, never had. I know they said they were very safe, but I didn't care, I hated leaving anything plugged in at night. Johnser used to make a laugh of me hot-water bottle, but yet, his feet always ended up on it.

As I sat in bed, with me feet on the warm rubber and me vodka in hand, I thought back over all that had happened to me in the last month. I cursed everything and everyone. I cursed God for me horrible life, I cursed me job, I cursed Jeffrey for being such a good liar, I cursed the police, the media, the killer. But, most of all, I cursed Johnser for leaving me on me own.

I woke to the sound of the phone ringing. It was Ger Byrne, the supervisor. She wanted me to go in on the early shift on Monday. Well, I thought, at long last something is working to my advantage.

STAN

Chapter Fifty-Three

I tried to stay out of Frankie Fitz's way, I still owed him ten grand and, with every week that passed, the interest was building. And Frankie didn't like people to renege on him. I should know, I'd been a collector for him. He had a reputation to uphold and that usually meant hurting anyone who failed to pay. Sometimes he'd string a fella along, just for the fun of it. If things were a bit tight and you couldn't afford to pay him, well, he'd give you another loan, and another, until you were in way over your head. With the result, you ended up either mortgaging your house or selling your business in order to pay him off. And, if you didn't have a house to mortgage or a business to sell, you ended up in hospital. He was a bollox. He was always ready to capitalise on other peoples' misery. And as well as his money-lending business, he also had his drugs. He was in control of a vicious circle, one that was hard to get out of. So like I say, he wasn't the kind of person you wanted to owe money to.

Hopefully, I wouldn't have to avoid him for much longer. Tara was gone over to Pat, so as soon as she got back I should be able to pay him off, and get rid of him, once and for all. While Tara was away, I had to mind Sally. I didn't want to but Tara wouldn't bring her with her cause she had an ear infection. I hated minding Sally, she was a real moaner. Her constant moaning cracked me up. And today was no different. She'd finally given up looking for attention and fell asleep. I took full advantage of me break. I got out me works and cooked meself a fix. Within minutes I was in paradise. A beautiful state of nothingness where I could plan me future, and everything seemed logical and achievable. Then from somewhere outside of paradise came the sound of Sally calling me. Her voice dragged me back to reality, a place I didn't want to be –

"OK, OK. I'm comin, yeh little fucker."

As I bent to put on me shoes, the phone rang, then someone knocked at the door –

"Ah, for fuck sake . . . "

I couldn't take this, I couldn't stand all the noise. I shouted at the door –

"Hold on, gimme a minute."

Then at Sally –

"Shurrup!"

I picked up the phone –

"Yeah?"

"Is that *The Gerry Ryan Show*?"

I slammed down the phone. Sally was still calling, I shouted at her –

"Will yeh wait for a fuckin minute!"

Suddenly, the door burst in. One of Frankie's men came flying into the room and landed in a heap on the floor. Frankie walked in after him –

"You'd want teh get a better lock on that door, Stan. There's some nasty people about . . . "

The phone rang again.

"Well, aren't yeh gonna answer it, Stan?"

I picked up the phone.

"Yeah? No . . . this is not deh fuckin *Gerry Ryan Show* . . . "

Sally came shuffling out of her room. Frankie tried to talk to her but eventually gave up –

"Here Corkie, feed this little darlin, will yeh?"

Corkie looked at Sally like she'd two heads.

"For fuck sake, Corkie, she won't bite yeh. Give her . . . give her . . . hey, Stan, what does she eat?"

"Biscuits an yogurt."

"For Jasus sake, Stan. Yeh can't only give her biscuits."

He turned back to Corkie –

"Here, Corkie, bring her teh that burger place on deh corner an get her a bag of chips."

As Corkie and Sally disappeared down the hall, Frankie cleared a place on the couch and sat down –

"Now, Stanley, let's get down to business."

I panicked. He was too cool, too controlled. And, he'd called me Stanley – that always made me nervous –

"Yeah, Frankie . . . I know I owe yeh a few bob, but . . . "

"A few bob?"

He laughed, sitting back into the chair.

"I think you owe me a bit more than a few bob, Stanley."

"Yeah, but yeh know I'm good for it."

"Do I?"

"Course yeh do." I sat down and gave him a friendly dig on the shoulder, "We're mates . . . right?"

He brushed his shoulder, as if removing dust –

277

"And yeh know what they say about lendin money teh friends . . . ?"

"But, I'll pay yeh back, Frankie. No worries."

"I'm not worried, Stan. It's the effect you're havin on other people that bothers me. When they see you gettin away with things . . . well, they think they can do the same."

"Ah, com'on Frankie. How deh fuck would anyone else know bout our arrangments?"

"When people talk, Frankie, other people listen. But, unfortunately, the people who listen only hear what they want teh hear . . . They put two an two together, an get ten. Next thing I know, I'm hearin rumours about how I'm losin me touch."

"Frankie . . . all I'm askin for is one more week. That's all, one more poxy week!"

He lit a cigarette –

"OK then Stan, I'll tell yeh what, I'm prepared teh make a little deal. You owe me ten grand, plus interest . . . now this is the point where I should break your legs . . . "

I could feel the blood draining from me face. When Frankie talked about breaking legs, that usually meant it was about to happen.

"But," he continued, "I'm not gonna do that. Cause, like you say . . . we're friends. So, with that in mind, I'm prepared to wipe the slate clean."

"Com'on, Frankie . . . what's deh catch?"

"Stanley, I'm surprised at you. Why should there be a catch? We're friends. I do a little somethin for you, and then some day, when I need it . . . you do a little somethin for me."

Now I was really worried. Frankie didn't do favours for

people for nothing. Sure look at Peter Brady. He got into a bit of bother with Frankie and in order to even things up, he had to do a little something for Frankie. And, that little something was, shoot Johnser Kiely.

Jasus Christ, I dreaded to think what he was going to expect me to do for ten grand.

I soon found out.

"I want you to give me the paintings."

"Are yeh fuckin mad? Give yeh deh paintins, they're worth more than ten grand . . . they're worth fuckin millions."

"Well, it's like I told you before, Stan, at the minute they're worth fuck-all. Now, I'm offering you a clean slate and no broken bones, for a few paintings that you couldn't offload in a year of Sundays."

"Jasus, Frankie, surely you'd be able teh throw in a few grand as well?"

I could see he was getting annoyed. He wasn't used to people arguing the toss –

"Stan, this isn't open for discussion. I want the paintings . . . you want to walk. There's no room for bartering."

Corkie and Sally were coming down the hall.

"I want them paintings first thing tomorrow . . . "

"I can't get them by tomorra, I'll need a bit more time."

He froze me with a look –

"Tomorrow, Stanley . . . don't let me down."

He got up and handed me a little package –

"A little something, to keep you going . . . while you work out how you're going to get my paintings."

On his way out he smiled at Sally and ruffled her hair.

The minute the door closed she started whinging again, then the phone rang –

"You," I shouted at Sally, "shut deh fuck up."

I picked up the phone –

"Yo . . . No, this isn't deh fuckin *Gerry Ryan Show* . . . Listen, mate, I don't give a bollox what fuckin number yeh rang . . . this isn't fuckin him."

TARA

Fifty-Four

I was still in a heap when I got back to the apartment. The taxi had cost nearly a tenner, I hadn't got enough. The taximan was going mental, threatening to call the police –

"Lookit, missus . . . this is the third time this week."

"The third time for what? All I wanna do is go up teh me fuckin apartment an get yeh yer poxy money!"

"Yeah, that's what they all say, an they never come back. So, I'm ringin the police."

I was starting to panic, I didn't want the police coming to the apartment. I grabbed his CB –

"Listen, there's no need for this . . . I'll leave me daughter here, I'm hardly likely teh run off without her, now am I?"

He looked at Tina, then back at me –

"OK, but make it quick, the clock's still runnin an . . . "

"Alrigh, calm fuckin down." I turned to Tina. "Tina you stay here, Mammy'll be back in a minute, OK?" I told her, fumbling with the taxi door.

"Fuck, fuck, fuck." The lift wasn't working.

I made for the stairs, running at first but I soon slowed

281

down. Jasus, that aul smack certainly fucked your lungs up. I remembered a time when I'd have run up and down them stairs all day, no problem. I got to the door and banged on it with me fist –

"Stan, Stan, open deh fuckin door." It pushed open.

Jasus, I could hardly breath, me lungs felt like they were about to burst. I went in but, there was no one there. The bastard was probably flaked out on the couch.

"I'll fuckin kill him for fallin asleep an leavin deh door open," I swore, barging into the front room –

"Stan! Stan! gimme some money . . . QUICK."

I was shouting at the top of me voice but he still didn't answer. I ran into the bedroom –

"Stan, yeh lazy fuckin . . ." The bedroom was empty.

There was a load of change on the dressing-table, I searched it for pound coins, then ran all the way back down the stairs again.

The taximan was staring straight ahead, tapping his steering wheel –

"I'd just about given up on you," he told me narkily.

I threw the money into his lap and grabbed Tina –

"It's all there."

"Yeah, well, if it's all deh same teh you . . . I'll count it."

"Yeh can do what deh fuck yeh like with it." I told him, grabbing Tina's hand.

Tina moaned on every stair. At first I tried to coax her – after all, it had been a long day. But, then I got fed up listening to her and slapped her hard, on her bare legs –

"Yeh little wagon! Move them fuckin legs."

She started to cry –

"Maaa . . . I can't . . . der painin me."

"I'll give yeh fuckin pain," I shouted, slapping her again, "OK, OK, yeh can fuckin stay there, then."

Temper gave me the energy I needed to get up the rest of the stairs. The door was still open, I stormed in –

"Stan! Where deh fuck are yeh?"

Tina appeared in the hallway, still fucking crying. I lifted me hand –

"If yeh don't shut fuckin up . . . "

I went from room to room, screaming now –

"STAN . . . STAN . . . "

He was nowhere to be seen. I went into the girls' room, Sally was the only one there, asleep. I leaned over the bed to cover her up, when I noticed a mark on her arm. I grabbed her arm up, and I seen it . . . I knew what that mark was. I grabbed her up and slapped her face –

"SALLY, Sally, wake up . . . SALLY . . . SALLLLYYY . . . "

"What deh fuck's all deh shoutin about?" Stan was standing in the doorway.

I flung meself at him –

"What deh fuck did yeh do teh her?"

I was trying not to panic.

He walked out of the room, ignoring me. I ran after him and grabbed his jumper –

"I asked yeh a question . . . now, tell me . . . what did yeh do teh her?"

"Where's deh gear?" He asked, pushing me away.

"STAN . . . what did yeh do . . . " I was becoming hysterical.

He grabbed me by the throat, lifting me off me feet –

"Where's deh fuckin gear?"

I couldn't speak, there was too much pressure on me throat. I croaked but nothing came out. I pointed towards the haversack, he looked round, seen it and, dropped me to the floor. He tore it open, breaking the buckles.

Tina started to cry –

"Daddy broke me bag . . . "

He turned on her –

"I'm not yer fuckin da."

He pulled out the dirty clothes, he didn't seem to notice their smell. He found the parcel, ripped it open, and started cooking up a fix. I was on me knees beside him, crying –

"Stan, what did yeh do teh Sally?"

"Nothin."

"Stan, don't lie teh me, just tell me, what did yeh do?"

He started talking about Frankie, and the paintings, and about how his slate had been wiped clean. He told me that Sally had been crying but, he couldn't stay with her, he had to get the paintings for tomorrow. But, that everything was going to be OK now. I hadn't a clue what he was on about, nothing was making any sense, but I thought it better to humour him –

"Yeah, OK, Stan, that's great . . . but, yeh have teh tell me, what happened teh Sally?"

He was rambling again –

"Couldn't brin'er with me . . . she was cryin . . . justa bit a gear . . . just deh ends . . . noth . . . "

He conked out. I ran back to Sally and started slapping her again –

"Tina, Tina, get Mammy cold water, a bucket, hurry Tina . . . hurry luv."

I kept slapping her and calling her name but, nothing. Tina came struggling in with the bucket. I picked Sally up and dunked her head in. Once, twice, three times, she coughed. I dunked her again, and this time she swallowed water, I pulled her out, she was crying. I pulled me two little girls close to me and squeezed them tight –

"Oh me poor little angels, I'm sorry. I'm so so sorry."

284

* * *

The girls couldn't sleep, neither could I. So, I brought them into the kitchen. They wanted drinking chocolate but we hadn't any so I made them hot milk instead. We sat in silence. I felt feverish, like I was coming down with the flu, but I knew that wasn't it. I knew what was wrong with me had more to do with the little parcel on the table in front of Stan. It kept calling me, calling me to come and party. I looked at the girls. Tina was being very protective about Sally, she was sitting with her arm around her, holding her tight and humming a lullaby very low. Sally obviously liked the song cause she was swaying slightly to the sound. God, Tina seemed more like a mother to Sally than I was.

From where I was sitting, I could see Stan, he looked so peaceful. The only time I ever seen him peaceful was when he was stoned and asleep. Once he was awake, his mind was so preoccupied with his next fix that he was like a bear with a sore head. But, for now, he was happy. Happy with the marks on his body, happy with the state of his body, the skinniness. Jasus, he'd lost so much weight lately it was unreal. But, he didn't care, all he cared about was finding a vein he could inject into.

I looked around the room. It was hard to remember how it had looked when we'd first got it. Hard to remember the paintings, the lovely ornaments, the marble chessboard, the cooker, the microwave. They were all gone. Even the furniture and the carpets were gone, gone into our veins. I looked back at Stan and, for the first time in ages, reality hit, all we were were a couple of

285

junkies. A couple of hopeless junkies. I looked at the table again, the parcel was still there, it was calling me, louder than ever –

"Com'on, Tara. Let's P-A-R-T-Y."

The needle sat beside the parcel, beside the lighter, beside the spoon –

"Com'on, Tara."

Tina hummed, Sally rocked.

"Paradise calling Tara, com'on in, Tara."

Tina sucked her thumb.

The parcel was getting annoyed –

"Bitch . . . I'm calling you!"

I looked at the girls, at Stan, at Stan's arms, at me own arms, at Sally's arm –

"Right girls, I want yous teh do exactly what I say."

Tina looked at me nervously.

"It's OK, Tina. I just want yous teh go an get yer coats . . . we're goin teh Nana's."

Tina took Sally by the hand and led her towards their bedroom. While they were out of the room I went over to Stan and picked up the parcel of heroin. When I bent to get Tina's haversack, I noticed a holdall on the floor. I picked it up, it was full of poster tubes, I opened one, "What deh fuck?" I was looking at a painting of some fat aul one. "Holy Jasus," I whispered, suddenly realising what I had. These were the paintings that Johnser had gone to prison over. The ones Stan had been talking about selling to Frankie Fitz –

"Thank you, God . . . thank you so much."

"What didyeh say, Ma?"

The girls were back, coats on, rag dolls in hand.

"What? Oh, nothin Tina. I was talkin teh meself."

I grabbed me bag and led the way out of the apartment. We were down the first flight of stairs before I remembered something –

"Oh, hold on girls, I forgot somethin . . . stay here . . . I won't be a minute," I told them as I ran back up the stairs.

Our luck was in. We got a taxi immediately, thankfully it wasn't the same one I'd had earlier. I gave the driver Ma's address and we headed off. When we arrived I left the kids in the taxi and ran up the drive. I kept me finger on the bell. Da's head appeared at the bedroom window –

"What deh fuck's goin on . . . oh, Tara, it's you . . . hold on, I'll be down in a minute."

There were more locks on their front door than there was in the Joy. Eventually, the door opened, Ma was first to speak –

"Tara, is everthin OK?"

"Yeah, Ma, fine. Can yeh mind the kids for a while?"

"Course I can, where are they?"

"Oh, they're still in deh taxi . . . Da?"

He fumbled in his pocket and took out twenty quid –

"Thanks, Da."

I ran back to the taxi, gave him the twenty and told him to wait. I hurried the girls up Ma's drive –

"Say hello teh yer Nana."

She didn't give them a chance to say anything –

"Com'er me little sweethearts, com'on, Nana has yer room all ready for yous."

"I'll be back as soon as I can," I said as Ma led them down the hall.

"Tara?" Da said warily.

"It's a long story, I'll tell yeh later . . . yeh wouldn't have a few . . . ?"

He took another twenty out of his pocket.

"Thanks, Da, yer a star."

"But, Tara, just tell me where yer goin?"

"Somewhere I should've gone a long time ago."

STAN

Chapter Fifty-Five

God, it was the best ever. Good aul Uncle Pat, his gear was pure dynamite. Tara was giving out shite about Sally, but it didn't bother me, nothing bothered me any more. Me day passed before me as I sailed away on a wave of oblivion. Christ, what a day.

When Frankie Fitz had left, I couldn't shut Sally up. I had things to do, things to remember, like where the paintings were. But, I couldn't do anything, not while she was crying. I couldn't take her with me, and I couldn't get anyone to mind her. I mean to say, who in their right mind would mind a crier like Sally?

I needed a fix . . . Sally cried.

I cooked up . . . Sally cried.

Found a vein . . . Sally cried.

I took the needle out . . . Sally cried.

I took Sally's arm . . . she cried.

I went into a vein . . . she settled.

I withdrew the needle . . . Sally slept.

Now, at long last, I could leave the flat.

It took me ages to find where we'd hid the paintings. Once I'd taken the turn at Bornabreena everywhere began to look the same, nothing but fields. Eventually, I seen a field that I recognised, well, it wasn't actually the field, it was the little white gate that I recognised. I couldn't drive in, so I got out and jumped over the gate. There was a forest straight ahead of me. Yes, this was the place all right. I remembered the reason we'd picked this place was because the trees were small, not small enough to let us be seen by a passer-by, but small enough to ensure they wouldn't be getting cut down for at least fifteen to twenty years. I found the trees we'd marked, easy enough, it wasn't an obvious mark, just a very faint red spot that you wouldn't notice unless you were looking for it.

Anyway, I made me way through the undergrowth, it was tough going but I finally came upon the clearing where we'd buried the paintings. I opened the bunker, they were still there. *"Eureka!"* I shouted, throwing me hands up to Heaven.

So like I say, it had been a great day, the best in a long time. As well as having the paintings, I also had me own supply of decent heroin. No more depending on Frankie Fitz's shite, I was me own man now. For the first time in ages, I felt relaxed and I just knew that everything was going to work out fine. Stan the Man was back.

As I drifted out of me dream and back to reality, I called Tara –

"Hey, babe, where are yeh?"

There was no answer, she knew that always annoyed me –

"Tara, get in here now! I wanna talk teh yeh."

I staggered to me feet, trying hard to focus. I went into the bedroom, no sign of her. Maybe she'd fallen asleep in the girls' room, no, she wasn't there –

"Where deh fuck's she gone?" I said to the doll sitting on Tina's bed.

I went back out to the sitting-room, I noticed the gear was gone . . . I was beginning to panic. I looked for the paintings, they were gone too . . . I panicked a lot.

I ran from room to room, pulling out drawers, emptying cupboards, looking under beds, in old handbags, I even searched the dirty laundry bin, but still nothing. I ran back to the kitchen and got the hammer out from under the sink, I started pulling up floor boards, I knew it was pointless, but, I was desperate. With every floorboard that came loose, I cursed Tara –

"Bitch . . . Slut . . . Whore . . . Cunt . . . Wagon . . . "

I gave up, it was hopeless, and I knew it. I threw the hammer at the fireplace, it hit the wall, leaving a hole. I looked at it . . . something was missing –

"Yeh dirty little slut." I roared at the empty mantelpiece. I knew now where she was gone.

JACKIE

Chapter Fifty-Six

It was a Godsend having Ma back on me side again, especially now that I'd started back on the early shift. The week flew by, everything seemed to be going just great, then Friday the 13th dawned.

I knew I shouldn't have got out of bed this morning. Me horoscope had said I'd have an eventful day and whenever they say that, it's guaranteed to turn out shite. The first thing that happened was the alarm didn't go off, or maybe it did and I hadn't heard it. Whatever, it was ten to nine when I woke up and the kids had to be in school by nine. I knew Jonathan would throw a wobbler, he wouldn't leave the house without his brekkie and then of course he'd have to have his shower and that took an eternity.

He was in secondary school now, and was up to ninety mumbling about how I was ruining his life and making him the laughing stock of the school. I felt like screaming. Here I was trying to make lunches (cause I couldn't afford to give them money for chips) organise breakfast and iron uniforms. Yes, I know I should have done all that the night before but I hadn't. Meanwhile, all Jonathan could think about was me ruining his life. Honest to God, his life was the least of me worries.

Despite all his moaning, we made the school by a quarter past. I offered to go in and explain to his teacher but he nearly had a heart attack-

"Oh, yeah, you'd love that, you'd really make a show of me then."

Edward, now he was different, he still held me hand and insisted that I explained to his master. God knows I hadn't time to chat to Mr Knowles, he was so fussy. I needed to be gone, to be at the bus stop or I'd be really late. And since all that stuff with Johnser I hadn't got many friends willing to cover for me.

So, I hurriedly explained to Mr Knowles what had happened then legged it out of the school and down to the bus stop –

"Fuck."

The poxy bus was pulling away from the stop. As it sailed passed me I stuck out me hand, but of course the driver didn't stop.

"Shite, shite, shite."

A taxi slowed looking at me, hoping I was going to hire him. I think they had a set-up with CIE. It couldn't be a coincidence that whenever you missed a bus, a taxi just happened to show up behind. But I hadn't got the money for a taxi, so despite being out of breath I started running again. I was aware that me chest was bouncing up and down, and I cursed the cheap bra I was wearing.

A van passed and the driver was hanging out the window, gawking and holding his middle finger in the air –

"Great tits, luv."

His mates broke their shite laughing. I wanted to tell them to fuck off but I knew if I did they'd have thought it was a victory for them. I could feel meself going scarlet but I kept running.

So that night, when Tara Coyle phoned me, I shouldn't have been surprised. It had been one of those days. And the fact that someone was hammering down me door just seemed like the perfect end to a perfect day . . . not!

"OK, OK. Keep yer hair on, I'm comin."

TARA

Chapter Fifty-Seven

At first she didn't want to talk to me but, once I told her it had something to do with Johnser she changed her mind. She'd asked me where I was and when I explained that I was in the phonebox across the road, she told me to come over.

I was just about to walk across to her house, when his car pulled up beside me. Jasus, he didn't waste any fucking time. I backed into the phonebox, and dialled her number again –

"Please, Jackie, answer deh fuckin phone."

While I waited for her to answer, I watched Stan to see where he was going, he was heading towards her house. The phone was still ringing –

"Why aren't yeh answerin, Jackie?" I asked the receiver.

Stan was knocking . . . banging . . . kicking her fucking door down –

"Oh, no! Don't answer the door . . . "

It was too late, the door was open, he was in.

STAN

Chapter Fifty-Eight

So she thought she could get away from me.

She thought she could just up and run with me paintings and heroin under her arm. And, I was just going to sit back and let her go. What kind of a fucking eejit did she take me for? Did she honestly think I was just going to forget all about her, and let her get on with the rest of her life? Yeah, right.

When I realised where she'd gone, I have to admit to being a bit confused. After all, they were supposed to hate each other . . . weren't they? But, anyway, despite all this I knew I was right.

"Small world," I thought, as I jumped into me car.

* * *

People should know better than to keep me waiting, they know how much it pisses me off. Besides, I'd no gripes with her, it was Tara I wanted.

I knocked on the door and waited as the minutes ticked by. It was probably only seconds but it felt longer to me. I started kicking the door, I wanted in so as I could get this whole fucking mess sorted. And me life back to normal. I didn't need all this hassle.

I sensed curtains twitching and knew that some nosy neighbour, with nothing better to do, would be ringing the police. It wouldn't be long before they arrived with sirens flashing and batons at the ready. I didn't need it. All I wanted was the door to fucking open, and if that meant kicking it open . . . then I would.

I heard a voice –

"Keep yer hair on . . . I'm comin."

Stupid cunt. We'll see who keeps their hair on when I get in.

This wasn't a fairytale, I wasn't a wolf huffin an puffin at her door. This was real, deadly real.

The door opened, ever so slightly, but enough. I'm sure she would have liked to just peep out the crack and tell me to piss off but, me boot put an end to that idea. The door burst in, and sent her flying across the floor on her bony arse. I closed the door and dragged her down the hall, no words spoken. I always found that more effective, it scared the shite out of them. And, by the time you did decide to talk, you found them more than willing to answer. No coaxing needed.

A simple but effective method. Answer me truthfully and you live, probably in a lot of pain, but you still live. Lie, and you die.

JACKIE

Chapter Fifty-Nine

Before I had a chance to open the door, it burst in on top of me –

"What the fuck deh yeh think yer doin . . . "

I didn't get to finish the sentence. As he pushed me away from the door, I stumbled and fell flat on me arse. He was so matter-of-fact about the whole thing, closed the door and walked towards me as if nothing was wrong.

I tried to be brave –

"Get the fuck outta here. Yeh have no right teh barge . . . aah . . . "

He grabbed me by the hair and dragged me like a caveman to the kitchen. I could feel me hair coming out of me scalp. He threw me against the table. As I fell I hit me face on the side of it. I knew me cheek was open, I could feel the warmth of the blood running down me face. He was mad, stone mad, and he wasn't finished yet. I tried to crawl under the table but he dragged me back out, kicking me in the stomach as he did. The pain was worse than having a thousand period cramps all at once.

I wanted to tell him to stop, to stand up and reason with him, but me mouth wouldn't say the words and his boot connected even harder. I was going to die, right here on me kitchen floor. On the floor that I was going to mop after dinner but hadn't got around to yet. And when they found me, they wouldn't think about who'd killed me or why. They'd just look at the dirty floor and the sink full of dishes and the washing-basket full of kids' dirty tracksuits and they'd say –

"No loss."

And Jonathan would tell them what a lousy mother I was and the neighbours would tell the story of gunmen at me door, and on me headstone they'd write –

"Waste of space."

And they'd be right.

JACKIE'S HOUSE

STAN

Chapter Sixty

She was scared shitless, wriggling like a maggot. But, the more she wriggled, the more I hurt her. Her hair was coming away at the roots, I spoke –

"Where's deh fuckin bitch?"

"What . . . ? Who . . . ? I don't know what yer on about."

I hit her again –

"Don't play fuckin games with me."

She looked confused, like she really didn't know what I was talking about. But, then again, maybe she was just a good liar –

"Are yeh fuckin stupid or . . . "

There was a noise behind me, I spun round, it was a young fella, I hit him. She screamed –

"Leave him . . . "

"Where is she?"

"Where's who? I swear . . . I don't know who yer talkin about."

I hit the young fella again, he fell to the floor, she grabbed me leg.

JACKIE

I thought I was going to die. He kept kicking me, and he was pulling out lumps of me hair. He kept on asking questions I couldn't answer and, when I told him I didn't know what he was talking about, he hit me again. Then Jonathan came into the room.

He hit Jonathan, knocking him to the floor. He raised his foot to kick him but, I grabbed his leg and unbalanced him. He shook his leg, trying to dislodge me but, I wasn't letting go. I screamed at Jonathan –

"Jonathan, run . . . quick, run."

Jonathan didn't move.

I bit his leg and he kicked me again, this time sending me flying across the room. I hit the back door and closing me eyes, I curled meself up into a ball. I waited for him to come at me again but, he didn't. After about ten seconds, he let an unmerciful roar that made me blood run cold.

TARA

I ran across the road, the door was closed over but the lock was broken. I pushed it open. From down the hall I could hear screaming. I ran towards the sound. Stan was kicking the life out of Jackie. One of the kids was sitting on the stairs, looking through the bannisters, the other was pulling himself up off the floor.

STAN

I was really starting to lose it, I was out of control, screaming –

"I'll fuckin kill yous all . . . I swear teh Jasus, if yeh don't start givin me some answers . . . I'll fuckin kill yous."

I lunged towards the back door, she was lying in a ball, pretending to be dead. Well, if she wanted to be dead, I'd help her on her way. I was just about to lay into her when something landed on me back. I spun round, trying to shake it off but I couldn't.

TARA

I was on his back, he was trying to shake me off but he couldn't. I had me arms locked tight around his throat. He ran backwards and squashed me against the wall but I still wouldn't let go. I freed one of me hands and clawed the face off him. I must have connected with his eyes cause he covered his face with his hands and screamed out, in agony. He went fucking mental. He pounded me against the wall so hard I was finding it difficult to breathe but I still wouldn't let go. I bit his ear as hard as I could.

JACKIE

I looked up. A first I couldn't make out who it was, who'd come into the kitchen but, as me vision cleared, I realised it was Tara. Seeing her gave me strength. I knew that if I didn't get up off this floor, he'd kill us both. I dragged meself across the floor and once again grabbed him by the leg. I bit into his flesh like it was a piece of steak.

* * *

Suddenly, the room was packed, there were people everywhere. Stan was roaring –

"Get them fuckin offa me . . . get them mad cunts away!" A policeman was trying to seperate me from Stan's leg. Two others were trying to get Tara off his back but they were finding it difficult. She was screaming like a woman possessed –

"Bastard . . . yeh fuckin useless bastard . . . I'm gonna fuc . . . "

TARA

The police were everywhere. Two of them were trying to get me away from Stan but I wasn't letting go, I didn't trust the bastard, police or no police. Only when he was in handcuffs, could they persuade me to let go.

A police woman was trying to get a bit of order –

"OK, OK. Now, let's all calm down. Someone has to tell us what's been going on here?"

Jackie started talking, a mile a minute. She told them about how he'd just burst into her house and started beating and kicking her, for no reason. And she told them about how he beat up her son, an innocent child. She was rattling off in all directions but they seemed to get the gist of what she was saying, cause they took Stan away. As they led him out to the car, I called after him –

"Hey, Stan . . . don't forget yer bag . . . "

I handed it to one of the policemen, he looked inside –

"What's this . . . then?"

Stan looked straight at me –

"Yeh fuckin bitch. Yer dead . . . deh yeh hear me? DEAD."

JACKIE

When Stan was safely out of the way one of the policemen put his arm around Jonathan and tried to lead him out of the room. Jasus, the poor child, he looked like someone who'd just gone three rounds with Mike Tyson. And, even though he must have been in agony, he wasn't going anywhere until he was sure I was all right –

"Ma? Ma, are yeh OK?"

I tried to smile, but it hurt too much –

"Yeah, Jonathan, I'm fine."

Tara stood looking on, our eyes met, she smiled –

"Well, there doesn't seem teh be any lastin damage there."

The policewoman wanted me to go to the hospital and get me face looked at but I wouldn't –

"No, it's OK . . . really. It looks worse than it is."

There was no way I was going anywhere near a hospital, I'd had enough of them in the last month to do me a lifetime. She persisted –

"But, I really think it would be better if a doctor had a look at you . . . both."

"Look, miss . . . I'm fine, I swear . . . it's nothing that a drop of Dettol won't fix," I reassured her again.

She wasn't giving up –

"What about the child, he'll need to see a doctor. You did say he was hit on the head?"

"Yeah, OK. But, we're not goin in a police car . . . I'll get me friend teh bring us."

"Well, if you're sure?"

"I am."

When she'd gone, the boys came back into the kitchen –

"Ma, I don't wanna go deh hospital."

"I know yeh don't, Jonathan but yeh have teh. Yeh got a bad bang on yer head. So, we have teh make sure yeh didn't damage that brilliant little brain of yers."

He gave me a watery smile.

"But first I have teh clean meself up."

I went over to the sink and filled a bowl with warm water –

"Edward, will yeh run up stairs an get me deh Dettol?"

When he came back with the Dettol, I poured some into the water and set about cleaning me face. I kept wincing, it stung like hell.

"Ah, here, gimme that. I'll do it for yeh." Tara pulled her chair close to mine.

She dabbed at me face for a minute or two then said reflectively –

"Well, that didn't turn out too bad, did it?"

I looked at her in amazement –

"Tara, he nearly fuckin killed us."

"Yeah, but he didn't . . . did he?"

I wasn't even going to try and understand her logic.

* * *

Someone started hammering on the back door. We all jumped.

"Jackie . . . Jackie . . . open deh door."

It was Ann.

305

Jonathan opened the door and she came flying into the kitchen –

"Oh, Jasus, Jackie . . . are yous OK?"

"Yeah, Ann, we're all grand."

She looked at Tara –

"What's she doin here?"

Tara turned on her –

"An who's she? The cat's fuckin mother?"

I jumped up –

"Now, hold on yous two, I've had enough fightin for one night . . . "

Ann turned back to me –

"Jackie, I think yer face needs teh be stitched."

"No, Ann, I'm grand . . . it's Jonathan I'm worried about. He got a terrible bang on the head."

"Well, don't worry, I'll get Tommy teh get deh car out. An I'll look after Edward till yeh come back."

"Thanks, Ann."

I turned to the boys –

"Yous go with Ann, I'll be out in a minute."

Ann put her arm around the boys' shoulders, and giving Tara a dirty look said –

"We'll be waitin outside . . . "

* * *

When they'd gone, I took out me bottle –

"Do yeh wanna drink?"

Tara nodded.

I poured two large vodkas and sat down –

"Well, Tara, are yeh gonna tell me why yeh came here?"

"Jasus, Jackie! Let me have a drink first."

She knocked back her drink –

"Nothin like a bitta Dutch courage, eh?"

306

"Tara!"

"Alrigh, alrigh, I came cause I thought there was a few things yeh should know . . . "

"Like?"

"Like, when you an Johnser got back together . . . he never sold drugs . . . "

"But, yeh said . . ."

She was getting annoyed –

"Lookit Jackie, forget what I said before . . . I lied, OK?" She picked up the bottle and poured herself another drink –

"I'm sorry for all deh things I did teh yeh. Yeh know . . . his funeral an all that."

"Yeah, well, forget it, Tara. It's in deh past, there's nothin we can do about it now."

"No, maybe not, but . . . " She leaned down and reached into her bag. "Here," she handed me what looked like a biscuit jar –

"What is it?"

"It's Johnser . . . well it's not actually him, it's his ashes." I hesitated.

"For fuck sake, Jackie, take it. It's not gonna bite yeh."

I took the jar out of her hands, I had tears in me eyes –

"But . . . why, Tara? Why after all this time . . . "

"Because I know that he really loved yeh . . . and you him. This is where he belongs . . . with you an yer kids."

She finished her drink and stood up –

"I'd better be off."

"Yeah, me too," I said getting up and putting on me coat.

When she reached the door she hesitated for a minute, and looking back at me said –

"Jackie, yeh know that bag that I gave the police, tonight . . . "

"Yeah?"

"Well, deh paintins were in it . . . yeh know . . . deh ones that Johnser robbed?"

"Oh."

"Yeah, an yeh know them two people who were killed, well, Johnser didn't do it . . . it was Stan."

"Well, I kinda guessed that."

* * *

We walked out of the house together. Tommy and Jonathan were waiting in the car. I turned to her –

"So, what are yeh gonna do now?"

"Dunno, I suppose I'll probably go back teh me ma's."

"Well, Tara, whatever yeh decide teh do . . . take care."

"Yeah, you too, Jackie."

THE END